PIPER'S DISCOVERY
Bradford Hall, Book Two

BARBARA MCMAHON

1

Piper Morgan hung up the phone and crawled back into bed. She was more miserable than she'd ever felt in her life. Pulling the covers up to her ears, she closed her eyes, and tried to ignore her aching body and focus instead on the phone conversation she'd just had.

What a shock to hear from Cassie Hodges. They'd been closer than sisters while growing up as foster children in the small town of Bradford, Mississippi. Separated when they were teenagers, they'd had no contact in twelve years. Piper had put her childhood memories in storage—the good and the bad—and left the United States seven years ago to embark on a new life in Paris.

She'd thought she had it all back then—a wonderful husband, a promising career, a glamorous lifestyle.

One out of three wasn't bad.

She'd made it to the top in an increasingly competitive field. A well-known model who commanded high fees to showcase the latest creations of the world's leading designers, Piper had to partially credit her playboy second husband, Jean-Paul Sartain, for her success.

At least he'd done her some good before he'd broken her heart by turning to another woman.

Restless, she pushed away the covers, wishing someone was around to fix her some hot soup. But her friends all thought she was still in Marrakech. She should have called someone when she got back to Paris a couple of days ago.

But there was no way she was going to feel sorry for herself, not when Cassie had called her. There were several messages on her answering machine when she'd returned home. Now, at last, they'd actually talked to each other. The years had dropped away as if they'd parted only yesterday.

Piper smiled despite feeling so ill. It had been wonderful to hear from her. Not that Cassie's news had been good. Margaret Nunes, their former foster mother, had suffered a stroke and was in the hospital. While her doctor was cautiously optimistic, Margaret was still at risk for a second stroke. And recovery would be a long process.

Cassie urged Piper to return to her former hometown.

Piper's initial inclination was to say no. Even under the best of circumstances, she'd never envisioned herself returning to Bradford. She'd never felt she belonged there.

The longer Cassie talked, though, the more memories came rushing back. Margaret, Cassie and Fiona, Margaret's third foster child, were the only family Piper had ever known. Because of Fiona's lies, the family tie they'd tenuously shared had been shattered.

Now Cassie was doing her best to have them reconnect.

But return to Bradford? Piper wasn't sure she could face the ghosts.

She'd told Cassie how sick she was. When she felt better she'd make a decision. But how long would it take to get over this bug she'd picked up in Marrakech?

If she did go back to Bradford, she wouldn't have to stay for long, a few days at most. That would give her time enough to catch up with Cassie and pay a few visits to Margaret. Much as Piper had railed against the rules her foster mother had laid down when the girls were teenagers, she couldn't deny Margaret had done her best for the three of them. Piper could make a quick trip and then resume her life in France.

For years she'd missed Cassie and Fiona fiercely. Granted, she now had plenty of friends in Paris and Cannes, but not old friends who had known her as a child.

Not close friends to whom she could tell anything.

And if she were honest, she missed Margaret, too. The thought surprised her.

Piper remembered the endless arguments she'd had with Margaret about her hair, her clothes, her makeup. Margaret had been older than most of her friends' mothers and Piper had constantly brought up the age difference. Margaret was from the dinosaur age. She didn't have a clue what everyone was wearing.

Piper had also resented Margaret for a deeper reason. When she was very young, Piper had blamed the woman for taking her mother's place. Piper didn't know who her parents were, but she'd believed that if Margaret hadn't taken her in as a foster child, maybe her own relatives would have stepped up to claim her.

As an adult, Piper could see that possibility was unlikely. One foster home was as good as another to the state of Mississippi. If she hadn't been sent to Margaret's, she would have gone elsewhere.

Piper cringed a little as she thought back to all the arguments. Margaret had done her best in dealing with girls who resented her kindness and fought against the system, Margaret and even each other from time to time.

In retrospect, Piper had to admit that Margaret had been right. She would have regretted dying her blond hair purple or piercing her nose.

Snuggling back down beneath the warm duvet, she frowned.

Living with Margaret hadn't been awful. There were a lot of fond memories. Slowly she let the images unfold. The happy times when the three girls were younger, their early years in school, picnics along the riverbank, learning to ride a bike. First dates.

No, it hadn't been all bad, and Piper might have been happier if she hadn't focused so much on yearning to discover who her real family was instead of appreciating the one she had. She so desperately wished that one day a happy couple would drive up in a luxury limousine and claim her. They'd tell her the separation had been some horrific mistake, and they'd been searching for her all her life.

How many hours had she spent dreaming that fantasy? And resented Margaret for keeping her from her parents.

Cassie had known her parents were dead. Her mother had died when Cassie was four, and her father before that. Fiona's parents had been druggies, her father in jail for attempted murder of her mother. Maybe it was better to have the fantasy than reality, Piper thought.

She'd been abandoned as an infant. Margaret had taken her in when she was only three months old. Taken Piper in and raised her until the State of Mississippi had abruptly moved the three girls to separate foster homes in separate cities with strict instructions not to contact anyone in Bradford.

Piper had missed Cassie and Fiona so much when they'd been separated. Despite the edict, she'd tried to find out where they'd been sent. And had been shut down in every attempt.

She rubbed her fingertips, remembering the day they'd become blood sisters. Whose dumb idea had that been? Yet it had sealed their own friendship as nothing else could have.

How could she have let so many years go by without making an effort to find them?

Despite the close tie with her foster sisters and her

reluctant respect for her foster mother, Piper had always felt a compelling need to find her biological family. She was registered with several Internet sites of adopted children looking for biological parents. Not that she'd been adopted, but if there was a chance her mother might be looking for her, she wanted to be out there.

It was harder to do research from France. Her schedule was hectic, and beyond the adoption sites, her knowledge of tracing people was very limited. Over the years, she'd learned to deal with the disappointment of reaching dead ends, but always in the back of her mind was the question of why her parents had left her behind.

Maybe it was time to go back to Bradford and reconnect with the only family she'd known.

Now that she'd talked to Cassie, Piper longed to see her again.

Of course, if she decided to visit Mississippi, she'd have to rearrange her schedule, have her agent clear her calendar so she could spend a few weeks in the U.S.

Too exhausted to worry about details, she turned over and drifted to sleep, thinking about Bradford. Whoever would have thought she'd feel nostalgic for a place she'd never liked.

Two weeks later Piper stepped off the airplane in New Orleans, the closest airport to Bradford. Walking into the terminal from the gate, she glanced around. Cassie said she'd look for her at the baggage carousel.

"Piper!" An excited voice called her name.

A smile lit Piper's face as she turned and recognized her old friend, the sister of her heart.

"Cassie."

Piper rushed over to hug her. The years dropped away instantly, and they were once again like two teenagers, hugging, pulling back to look at each other, squealing. Piper felt close to tears.

"Oh my goodness, I can't believe you're finally here," Cassie said. "You don't look any different from the last time I saw you. You're gorgeous! It's so good to see you."

She hugged Piper hard.

"What have you been doing all this time? I like your shorter hair. You look fabulous. I can't believe I'm here, either."

Piper felt like laughing and dancing and holding on to her friend so they'd never be parted again. They'd had several transatlantic telephone calls to catch up on the highlights of their lives, but that hadn't been enough. Piper knew they'd be talking for days.

"Welcome back to Mississippi," a deep male voice said.

Piper looked beyond Cassie and saw Matt Bennett. He'd been Cassie's main squeeze when they were in high school. That ended right before the three teenagers had been separated. Now they were back together.

"Matt? Matt Bennett!" Releasing Cassie, she

reached out to hug him. "You're looking fine."

She'd always thought he was one of the best-looking guys in their high school. Cassie had been lucky to date him back then.

He hugged her back, then let go. A slow smile lit his face as he looked at Cassie.

"I drove Cassie in to get you," he said.

"We're engaged." Cassie flashed a diamond ring in Piper's face.

"I thought you said—"

"As of a couple of days ago," Cassie broke in. "Let's get your luggage and head for home. It's a long story. I'll tell you all about it later."

"Glad you're sparing my ears," Matt said, taking Cassie's hand in his, lacing their fingers.

When they were on the highway heading for Bradford, Piper leaned forward from the back seat.

"Tell me about Margaret. Your last phone call said she was out of the ICU and into a regular room. How much longer before she gets out of the hospital altogether?"

"Actually she's now in a convalescent hospital and has actually begun physical therapy. That could take a few weeks, according to her doctor," Cassie told her. "They're still trying to find the right dose of blood-pressure medication to reduce the chance of another stroke. The physical therapist is working to get her mobile again, and she also has a speech therapist. She really can't talk at all, only garbled sounds. It's called aphasia," Cassie explained. "But she seems to understand everything we say."

"She's doing so much better than originally expected," Matt added.

"I know," Cassie agreed, "but it's still awful to see her so ill. Remember how indomitable she seemed?"

"Of course, General Attila," Piper said drily.

Cassie smiled.

"She's older now. Seems frail. You'll be surprised when you see her."

She squeezed Piper's hand.

"But tell me about you. Are you better?"

Piper leaned back and sighed softly.

"Not entirely. I have no energy. The doctor said I'm fine, but what does he know. Anyway, I figure I can laze around and do nothing here as easily as Paris. My agent rearranged some of my assignments, got me out of a couple due to illness. I may have to take a few naps. Darn it, I hate being so lethargic all the time."

"There's not a lot to do here except visit Margaret," Cassie said. "It's when she comes home that I may need help. So rest up. You can stay awhile, right?"

"For a few weeks anyway. When are you two getting married?"

"When I know Margaret will be okay on her own."

"Unless we move up the date and take care of Margaret together," Matt said.

Piper watched as Cassie gave him a loving smile.

For a moment envy struck. She'd never had that kind of devotion from either of her husbands. When Matt's sister committed suicide, something had driven

Cassie and Matt apart, but it looked as if that rift was totally mended.

Piper couldn't picture anyone else with her friend.

She wondered what had happened to Cassie's fiancé from Boston as she let her head fall back on the seat cushion and closed her eyes. She smiled to herself. Maybe being married twice wasn't any more egregious than being engaged to two men in the same month.

"Piper?" Cassie shook her gently. "Wake up, we're home."

Slowly Piper came awake and looked out the window. They'd reached the old house she'd grown up in. She stared at the place, noting the riotous flower gardens, the freshly mowed grass. Surprisingly, tears came. She *was* home.

"It needs work," Cassie explained when Piper climbed from the car and cast an appraising glance at the front of the house. "Especially to get the clearances and approvals we need to open the home for unwed pregnant teens that Matt and Margaret are planning. Renovations have started inside. Not on the bedroom floor yet, but downstairs. It's a mess, but Matt assures me it'll look great inside and out when the work is finished."

Cassie had told Piper in one of their phone calls that Matt had a successful construction firm.

"I hope he knows what he's talking about," Piper said a few moments later as she stepped over drop cloths and dodged scaffolding.

The front room and hallway were crammed with

construction tools, wood and paint.

"You said Margaret took out a loan to look for Fiona and me. Couldn't she have used some of the money to keep this house up?"

"I think finding her girls was more important," Cassie replied. "Come on, you have your old room. It didn't take much to get it ready for you. Seems Margaret kept our rooms pretty much the way they were. Yours will soon have a bathroom between it and Fiona's room. In the meantime, we have to share the one bath at the end of the hall."

"Just like the old days," Piper murmured, following her up the stairs.

Once Piper's suitcases had been deposited in her room, Matt pulled Cassie aside.

"I'm heading out. You two can visit to your heart's content. I'll call you later."

"Don't leave on my account," Piper said.

Despite the nap in the car, the bed beckoned. She tried to figure out how late it was in Paris, but was too tired to do any calculations.

"I have things to do. And I know Cassie's been dying to talk to you. You two will do better with me gone."

"You don't want to listen to us reminisce?" Cassie teased.

"That, too."

He kissed her—a hot, erotic kiss, definitely that of one lover to another.

Piper looked away. It had been a long time since

anyone had kissed her like that. She'd been very popular with the boys in high school and had enjoyed a healthy physical relationship in each marriage. But there'd always been something just beyond her grasp.

Something that Cassie and Matt definitely had, she thought.

When Matt finally left, Cassie bounced on the bed and grinned at Piper.

"Okay, give. I want to know everything that you've done since we were separated."

"After all our phone calls, you know most of it already, but I can fill you in on the details. And I want to hear your news, too. All of it."

She sat on the bed, leaning against the headboard. Unpacking could wait. She wanted to catch up with Cassie.

"Deal. I probably know even more about you than you think. Margaret hired that private investigator I told you about to find you and Fiona. He succeeded with you. One of the things he was able to do was get clippings from the French newspapers. Margaret has a whole scrapbook devoted to you. Wait, I'll show you."

Cassie jumped up and left the room. Piper couldn't help smiling. It was hard to believe twelve years had passed since she'd last seen Cassie.

She hadn't changed that much. She looked a little older, and her clothes were certainly nicer than when they were kids. But her shining happiness hadn't dimmed at all. Piper wished she could be as happy.

Funny how three girls raised by the same woman

could turn out so differently. She wondered where Fiona was and what she was doing.

Cassie had mentioned on the phone that Margaret was the only mother she really remembered. But at least she knew who her real parents had been.

Maybe that private detective could help Piper find information about her own parents. Why had she thought she had to do it on her own? Given enough time and money, a detective could probably unearth anything.

And money was something she had plenty of.

Cassie hurried back into the room, carrying a scrapbook.

"Here, you can probably read it all. I can't believe you speak French."

"I took it in high school, remember? One of the few courses I did well in. I seem to have an ear for languages. Of course, there's nothing like living in Paris to perfect your French. I also speak German, Spanish and a little Italian from trips over the years. German was hardest to learn."

"I barely mastered English," Cassie said, plumping a pillow behind her back and sitting beside Piper. "I took these to Tulane University to have them translated."

She opened the book and Piper looked at the first clipping. It was six years old, when she was just starting out in modeling. Taped to the opposite page was a type-written translation.

"These clippings couldn't have been easy to get,"

she murmured, leafing through the scrapbook. "Some of them are ancient."

"The detective is very thorough. That's why he's so expensive. Is there any chance you could lend Margaret some money? Matt and I paid down the overdue amount on her bank loan so she wouldn't lose this house, but I'd love to get the whole thing cleared by the time Margaret's out of the hospital."

"I might," Piper hedged.

Over the years she had learned to be careful about money.

"What's wrong with just making regular payments?"

"I thought I told you on the phone. Maybe not. Remember the assistant vice president at the bank back when we were kids? Allen McLennon? He was dating Margaret right before we left."

"Vaguely. Wasn't he always staring at us? Like we had the plague or something."

"I don't remember that. Anyway, he's now president of the bank, and he was going to sell the house and property to some consortium that wants to build a golf and country club on Margaret's land. He's against the home for unwed pregnant teens that Margaret and Matt proposed. The City Council has granted provisional approval, so Matt has to make sure he can do all that's required to get final approval. We stalled foreclosure by bringing the overdue part of Margaret's bank loan as close to current as we could. But I don't have the money to pay off the loan and

Matt's money is tied up in his construction firm."

"How much are we talking about?" Piper asked.

Cassie told her. Piper shrugged. It was a relatively small amount compared with what she'd banked over the years.

"Sure, I can pay it off."

Her friend stared at her.

"You can pay it off? Really? That would be wonderful. But don't run yourself short. I was able to get work here to make sure I had an income, but I don't think there's much call for super-models in Bradford."

"Relax, I have enough. You said Margaret used the money for the detective. What did he do, gold plate every report?"

She wondered how quickly the detective had run up the bills. Maybe she'd rethink hiring him to trace her parents.

"He's been searching for you and Fiona for three or four years. I think the overseas connection probably added a lot to the cost. I'm not sure why Margaret got so far behind on the payments. Anytime I try to bring it up, she gets agitated, so I've stopped asking her. It really doesn't matter. Anyway, she can't wait to see you. I thought we'd go to the hospital later this afternoon. She has physical therapy in the morning and takes a nap after lunch. Then we can stop in and visit."

"I wouldn't mind a nap myself," Piper said.

"You're in luck. The construction crew isn't here today. When they are, it's bedlam."

"I bet. Still, the way I feel, I could sleep through anything."

"Traveling all the way from Europe must be tiring. Tell me how you wound up in France. And how you managed to get married twice. Oh, I want to hear it all."

"Too bad Fiona isn't here. We could take turns telling what we've done."

Piper remembered the day Fiona reported to the authorities that Margaret had beaten her. It had all been lies, but when Fiona finally told the truth, no one in authority had believed her.

As a result, Margaret had lost her foster care license and the three girls had been sent to different homes throughout the state. Everything had happened so quickly and Piper still didn't understand why. People in town had known Margaret all her life. How could things have turned as they had?

Especially in light of Cassie telling her recently that formal charges had never been filed against Margaret.

Piper considered where to begin.

"When we were separated, I got moved to Jackson. Where did you end up?"

Cassie told her briefly about her new foster parents in Biloxi, Mississippi, and how she'd moved to Boston with them when they were transferred. Even though Cassie had grown close to Al and Dottie Johnson, Piper could hear the old hurt in her voice. She herself had been inconsolable when she'd left Bradford Hall for another foster home, in Jackson.

"I came back here when I read about Margaret's stroke in the newspaper," Cassie said softly. "To reconnect."

Piper nodded.

"I know how you feel. I came back the weekend after I graduated from high school. Margaret was less than welcoming. She said she didn't know where you two were, so that was a dead end. I think I got on my high horse at her attitude and stormed away. I went straight back to Jackson and married Billy Bob Thompson."

Cassie looked startled.

"Because Margaret was difficult?"

"That was one of the reasons. He was also hot. And he asked me. Whatever, he and I were not soul mates. But I was scared of being alone. My foster parents couldn't wait for me to leave when I turned eighteen. I was lucky they let me stay until the end of the school year. Nothing had prepared me for finding a place to live, trying to get a job without any skills. Billy Bob seemed like a good idea at the time."

"Only he wasn't," Cassie guessed.

"You got it. His idea of a wife was someone to show off to his friends. And get him a beer while he watched football. His glory days were on the high school football team, and he's never done anything else. At least I guess he hasn't. He was still talking about all his touchdowns when I filed for divorce and headed for Manhattan. I haven't heard from him since."

She pushed aside the remembered hurt of being

wanted solely for her looks. There was more to Piper Morgan than a beautiful face, corn-silk hair and blue eyes, though most people never bothered to search for it. The few who did had become true friends.

Piper had grown used to the attention that came from being a model, but sometimes, deep inside, she wished she hadn't been blessed with such beauty. She wanted people to like her for who she was, not what she looked like.

"So you were in Manhattan when I was in Boston," Cassie sighed. "I could have driven down to see you."

"How did you like Boston?"

"Okay. It was as good a place as any other. How did you like New York?"

"I loved it. I worked as a clerk in a deli near the garment district. There's so much life in the city. I would still be there if I hadn't moved to France, which turns out to have been a good thing. I don't think I would have hit it as big modeling in the States."

Piper yawned and snuggled down onto the pillow a little more.

"Tell me how you got into cooking," she said, wanting to hear more about Cassie.

There was no hurry, she realized. She'd arranged her schedule so she could stay through the end of June.

"Later," Cassie promised. "I can tell you're half-asleep. I'm so glad to see you again, Piper. I've missed you so much."

"Me, too," she said. "Blood sisters, remember?"

She held up her finger.

Cassie touched it with her own scarred fingertip. Smiling, Piper closed her eyes and was soon asleep.

When she awoke, it was late afternoon. The sun shone in her window, dust motes dancing in the beams. She lay there for a while, letting her eyes roam around the familiar bedroom. It looked the same as the day she left. There were old rock posters on the walls, jumbled books in the bookshelves.

Piper loved to read. Books had taken her away from the small Mississippi town and swept her into adventure. Her grades in school had never been as high as Cassie's, because if a subject didn't interest her, she hadn't bothered doing more than the minimum to get by. She had excelled in English literature, however. And French.

Recognizing favorite books, she vowed she'd reread some of them while she was here.

As she got out of bed to freshen up, Piper was touched to see that Cassie had unpacked for her. Her clothes were put away and her suitcase tucked into the closet.

After she'd changed her clothes, Piper went downstairs. The phone sat on the table at the foot of the stairs. She remembered how she'd argued and argued for an extension, one located somewhere a little more private. Obviously, Margaret still felt that one phone was enough.

Wandering into the kitchen, she stopped in the

doorway. Cassie was cooking and the aroma made her mouth water.

"That smells divine. What is it?"

"Gumbo. We're having it for dinner, but I want it to simmer all afternoon. Matt's coming."

"Am I going to be in the way?" Piper asked.

"Not at all. We're mature adults," Cassie teased. "We can behave around others."

"Hmm, like that kiss earlier?"

Cassie beamed.

"I love him so much I ache with it."

"He seems to feel the same. Tell me what happened to split up high school's couple-most-likely-to-succeed."

"He blamed me for Dolores's death."

"Hey, wasn't that the same day Fiona got beaten so badly? And Margaret had a fit because I was caught smoking in school and was suspended? And you cut classes? The day we were separated."

"The worst day of my life," Cassie agreed, stirring the gumbo. "Matt and I have cleared things up...finally."

"Yeah, I guess so, from that kiss."

"Want something to eat before we go to the hospital?" Cassie asked.

"A sandwich will hold me. Maybe we should wait until tomorrow to go to the hospital." She felt oddly nervous about seeing Margaret again.

Cassie put down her spoon and shook her head. She went to the refrigerator and pulled out cold cuts and mayonnaise.

"Margaret is so looking forward to your visit. I told her the minute I knew you were coming. She can hardly wait."

"How do you know that? I thought she couldn't talk."

Piper sat at the table, in the place that had been hers so many years ago.

"She has limited mobility in her right hand, so she squeezes once for yes and twice for no. It's hard coming up with conversation that requires a yes or no response, but it's the best I can do. The speech therapist is working with her. She says Margaret's making progress, but I don't hear it."

Cassie quickly made a couple of sandwiches, cut them and handed one to Piper.

"Thanks. I'm still not sure about this."

It was silly of her to feel so nervous about seeing Margaret again.

"She wants to see you."

"I know. I want to see her, too, but I'm nervous."

There, she'd admitted what was bothering her. Their parting hadn't been amicable. Her aborted visit to Bradford a year later hadn't gone well. Would their reunion be any better?

Piper hoped so. Otherwise she wouldn't have made the trip from Paris.

"I'll pop in to say hi," Cassie said as they walked down the convalescent hospital corridor a little while later. "Then you're on your own."

Piper wasn't sure what she'd say, but her nervousness fled when they entered the room and she saw Margaret.

The woman had aged as Cassie said. Her hair was gray and thin, her cheeks hollow, her skin wrinkled and parchment like. But Margaret's eyes were bright and they seemed to light up when she saw Piper. One side of her mouth lifted up in a smile and garbled sounds came out.

"Hi, Margaret," Piper said softly.

How could she have been worried about seeing her foster mother again? This woman had taken care of her as an infant, a child and a teenager.

She leaned over and gathered the older woman into a hug, squeezing gently.

"I've missed you so much," she said, blinking back tears.

It was true, Piper realized. She'd missed Margaret. And Cassie and Fiona. Only now that she was back could she admit to herself it was good to be home.

Even if only for a visit.

2

"What I can't figure is what you're doing in this backwater town. If you had to leave New Orleans, why not choose a city that at least offered some diversions? What do you do here for fun—watch trees grow?"

Adam Saunders leaned back in the rocking chair—rocking chair, for heaven's sake—on Sam Witt's front porch. Maybe when he was eighty he'd want a rocker, but not now.

He looked at his friend in bafflement. What had happened to change the man so much? Sam used to have a fire in his belly that only constant work could assuage. Now he was content to sit on a blasted porch in a bucolic town as unlike New Orleans as Adam had ever seen.

Sam smiled.

"The town grows on you."

Adam sighed loudly.

"Maybe. I won't be here long enough to find out. I came to see you, hoping for some action. If I wanted to sit around and do nothing, I could have stayed with my parents."

"Why didn't you?" Sam asked.

He took a long drink of his beer and studied his friend.

"Too much coddling," Adam growled.

He'd hated every moment his mother had fussed over him. Sure he'd been injured by a land mine, but injured wasn't dead. And he was mobile. What more could they expect when he'd been covering the war?

"Probably scared them to death when they got word you'd been blown up," Sam said reasonably.

Adam wasn't in the mood for reasonable. He was antsy.

"I was injured, not blown up."

"The guy with you died," Sam reminded him.

He hardly needed reminding. Not a day went by that Adam didn't think about Pete and fate and that blasted mine. Why had he been spared and not his cameraman?

"Anyway," Adam continued, "until I'm one-hundred percent again, I'm grounded. No reporting."

"Relax, Adam. You'll heal at your own pace. Once you're fit, you can head back into the line of fire."

"In the meantime, I'm supposed to do what?"

"Did you visit your sister?"

"Yes. Alice said to tell you hi if I saw you. And her brood was wild. If she and Ed don't rein in some of that energy, they're going to have a pack of hellions by the time the kids are teenagers."

"So, can't stay at your mother's, can't stay at your sister's. I'm next best, right?"

"I thought you were still in New Orleans."

"I told you after Patty died that I was leaving. I should have done it before her death. She hated my job. She wouldn't have minded it so much here in Bradford. It's a quiet, slow-paced town."

"She'd have been bored to tears," Adam said, looking across the lawn at the street.

He hadn't seen a car drive by in twenty minutes.

"And you're happy here?" he asked with some skepticism.

"Content, I'd say."

Sam took another swallow of beer.

For a split second, Adam envied him the cold beer. Still on medication, he wasn't drinking. He'd tried to kick the pills a week ago, but the knife-sharp pain in his foot and ankle had kept him up all night long. He'd cut back, but sometimes the meds were the only thing that helped.

He hated being dependent on drugs of any kind.

Or on the hospitality of friends, no matter how far back they went.

And he and Sam went back to early childhood. They'd started elementary school together in Baton Rouge. They'd enrolled in college together and enlisted into the military as a team. Then their paths had separated. Sam had married Patty and become a New Orleans cop.

Adam majored in journalism in college, and used his military experience as a springboard to reporting news in foreign countries. Lately, all he seemed to see was death and destruction.

He rubbed his hand across his eyes. He continued to see it in his dreams at night. But if he didn't keep going, he might take time to rethink things. Who knew where that would lead?

Look at Sam. From a detective in New Orleans to a sheriff in a backwater town in Mississippi.

Losing his wife must have been hard. Adam had liked Patty a lot. How had Sam stood it?

"Contentment?" Adam said, just to prod his old friend. "You sound like you're ancient. What happened to the fire you had for righting wrong?"

"Hey, I can right wrongs here as well as in New Orleans," Sam replied easily. "I know my neighbors. I've made some good friends over the last couple of years. And I don't see the drug dealers or killers like I used to in the city. It's realigned my thinking about mankind."

"Don't you get bored?"

Sam shrugged. "Not as much as I thought I would."

"So what am I supposed to do while I'm here?"

Adam knew he was whining, and didn't like it. The thought of moving elsewhere didn't help. Who else would put up with him while he convalesced?

"I'd suggest we go dancing, but with your bum leg, I don't think that would work."

Sam laughed at Adam's dour expression.

"I don't go dancing even when my leg isn't banged up," he groused.

"I know. Tomorrow you can ride shotgun with me,

see the town, meet some folks. Maybe you'll find something to do. If not, you're on your own. I'm not your keeper."

Not like his mother or sister, Adam thought, who fussed over him every moment he was awake. They hadn't wanted him to do anything more than sit in front of a television all day to rest his leg. That had driven him nuts. He wasn't an invalid, just temporarily sidelined.

Maybe he was still a little nuts. He couldn't settle down for a minute. He was restless sitting on the porch. Sam, on the other hand, seemed content to linger in the twilight and talk with an old friend.

Was he destined to seek that adrenaline rush all his life? If he didn't find some diversion soon, he'd head back to New Orleans.

To what? A motel room and television? He didn't even have an apartment to call his own. Since he traveled all the time, it made no sense to have one. Mail was sent to his folks' house, where they held it until he made one of his infrequent visits, or to the office in Atlanta to be forwarded to his latest posting. Any bills were paid automatically through his bank.

He looked at the porch, at the yard. Not a lot to see in the gray of evening.

"Did you buy this place?" he asked.

"Yep," Sam said.

"So you're staying."

"I've been here a couple of years. I like what I have. I'm staying."

Two years in one place. A house. Adam looked at his friend, feeling the gap widen. They'd been close as boys, even as young men, talking big, living for adventure. But their paths had diverged, and now Sam seemed to belong to another world, unlike the one Adam was familiar with.

Or was he the one who lived in another dimension? Risking life and limb daily to get the story. Seeing the hot spots in the world. Making a difference. Man, he couldn't wait to get back.

He stretched out his left leg, wincing at the pain that shot through it. His foot had all but been blown off. Only the skill of the surgeons at the military hospital in Germany had saved it. Whether he'd ever regain full function was still questionable. He could walk, though, using a cane. That was what mattered now. He'd work on the mobility once the cast came off. With any luck, he'd be back on the front lines in only a few months—if he survived this interval in Bradford, Mississippi.

"Okay, I'll give it a shot," Adam said, knowing he didn't have any choice.

They were silent for a while. Then Adam looked at Sam.

"Been dating lately?"

Patty had been dead for more than three years. He was curious as to whether Sam was moving on.

Sam shook his head. "You?"

Adam shrugged. "The front lines of a war aren't exactly conducive to meeting women. Any prospects in

Bradford?"

Sam laughed softly.

"Not unless you like them really young. Anyone our age is already married, or has long left for brighter lights."

"See, I was right. This town is dead. No one stays here if they can go elsewhere."

"So I'm getting to be an old fogy, is that what you're saying?"

"If the shoe fits."

"I'm not ready," Sam said softly. "I still miss Patty like she died yesterday."

"At least you had five years together. I'm sorry as hell, Sam. She was the best."

"You ever think about settling down?"

"Never. I'll be reporting to you live from the next trouble zone when I'm in my eighties."

Adam hoped it was true. If his foot didn't heal properly, he might never go on that kind of assignment again. He didn't want to think about it.

"I told Etta Williams you were coming to visit," Sam said.

"Who is Etta Williams?"

"The local librarian. She wondered if you would do a couple of talks at the library about being a foreign journalist."

"I don't see myself talking to a bunch of gray-haired old ladies about the death and destruction in Ukraine."

"Etta seems to feel younger people would be

interested in how to get into journalism, how to get into foreign reporting. The basics of the business, with an occasional personal story thrown in to showcase your unique style."

Adam laughed. "My unique style?"

"Standing in front of firing artillery to report the latest developments," Sam said drily.

"Heck, why not? It's not as if I have a lot of other pressing engagements."

"Yeah, I thought you'd feel that way."

"So you already accepted for me?" Adam asked.

"No, it's still your choice. But it'll give you something to do. How about Wednesdays for a few weeks."

"If I stay here that long."

Adam wondered if the medication was dulling his senses. He wasn't used to giving speeches or answering questions. He reported news—hard news. He wondered when the last thing of any interest had happened in Bradford. Probably during the Civil War.

"Stay, or go," Sam said. "But if you stay, try to fit in, don't find fault with everything you see. I know we're not Kyiv or Somalia. But this is a nice town. The people are real. These are the folks the soldiers are fighting for."

"So maybe I can do a human-interest story."

"Or maybe you can just live here for a while and not do a story," Sam suggested. "When was the last time you lived your own life and not a news story?"

Adam frowned. It was what he was made for—

getting the news out to the rest of the world. He couldn't imagine doing anything else. Especially sitting in a rocking chair and gazing at grass growing.

Until then, he might as well regale people with the realities of reporting. It wasn't all glamour and excitement. A lot of it was drudgery—digging for facts, verifying each one, cross-checking references and sources. Making sure the report was as unbiased as possible.

"I'll tell Etta in the morning," Sam said.

A pickup truck drove down the street, passed the house, then braked. After backing up, it parked in front of Sam's place. When a man got out and headed for the porch, Sam rose and went to the steps.

"Evening, Matt," he said.

"Sam." He glanced at Adam. "Am I interrupting?"

"Come on up. This business?"

"Not really. Just wanted to see if you had any new leads in the search for Fiona Hunter."

"No."

Sam made introductions and offered Matt a beer, which he took as he settled another rocking chair.

"Piper showed up today," he said. "She and Cassie are talking a mile a minute, so I left right after dinner. It'd be great if we could find Fiona while Piper's here. Those girls were close. I know Cassie's talked about nothing else since Piper said she'd come."

"I'll see about sorting through the lists we have and narrowing the search," Sam said. "I didn't think it was urgent."

"Someone missing?" Adam asked, his curiosity aroused.

Was there a story in this?

Matt explained about three girls who were raised by one of the local residents.

"They lost touch when they were sent to separate foster homes twelve years ago. Two of the girls are back in town now and would like to locate the third."

"One's engaged to Matt," Sam interjected. "Cassie Hodges."

"Yeah, guess that's my main reason for coming by," Matt admitted. "I'd love to have Fiona show up and surprise both her and Piper."

Sam told Adam about the search he'd started for Fiona Hunter and the lack of leads he'd turned up so far.

"She could be dead for all we know," he finished.

"Or married or living underground," Adam said.

Maybe there was no story after all.

"Do I know you from somewhere?" Matt asked. "You look familiar. Not from Bradford, but New Orleans maybe?"

"From CNN, probably," Sam said. "Adam's been in Ukraine until recently."

"You're that Adam Saunders. I should have recognized you immediately. Sorry about that."

Matt looked at Adam with new interest.

"Sometime, if you're in the mood, I'd like to hear more about what's going on over there."

"Adam plans to give a series of talks at the library,

starting on Wednesday," Sam said.

"A series sounds long-term," Adam growled. "I don't know how long I'm staying."

"Okay, one or two talks," Sam amended. "I want to hear them myself."

"Let me know the time, and I'll do my best to be there." Matt stood up to go. "Thanks for the beer. Call me if you hear anything that might help us locate Fiona."

Adam needed to rethink his approach to the library talks. Maybe his audience wouldn't only be gray-haired ladies after all.

By Wednesday morning, Piper was feeling more acclimated to the Mississippi spring. The hot, humid days zapped her energy—what little she had—so she rested as much as possible. The nights were cooler, and she and Cassie stayed up late talking. They had so much to share. Piper couldn't believe she'd been here several days and they still talked nonstop from dinner to bedtime.

This morning she'd helped Cassie dust and vacuum the rooms they were using. The renovations seemed to spread dust everywhere.

There'd been four men working on the project the past couple of days, and every time she walked by, they stopped to stare, strike up a conversation, make an excuse for her to stay and talk. She didn't mind talking with the workmen, but whenever she was around they seemed to compete with each other for her attention and completely forget about work.

Maybe she should mention it to Matt, but on second thought she decided against it. There was no sense making a big deal this time, and she'd do her best to be friendly but not encourage their flirting. She'd had to deal with situations like these before.

She'd gone to visit Margaret every day. Piper wasn't sure who had changed, her or Margaret, but their visits were going well. Maybe that was partly due to the fact Margaret couldn't talk, but Piper didn't think so. She skimmed over her marriages, focusing on her life in Paris. Margaret seemed to love hearing about her flat, about the fresh baguettes from the boulangerie, and the lively cafés on the Left Bank.

Piper tried to give her career a bit of a spin, glossing over how hard it was to maintain her slim figure by constantly watching what she ate, and getting enough sleep to keep circles from beneath her eyes.

Today Margaret had been tired from her physical therapy, so Piper had stayed only a few minutes. She should stick to late afternoon or evening visits, rather than right after lunch. With nothing else to do, she walked down the main street of town, reminiscing as she went. Passing Ruby's Café, she glanced inside, debating whether to stop for a cup of coffee or not.

Before she made up her mind, the door burst open and a waitress came rushing out.

"Piper Morgan. Cassie said you were here. I'm glad to see you."

Piper was embraced in a friendly hug.

"Betsy?"

She hugged the woman back. Betsy had been more Cassie's friend than Piper's. She and Cassie had embarked on a fledgling catering business in Bradford, though Betsy was keeping her regular job until their new company was financially secure.

She was the first friend from school other than Matt that Piper had seen in the two days she'd been in town.

"You look fantastic," Betsy said. "I can't believe you're a super model in Europe. All I've ever done is stay in Bradford and marry Dexter Bullard."

"Sounds like as good a way to live as any," Piper said diplomatically.

Truth to tell, she'd once hoped to do something very much like that. After two failed marriages, those dreams had changed.

"Come in and have something to eat," Betsy said.

"Not just now. Maybe tomorrow. I ate lunch before I went to see Margaret."

No matter how glad she was to see Betsy, Piper didn't feel up to talking with an old acquaintance. Tomorrow, she promised herself.

"Okay, then. Maybe I'll stop by the house later and we can catch up."

Piper nodded. She'd heard a lot about Betsy from Cassie already. She'd have to look up some of her own friends—if any had remained in Bradford.

But not today.

Continuing her walk down the main street, she passed the library, noticing a poster with a picture of Adam Saunders, CNN correspondent, prominently displayed on the door.

She did a double take. Adam Saunders here in Bradford? She often saw him on television at home, where her satellite connection pulled in both CNN and his feed to the BBC. What in the world was a reporter of his reputation doing in Bradford? According to the poster, giving a series of lectures starting today.

Intrigued, she walked into the cool building. The scents of old books assailed her and she smiled at the once-familiar smell. She'd spent many afternoons in this place as a child. Fewer afternoons as she grew older.

Following the signs to the public meeting room, Piper wasn't surprised to find it almost full. Glancing at her watch, she saw Adam was scheduled to begin his talk in a few moments. Taking a chair in the last row, she leaned back. She was tired, but she might as well rest here as at home. At least she'd be entertained and feel less guilty for not helping Cassie more.

Adam hobbled to the chair behind the small table and sat down. He'd walked over from Sam's place and his leg was throbbing. The librarian introduced him and he nodded, letting his gaze travel around the room. It was crowded. He wouldn't have thought this many people in Bradford would be interested in anything he had to say. Or that this many didn't have jobs to be at.

There were the older people he'd expected. Sam had stopped by. He saw several other men their age, and some teenagers. In the back of the room his regard paused a moment on one of the most beautiful women he'd ever seen. Blond hair seemed to float around her head. Even from this distance he could see the deep blue of her eyes. Probably a wife of one of the town's leading citizens.

"Thank you for coming," he began. "I didn't expect such a turnout. Television often portrays news reporting as glamorous and exciting. I can attest to the exciting part, on occasion. But glamour is often missing."

He launched into the talk he'd roughed out the night before. He didn't need notes. He knew what he had to say. He wanted these people to know how difficult it was to get unbiased information, and the hardships reporters and camera crews faced.

He provided insights into what drove the men and women who reported the news, interspersing his lecture with incidents he or one of his friends had experienced. Sometimes he drew laughter. Sometimes he saw tears in the eyes of his audience. One teenager seemed to hang on his every word.

Finishing up, Adam asked if there were any questions.

"When are you giving another talk?" the teenager asked eagerly.

"Same time next week. I'll cover a different aspect,

so if you come back, you won't hear the same thing."

"Awesome," the kid said, grinning.

He quickly answered other questions. Until Etta Williams announced the talk was over and the audience began to rise from their seats.

The librarian hurried over.

"Thank you so much, Mr. Saunders. That was fascinating. I do appreciate your coming today. I can't wait for next week."

Adam nodded, wishing his foot didn't hurt so much. Sitting still for so long only made it worse. Next week, if it wasn't better, he'd have to request a stool or something to elevate it.

Sam came over to the table.

"Need a ride home?"

Adam nodded, and Sam said he'd pull the car around in front. Once he left, Adam rose and prepared to hobble outside. The teenager who had hung on his every word came up to ask more questions.

Then one of the older men stopped him to talk about the way news was reported these days. Another woman thanked him for risking his life so Americans could know what was really going on.

The blonde from the back of the room hovered near the door. Adam made his way slowly toward her.

"Mr. Saunders," she said, when he drew level with her.

He nodded. By this time, the two of them were the only ones left in the room.

"Yes?"

He leaned heavily on his cane, willing the pain to go away.

"I was wondering if you'd like to have coffee with me. I want to talk to you about something."

"Someone's waiting to give me a lift home," he said, wondering how anyone could have eyes so clear and blue. She was on the thin side, almost as tall as he was. Was she interested in a reporter's job? With her looks, she could be a TV anchor even if she didn't have two thoughts to rub together. If she only read the reports, audiences in America would lap up the news.

"Another time then?" she said.

"What's this about?"

Despite her beauty, he couldn't help her get a job.

"I'm Piper Morgan."

"Friend of Matt's?" he asked, making the assumption.

How many Pipers lived in Bradford? He'd noticed how people in the audience had eyed her, as if she wasn't quite one of them. A certain level of curiosity would be normal if she'd been gone for twelve years and only returned for a visit.

"That's right. How did you know?"

She seemed startled.

"Instinct. What can I do for you, Miss Morgan?"

"Call me Piper—everyone does. I want help in finding someone."

"Fiona?"

He couldn't do more than Sam could.

"You *are* tapped into the local grapevine. No, not

Fiona, as it happens. I understand Margaret already has a private detective working on that. I want help finding my birth parents."

Piper made the decision to ask for help as she listened to Adam Saunders describe some of the ways he researched facts. She knew he reported from foreign locales, but the basics of investigative methods would be the same.

Maybe he'd have some pointers for her on how to expand her search for her parents. She wasn't sure what contacts reporters had, but if he could tap sources unavailable to the general public, it might help with her search.

She could tell from his expression she'd surprised him. What—had he thought she was some groupie wanting to cling to a famous reporter?

"I'm not into finding missing persons," he said abruptly. "Try the sheriff's office or Social Services. A private detective. Those are the kind of agencies who can help."

He headed out the door.

Stung by his curt response, Piper watched him go.

"Don't you think I've already thought of all those avenues?" she muttered.

She was annoyed she'd asked him for help. He probably thought she was some dumb blonde who didn't have a clue about anything. If so, he wouldn't be the first to misjudge her that way.

As soon as he was out of sight, she left the meeting room. Returning to Bradford had awakened her longing to find out about her parents. She thought she'd dealt with that issue years ago, yet here she was again, hoping for some clue that would lead to their identity. She realized now that the only closure would come from finding them.

She had her birth date to start with. It was listed on the state-issued delayed birth certificate she'd had to get when she first applied for a passport. Social services had registered it. The parents' name fields had been "Unknown." But from some of the stories Adam had told, he'd often started with less.

Maybe she should reconsider contracting the private detective who had traced her for Margaret. She'd have more confidence in the man's abilities if he'd found Fiona.

Piper headed for the main desk of the library. While she was here, she'd stop to speak with Etta Williams. The librarian had recommended books for Piper to read when she was younger. Would Etta remember the little girl she'd befriended so many years ago?

Etta was delighted to see her.

"I recognized you the minute you walked into the room, but didn't have a chance to greet you. You look lovely, Piper. What have you been doing?"

Piper filled her in briefly and said she had come back to be with Margaret.

"It's a shame about Margaret Nunes. She didn't

deserve all the hardship she's had in her life. I'm right glad you and Cassie have rallied around when she needs family. I do hope she makes a complete recovery. Tell her I asked after her, will you?"

"I'll do that."

"Need any books today?" Etta asked with a smile.

"I have a bunch of classics on my old bookshelf at the house," Piper said, "so I thought I'd start rereading them. But if I get the urge for a mystery or something more recent, I'll come back."

"Anytime." Etta smiled warmly. "I'm always glad to see you."

Feeling a bit as though she'd stepped back in time, Piper left the library and continued her walk home.

Family, Etta had said. Cassie had said that, as well. The three girls and Margaret made a family. Not a conventional one, not a biological one, but a family nonetheless.

Piper had railed against Margaret's restrictions when she'd been a teenager, longing to see what was beyond the horizon. Now she'd done that, and found it was pretty much the same as anywhere else—and lonely without family.

All her life she'd missed having relatives of her own. Why hadn't she just appreciated the family she did have? The old saying, blood was thicker than water, wasn't always true.

As she approached Bradford Hall, her annoyance with Adam Saunders grew. He didn't have to be so rude, dismissing her before he'd heard her out.

Okay, he had no obligation to help her. And at least he hadn't tried to put the make on her the way most men did. She could respect him for that. But his attitude sucked.

Cassie was out when Piper reached home. She tried to remember whether her friend had a catering event, but there were so many she couldn't keep them all straight. Bypassing the men working in the hall, she headed for the kitchen. An iced tea sounded perfect.

As she was getting a large glass, she saw the note on the counter. Cassie and Betsy would be back soon and cook dinner on the grill. They'd gone to scope out the location for their next assignment.

Piper shook her head, still amazed her friend had started a business in Bradford when she'd only come back for a visit. She took her tea and headed for her room, doing her best to ignore the construction workers.

She could start reading one of her books, but she knew she'd fall asleep. If she didn't get back to feeling like normal soon, she was going to see a doctor here in Bradford or a specialist in New Orleans. She hated not having any energy.

Starting up the stairs, she glanced at the phone. Maybe she should try that private detective. It wasn't as if she couldn't afford him. And there was a chance he'd be able to help her. It was worth a shot.

3

Matt was the first to show up later that afternoon. He rang the doorbell, but before Piper could get downstairs, he opened the door and walked in.

"Hi, Cassie home yet?" he asked when he spotted Piper.

It was late afternoon. Work had stopped on the renovations. The house was quiet and covered in dust.

Piper shook her head.

"No, she and Betsy had to check out the location of some job coming up. She said they'd be home for dinner."

"Sounds good. I think we're grilling outside. Maybe I'll start the coals."

Piper followed Matt out to the backyard. There was a new stainless-steel barbecue grill on the worn, uneven brick patio. She knew Cassie or Matt must have bought it. Margaret would never use something like that.

"What did you do today?" Matt asked as he began to work.

"I went to see Margaret, then stopped at the library to hear Adam Saunders."

"I wanted to get to that but got caught up in a meeting in New Orleans. I met him at Sam's the other night."

"Sam's the sheriff?" Piper remembered the old sheriff who had questioned Cassie and her years ago.

"Right," Matt said. "He's been here two years. Came from New Orleans."

"Quite a change. Is he as stupid as Sheriff Halstead was?"

Matt glanced over.

"Cassie doesn't hold the old sheriff in high regard, either. Sam's younger, seems smart enough to me. After he read the files, he told Cassie he thinks Margaret got a raw deal."

"Well, duh."

Matt laughed softly. "Can I get you something to drink?"

Piper looked at him and smiled.

"Sure. I'll go in with you. I'd love some iced tea."

It was obvious Matt knew his way around the kitchen. He took down four glasses, filled two with ice and then poured tea from the large pitcher in the refrigerator.

"Sugar already in," he said, handing her the drink.

Taking a long sip, she sighed. "Delicious. Hard to get it this good in France." She glanced around. "How long will this renovation take?"

"The men should be finished with the first floor by the end of next week. We're starting the second floor next. Depending on how much work we find we need to do on the plumbing, that could take a while. Sooner or later you and Cassie are going to have to vacate your rooms so I can have bathrooms built. I want one en suite between every two bedrooms."

"So tell me more about this project and why Margaret is involved."

"Remember my sister?" Matt asked.

Piper nodded. She was the one who had committed suicide the same day Fiona had been beaten so badly.

Matt explained something that hadn't been common knowledge at the time. His sister Dolores had been pregnant when she killed herself. He thought part of her desperation was due to fear of the future and lack of support. She'd kept her condition secret and he'd forever wonder if she'd told him if things would have turned out differently.

He surprised Piper when he said he'd told Margaret about his proposal for a home for pregnant teens and the older woman had immediately latched on to the idea, offering Bradford Hall as the perfect facility.

"Not everyone in town wants the home," he added.

"Like the banker. Cassie told me about him. What I don't understand is why he's opposing Margaret. They were dating when I last lived here. What happened?"

"No one seems to know. Remember Edith Harper, Margaret's friend?"

"I do."

"She might know more, but if she does, she hasn't

told Cassie. Maybe you can get something out of her."

"I'll have to go visit her," Piper said, looking at her glass. "It's funny a lifelong spinster like Margaret would be interested in a home for unwed teens."

"I think it gives her a purpose again. I want her to run it."

"Even now? After the stroke?"

"If she recovers enough, sure. If not, then we'll have to cross that bridge when we come to it. The place should be ready by end of July. I'm hoping to get all the permits and approvals by August, so we can open for business."

Piper asked him a few more questions, trying to get clear in her mind the scope of the project. She thought of Margaret raising three girls all the same age. Almost like raising triplets.

Had she wanted to foster more children? Would the past accusations prevent her from taking charge of the home? She and Cassie were adults now. They could make new statements to clear Margaret's reputation.

She hoped the stroke wasn't permanently incapacitating and that Margaret had her chance to run the home, but she had a long way to go before she'd be up to the task.

Piper heard a car in the driveway and went to see who it was. It was a sheriff's vehicle, pulling to a stop as she reached the screen door. A tall man climbed out, his dark hair gleaming in the sunshine. He looked tanned and fit. A deputy or the sheriff himself, she wasn't sure, but a far cry from Sheriff Halstead and his paunch.

Matt joined her.

"It's Sam. I asked him if he could speed up the search for Fiona. I hoped maybe he'd locate her while you were here."

"Cops are looking for her?"

"As a favor only. They've got contacts unavailable to the rest of us."

Matt went out to meet the man.

Piper stood in the door and watched. She glanced at the patrol car. Adam Saunders sat in the front seat. She turned and went back to the table. She'd had enough of that man to last her forever.

A moment later Matt and the sheriff entered the kitchen.

"Piper, Sam Witt," Matt introduced. "Sam, Piper Morgan."

"Pleasure, ma'am."

"Hello," she said, wondering what his relationship was with Adam Saunders.

The reporter had been in the front seat, so he couldn't be under arrest. Too bad.

Sam put his hat on the table and pulled out a chair. Matt placed a full glass of iced tea in front of Sam a moment later.

"Guess you heard I'm searching for Fiona Hunter," Sam said to Piper after taking a swallow of the tea.

She nodded.

"Got any ideas where she might be?"

"I don't even know where she was sent when we

were split up."

"She went to Meridian," Sam told her. "Seems strange all three of you were sent so far apart, especially after being raised together most of your lives."

"Seems strange we were sent anywhere," Piper returned. "Fiona blamed Margaret initially, but she said she told the truth later and no one would believe her."

"Who did beat her?" Sam asked.

"I don't know. She never told us, but she was really angry with Margaret. The next day Social Services came in and we were shipped out. I never knew what happened to either of the others until Cassie called me a few weeks ago."

"Doesn't the official report say?" Matt asked, straddling a chair and studying Sam.

The sheriff shook his head.

"The entire file is skimpy. Poor practices seemed to have been the norm with my predecessor. The notes only say Fiona's accusations grew more outrageous the more she talked."

"Did anyone contact her foster family in Meridian?" Piper asked.

Sam nodded. "Seems Fiona ran away within two months. They thought she'd tried to return to Bradford, but there isn't anything in the records I could find to show that."

"Margaret said she didn't," Matt said.

He looked at Piper.

"We talked about you girls a bit before she had her stroke. I didn't know she'd hired a detective to find you, but I knew she regretted the way things had turned out. And she wanted to see all three of you again."

"Any special place Fiona talked about, where she might have gone?" Sam asked Piper.

"We all talked about leaving Bradford when we were younger. But New Orleans was our mecca in those days. Could she have gone there?"

Sam shrugged. "Maybe. But if she did, she changed her name or married or something. There are no records for a Fiona Hunter in New Orleans that come close to Fiona's description or age. Or anywhere in Mississippi or Louisiana for that matter."

"So where does that leave us?" Piper asked.

"Guess we'll keep trying."

Sam finished his drink then rose.

"Thanks for the tea, it hit the spot."

"Sorry Adam didn't want any," Matt said.

"I need to get him home. He gave that talk today, and then did rounds with me. I think he's tired, though he'd never admit it."

"From a talk?" Piper asked.

"He was injured pretty badly in a skirmish recently. He's still recovering, so he tires easily."

That explained the cast and cane. She could relate to getting tired easily. Her own recovery from this bug was taking longer than she'd expected.

The sound of tires crunching on the shell driveway

could be heard. Matt went out the back door.

"See you around," Sam said to Piper as he prepared to leave.

"I hope you can find Fiona before I have to return to Paris."

"I don't hold out a lot of hope," he said, "but we'll keep looking."

Cassie and Betsy came into the kitchen, laughing. Cassie was holding Matt's hand.

"Sam, I thought that was your car. Stay for dinner. Matt's cooking on the grill, and Dex is coming over. We'll have a party."

"Thanks, but I have company."

"I saw the guy in the car. He's invited, too. The more the merrier. We're having barbecue chicken, ribs and plain steaks. I'm whipping up a terrific salad and Betsy has the most delicious yeast rolls. And there's chocolate torte for dessert."

"I've heard about that dessert from Suzanne Canaday," Sam said with a grin. "I'll ask Adam."

Piper frowned. She didn't feel up to a party of any kind, much less one where that man would be present.

"Piper, be a sweetie and help me," Betsy said, already pulling flour from a cupboard. "I need the oven set at three seventy-five and some muffin tins, please."

As she rose to help, Piper hoped Adam would refuse the dinner invitation.

Unfortunately, her luck wasn't running that way. A couple of moments later he entered the kitchen, leaning heavily on his cane. From the frown on his face, she didn't think he was enthused about staying, but had gone along for his friend's sake.

Sam made the introductions and then gestured to the table.

"Take a seat and put your foot up."

"I'll get you some tea," Matt said, going to the counter and stopping to give Cassie a quick kiss on the way.

For the next few minutes confusion reigned as Matt and Cassie prepared the meat for the grill, Betsy and Piper worked together on the rolls and then carried dishes, silverware and citronella candles outside to the picnic table on the flagstone patio.

Glad to have something to do, Piper was conscious of Adam's dark mood as he sat and watched the others. He didn't contribute to the conversations flying around, and looked as if he wished he were anyplace but here.

Feeling perversely uncomfortable about his isolation, Piper went to sit at the table. She didn't like the man, but felt sorry he was so alone.

"Need anything?" she asked.

"No."

He didn't even look at her.

"I have some pain meds if you need them for your foot," she offered.

"I'm fine."

The bracket of lines on either side of his mouth belied that statement. The man was in major discomfort. But if he wanted to macho it out, let him.

Piper watched as Cassie and Betsy worked together in harmony—as if they'd been doing it for years instead of a few short weeks.

She'd have to call some of her old friends in the morning, see if any were still in town. None of them had been as close as Cassie and Fiona, however.

By the time Betsy's husband, Dex, arrived, the preparations were well underway and the group had moved to the patio. At this time of year, the mosquitoes weren't as bad as later in the summer. Adam leaned heavily on his cane as the men stood around the grill and the women set the table.

"Reminds me of my folks," Betsy said, glancing at the grill. "As long as I can remember, whenever Mom and Dad had friends over, the men all stood together talking about fishing or bowling or something, and the women got together to talk about children."

Piper looked at Cassie. Their childhood had been very different from Betsy's.

"Reminds me of junior high school dances, boys on one side, girls on another," Piper said.

Betsy laughed.

"That, too. But they'll join us when it's time to eat. I can't believe Adam Saunders is recuperating here in Bradford. You'd think he'd be in Manhattan or somewhere more exotic than this town."

"*Monique* is recuperating here, Bradford, Mississippi, is the best place to be," Cassie said dramatically, referring to Piper's professional name, making Betsy and Piper laugh.

True to Betsy's prediction, once the meal was ready, the men joined the women at the table. Matt sat next to Cassie, Dex next to Betsy. Piper was grateful Sam and Adam sat at the opposite end of the table from her. If she grew too tired, she'd slip away to her room. But to her surprise, she enjoyed the lively conversation, which focused on all the changes in Bradford over the past decade.

At one point Matt leaned over to address Adam.

"Sorry I missed your talk today, Sam said it went well."

"Good enough."

He flicked a glance at Piper.

"Or would you disagree?" he challenged.

"The talk was excellent. You brought the entire situation alive for all of us."

There was no denying he was an inspiring speaker. It was his personality that could use some improvement, Piper thought.

"I admit I was surprised to see the mix in the audience," Adam said. "The crowd ranged from old-timers to teenagers. They probably cut classes to attend."

"Probably worth it," Matt said. "What did I miss?"

"Tell us the highlights," Betsy urged. "We couldn't be there, either."

Adam hesitated a minute, then nodded and began to repeat some of the things Piper had heard earlier.

A wave of fatigue hit and she whispered to Cassie, "I'm going inside. Stay and listen—he tells a powerful story."

Cassie nodded, her attention on Adam.

Piper picked up her dish and utensils and headed for the house. She wanted to get to bed before she collapsed. Ten minutes later she was under the covers, lights out. She could hear the soft murmur of voices from the backyard. It had been an interesting dinner, unlike the ones she'd shared with friends in Paris in recent years. No loud music, no fancy clothes, just friends sitting down to eat together.

It had been nice.

"You okay?" Sam asked Adam as they drove away from Bradford Hall.

"Tired, that's all."

"Leg okay?"

"Yeah."

It wasn't, but that wasn't Sam's fault. He'd done too much. Dammit, how much longer before he was back in shape?

"Thanks for giving your talk again. I know Dex and Matt appreciated it. Betsy asked some intelligent questions, I thought."

"Yeah."

Piper had left as soon as he started. Was that because she had already heard it?

"What's the story with Piper?" he asked.

"She and Cassie grew up together. The detective Margaret hired to find the girls located her some months ago. When Cassie contacted her, she came home. She's a model in Paris. Ever hear of her?

Monique's her French name. She apparently is a big hit in Europe."

Figured. With her looks, modeling was right up her alley.

"I don't associate with models," Adam said.

"Far as I can tell, old son, you don't associate much with anyone," Sam said easily.

"Never in one place long enough."

Sam turned into his driveway, his headlights briefly illuminating the house. Adam could count the minutes now until he'd be prone and could take the medication that would ease the pain in his foot. Today had proved how far he was from being ready to return to work.

When they got into the house, Adam said, "Thanks for including me. You have good friends."

"Settle down someplace and you'll make your own. What are you going to do tomorrow?"

Nothing, was the first thing to come to mind. But he wasn't going to get better by letting his muscles atrophy.

"Take a walk, check in with the news bureau. You don't have to entertain me, remember?"

"I remember. Stop by the office and I'll show you what I've done so far searching for Fiona. You might be interested and catch something I've missed."

"What is this? Do I look like a darn missing persons bureau?"

Sam's eyebrows shot up.

"Whoa, where did that come from?"

"Piper asked me earlier if I'd help her find her parents."

"Maybe with your background, we're hoping you'll have suggestions for digging out the facts we want. You have time to devote to the search. As far as I know, Fiona hasn't done anything wrong. Hard to justify spending taxpayers' money on an extensive search."

Sam looked at Adam with curiosity.

"What did you tell Piper?"

"No, of course."

"And my request gets a negative, too?"

"I'll stop by. But if modern police science can't find a person, I doubt I can."

Adam headed on to bed, glad to get off his foot. He lay in the darkness, though, unable to sleep. The ache was only part of the problem.

His wakefulness had to do with his future. Or perhaps lack of future. If his foot didn't heal properly, he'd never go on assignment again.

What would he do then?

Maybe he should give some thought to working on locating this Fiona Hunter. It'd give him something to fill the time until he was in fighting shape again. And keep him from dwelling on what the future might or might not hold.

The next morning Piper walked into town heading to the sheriff's office. She wanted to ask Sam if he could offer any help in her search for her parents.

To her surprise, Adam Saunders was ahead of her, ready to enter the building as she approached. She hesitated, but he turned and saw her and held the door for her to enter.

She walked past him into the dimness of the old building. The tall ceilings held lazily rotating fans. The walls needed to be repainted and the wooden desks were gouged and scarred. Artificial lights cast a yellowish gloom over everything, and the few windows were covered with closed Venetian blinds.

"Here to see Sam?" Adam asked Piper, following her to the counter where an officer sat.

"Yes."

Not that it was any of his business.

"He's in the back. I'm heading that way myself."

Adam gestured toward the rear of the building. He nodded to the man at the desk and held the swinging gate for Piper to enter.

She matched her stride to his halting one as they silently walked down the long hallway. Rounding a corner, they came into an open area with several more desks. Piper was surprised to find Bradford had such a large force. There had to be at least a half-dozen desks all told. The sheriff's department acted as law enforcement for the town and surrounding county. Still, she was surprised there'd be that much crime to deal with.

Adam approached the desk near a partially opened door.

"We're here to see Sam," he told the woman seated at the desk.

She smiled at him, then looked at Piper, her eyes

widening.

"Piper Morgan, as I live and breathe!"

She jumped up and came around thc desk to hug her.

"It's me, Marjorie Tamlin. How are you. Wow, aren't you gorgeous."

Piper felt Adam's gaze, but she avoided looking at him as she hugged Marjorie.

"It's been too long," she said, smiling at her former classmate.

"I'll say. Hold on, I'll tell Sam you two are here. I have a break at eleven-thirty. Have lunch with me and we can catch up. Remember Lulu? She told me she heard you were back. Staying long?"

"Just a few weeks. I came because of Margaret."

"How is she? I heard from Sam she's doing better."

"She is."

Piper didn't care to talk about her foster family around Adam, so she smiled brightly, promising to fill Marjorie in when they met for lunch.

"I'll see if the sheriff is free," Marjorie said, hurrying through the open door.

Piper eyed Adam. "You go first."

For a moment, she thought she saw amusement in his eyes.

"Afraid to say something in front of me? I'm not here to report Bradford's news."

"What I have to say doesn't concern anyone but me."

"You're looking for help locating your parents," he

said.

"Lucky guess. Didn't you suggest I try the sheriff?"

Marjorie came out of Sam's office.

"He's free. Come on in."

Neither Piper nor Adam moved.

"After you," she said.

"You go first," he countered. "I'm here to help look for Fiona, so I expect to be a while."

That caught her by surprise. So he'd help out Cassie and Matt, but not her. Fine, she didn't need his help!

Lifting her chin, she headed into the sheriff's office, aware that Adam Saunders followed right behind her.

Sam glanced at Piper then Adam. "You two working together?" he asked as they entered the office.

"No," Piper said quickly, frowning over her shoulder at Adam.

She looked at Sam and smiled.

"I was hoping to see you alone. But some people don't seem to know when they're barging in."

Adam leaned against the door frame and said nothing.

"What can I do for you?" Sam asked, looking back and forth between the two of them.

"I'm hoping you can help me in a search of my own—for my birth parents."

"Have a seat."

Sam waited until Piper sat down before resuming his seat. He flicked another glance at Adam, who had moved beside one of the file cabinets, leaning against it so he could see Piper better.

"It's personal," she said, glaring at Adam.

"Which means she doesn't want me here," Adam explained.

"If you don't mind, it *is* personal," Piper insisted, wishing she could ignore the man.

Or that Sam would kick him out.

"I'll do what I can, but we don't conduct family searches if no crimes have been committed," Sam said slowly. "What do you have to go on?"

"Just my birth date. It's from a delayed birth certificate—one I got when I first applied for a passport. No parents' names, only unknown."

"The date may not be accurate," Adam murmured.

"What?" Piper swung around. "You think that's not my birth date?"

"If you were abandoned, it's likely no one knew your birth date. They just estimated how old you were and assigned you the closest date."

She blinked. She'd never thought of that. So even her birth date could be a dead end.

"Seems to me a hotshot like you could handle this before lunch," Sam said to Adam.

He looked at Piper.

"You might try Social Services. They have the records of your particular case."

The phone on the desk rang. Sam picked it up. From the one-sided conversation, Piper knew he had to go somewhere—fast. He stood even as he was talking, and reached for his hat on the hatrack behind him.

"Sorry, I have to leave," he said as soon as he hung up. "Adam, take care of Piper, will you? And here's a copy of all I have on Fiona."

He thrust a slim folder at Adam. In a second he was gone.

Piper could hear him give rapid instructions to Marjorie as he left. A moment later there was only silence.

Adam tossed the folder on the desk. The slap it made startled Piper. Rising, she turned to the door.

"All right, I'll see what I can do to get you started," he said.

It was clear the news about her birth date had hit her hard.

She studied him for a moment. Adam could tell she didn't like what she saw. He'd been acting like a jerk and wouldn't blame her if she wanted nothing to do with him. But his skills made him a good bet for finding information about her past. And maybe she'd remember something about Fiona that he could check out for Sam.

"Don't do me any favors."

"Hey, I'm doing it for Sam."

She was quiet a moment, then rose.

"Thank you," Piper said primly.

He knew she didn't want to accept his offer. She must want to find her parents badly to put aside her animosity and agree to his help.

"Let's get a cup of coffee, start over and see where we begin the great parent search," he said, trying to lighten the mood. He grabbed the folder and headed for the door.

A few moments later they were seated in a quiet corner of Ruby's Café, Fiona's folder in front of Adam. Coffee had been ordered. He glanced around the room.

"People are staring," Piper said, her eyes on the folder.

"You're a beautiful woman. They probably like looking at you."

He would, if he didn't feel she was the type to trade on her looks. There was a certain something about her—an air of vulnerability—that had him looking despite his efforts not to.

When the coffee arrived, Adam pulled out a small notebook and tiny pencil. He never went anywhere without it.

"Do we start with Fiona?" she asked, looking at the notebook.

"No, I'll check out the folder later. See what Sam's done. Between his searches and the detective Margaret hired, I bet they've covered all bases. You and Cassie can help by reminiscing to see if you can remember anywhere Fiona really wanted to see. Sometimes when life gets too hard, people will bolt for a special place— even if they've never been there—in hopes it'll prove to be the one place on earth that's right for them."

"New Orleans was the only place we ever talked about. We couldn't wait to get there when we were teenagers."

"Yet neither you nor Cassie settled there after leaving school."

"True. Do you think there's a chance Fiona did?"

"Sam said he checked the neighboring states. Dead end."

Piper sipped her coffee, studying Adam.

"Tell me all the facts you know about yourself," he said.

"Margaret told me I was abandoned and she stepped in to act as foster mother. I was born twenty-seven years ago on May seventeenth. At least I always thought I was, until you put that doubt in my head."

"You have a birth certificate, you said."

She nodded. "A delayed registration they called it. I can dig it up if you need to see it. It doesn't give much information beyond my date of birth. No parents listed."

"Born where?"

"The certificate says Bradford."

He tossed his pencil down.

"Nope. If you were born here in town, we'd be able to locate your parents in no time. Even if the day is wrong, the month has to be close. We could check all live births from April through June of that year and see who's unaccounted for. Are you sure you were born here?"

"No. I told you it was a delayed birth certificate. Filled out when I was nineteen. Social Services filed it when I needed one for a passport."

"First stop, then, Social Services."

"I tried to get them to help me when I was a teenager," she said. She took another sip of her coffee. "Dead end."

For a moment he saw that vulnerability again. It bothered him, since it didn't fit the role he'd assigned her. Maybe he needed to do some more digging around to find out exactly who Piper Morgan was.

"First of all, I doubt they'd talk to a minor."

"They acted like they never gave out any information. I was totally stonewalled."

"I have a different technique," he said smugly.

"I can hardly wait to see the mighty reporter in action."

She fiddled with her cup, turning it around on the saucer.

"How long are you staying in Bradford?"

He shrugged. "Depends on how fast my foot heals."

"What happened?"

"Land mine."

"Ouch. You're lucky it wasn't blown off."

He saw the sympathy in her expression and frowned. He didn't want pity.

"I didn't step on it, I was just a bystander. But it did enough damage."

"You'll be fine again, right?"

"Yeah, as soon as it heals."

He hoped to God that was true.

4

"What are the chances the people we'll talk to at Social Services will just give me my file?" Piper asked. "They refused before. Maybe if Margaret had pushed, they might have done more, but she wasn't willing to."

He was quiet for a moment. Then he asked her about the decision to remove the girls from Margaret's care. She explained the matter had been handled quickly, with no input from the three of them. One day they were living with Margaret, the next they were in different homes.

"Odd," he said.

"Why?"

"You girls had been together for years, raised as sisters essentially. I'd think the court would initially try to place you together. Or if not, at least make sure you were able to maintain contact. It was cruel to make you sever all ties. Sam said the investigation was handled poorly. Now I'm wondering if there was more involved."

"Like a conspiracy?" She half smiled. "I doubt it. We were three foster kids. There aren't a lot of foster families in Bradford, or there weren't back then, and not many people are willing to take on three teenagers. Probably the easiest thing to do was send us to the first homes available, which just happened to be in different towns."

"Maybe. Maybe not. But why not tell you where the other girls were sent? Cassie said you couldn't contact each other. There was nothing in the file about that, according to Sam. Maybe Social Services will give us some information."

"If there was some hidden agenda, do you think they'll tell us at this late date?"

"Good point."

He was quiet for a moment. Piper could almost see his mind turning over all possibilities.

"Anyone there know you personally?" he asked.

"I haven't had any contact since my case was transferred to Adamson county years ago. Maybe they have new staff."

"Unlikely in this town. Seems to me the only chance for advancement comes when someone dies."

"So maybe Mrs. Savalak died. She looked a hundred and three when she was my caseworker. Even older than Margaret."

"What do you mean?"

Piper explained that she and the others had thought Margaret's ideas old-fashioned and considered her ancient.

"In retrospect, I think she just had high standards and tried to instill them in all of us," she said slowly.

"Would Margaret be any help to us?"

"I doubt it. If she could talk, she might tell us how she came to get me, but unless you can word all your questions to take yes or no answers, we're out of luck. Besides, I tried to find out more when I was a child and she wasn't any help then."

"Asking yes/no questions is easy enough to do. But let's see what else we can find out first. You finished?"

"Just about."

She drained her coffee cup.

"What about Fiona?"

"I'll see if there's anything else I can come up with, but if people don't want to be found, they usually aren't."

"Why wouldn't she want to be found? I'll bet she'd like to know Cassie and I are looking for her."

"If she ran away, she might have thought the law was after her. Which it should have been. From what Sam said, that was something else that wasn't handled according to policy. If she changed her name to avoid detection, she could still be living under that name. Did she have any other family?"

Piper shook her head.

"Her mother died when we were all about thirteen. Fiona's father was in prison. Still is for all I know. Or maybe he died, but she sure wouldn't have gone to him."

"Why not? What was he in prison for?"

"Trying to kill her mother."

Adam whistled. "Okay, let's go check out Social Services."

As they were ushered into the office of the director of Social Services a short time later, Piper held back, letting Adam run the interview. She'd smiled when he'd flashed his reporter's card at the receptionist and asked for an appointment. The woman had recognized him immediately. Apparently lots of people watched CNN.

"Adam Saunders, I'm Roberta Nelson," the director greeted him when they entered her utilitarian office.

"Thank you for seeing us without a prior appointment, Ms. Nelson," he said smoothly, shaking hands and introducing Piper.

"How do you do?" she said to Piper, then gestured to the visitor chairs. "Please, sit down, both of you. I can't imagine what I can do for you. I've seen you so many times reporting from so many hot spots, Mr. Saunders. You will be going back, won't you?" She eyed Adam's cast and cane.

Roberta Nelson was an older woman with graying brown hair. Her dress was more functional than stylish, and a pair of glasses rested on the desk in front of her.

"That's still up in the air," he replied as the three of them were seated. "Until then, I'm keeping my hand in. I'm doing a proposal for a story idea to my boss about foster care, how it works, and the benefits it affords children who would otherwise have to go to an orphanage. I want to research what happens to some of these children. How many make a success of their lives, how many end up in trouble."

Piper looked at him. What a cover. The man was good.

"Oh?"

Roberta was caught, Piper could tell.

"I'm staying with Sam Witt, Sheriff Witt. I thought I'd get started right here in Bradford. There are several local success stories that piqued my interest. Combined with those from other locales, such as New Orleans, Atlanta, even New York, we can present a broad canvas that will capture America's attention and give credit to hardworking foster parents who open their doors to homeless children."

"Why, I think that's a wonderful idea," the director enthused. "We only have a few qualified families here. But then, we don't have a lot of homeless children, either."

"Actually, Piper Morgan is a foster child who was placed here in Bradford. She's now a successful model in France. She's agreed to allow me to start my interviews with her while she's here visiting."

"I see." Roberta looked at Piper and smiled. "You're certainly beautiful enough to be a model. In Paris?"

"I've lived there for seven years. But Bradford will always be home."

She hoped her tone was the one Adam was looking for. Would the woman really buy his story?

"How can I help you?" Roberta asked.

"We'd like to discuss the basics of how the foster-care system works," Adam explained. "How you place children, maybe look at Piper's history as a case study. Of course, once we're further along and know if this will make it to the network, we'd ask if you were willing to be taped for broadcast on national television. The film crew would do its best not to disrupt your daily routine," Adam assured her.

"National television. Oh, my."

Roberta Nelson seemed to have stars in her eyes.

"The whole concept is still in the planning stages, right now," Adam added.

"Of course. I'm happy to help however I can."

Adam settled back and pulled out his notebook. "I thought I'd ask a few questions to get the ball rolling, jot some notes, if that's okay with you?"

The director nodded eagerly.

"Then we'll formulate how we wish to proceed. And maybe you can go over Piper's file with us, to show us an actual example of how the system works."

"Oh, I don't know about that. We don't make that information public."

She looked apologetically at Piper.

"I understand," Piper said. "But if I'm here to give my permission, wouldn't that make a difference?"

"For the broadcast, we'll blank out any personal details," Adam added.

"I've seen how that works," Roberta told him. "Everything gets fuzzy inside a certain area."

"Exactly," Adam agreed. "Now, can we begin with a brief history of your own background and how you got started in Social Services?"

Piper listened as Adam asked question after question, taking down notes, encouraging Roberta to talk. The woman was flattered by the attention of a reporter of Adam's stature and ended up giving all the information he requested, even sending for Piper's file.

Piper almost held her breath when a woman brought in the folder and handed it to Roberta. Was the director truly going to show the file to them?

Adam glanced at Piper with a warning in his eyes. She looked back at the director. Didn't he know models were in large part actresses? She had to look happy, carefree and beautiful whether it was a hundred degrees in the shade or below freezing when she was modeling a bikini. She had to appear genuinely happy when she had just had a fight with the photographer or was coming down with a cold. Her features wouldn't give anything away—no matter how elated she was to have the folder so tantalizingly close.

Roberta Nelson opened the file and lifted the top pages to get to the earliest one in the stack clipped to the back.

"We don't use these forms anymore," she murmured. "Actually, in the past eight or nine years, we've put most of our records on computers."

She smiled at Adam and Piper.

"This case, of course, started long before we became automated. And it looks as if Piper transferred out of our care about a dozen years ago." She skimmed the early pages. "Oh dear, this is odd."

Adam reached out and caught Piper's arm, squeezing lightly in warning, then released it.

"What is?" he asked.

"Piper came to us from another state. That is most unusual."

"Another state?" Piper said involuntarily.

"Ah, a less routine case than we were expecting," Adam said smoothly.

Piper was grateful he seemed to keep his wits about him. In contrast, she was floored by the statement. She had always thought she'd been born in Bradford.

"Florida—Orlando specifically. Margaret Nunes took her on as a foster child, and then applied for the license for foster care, which registered her in our system. That's highly irregular."

The woman read a little further, then looked up, smiling apologetically.

"I'm sorry, I got caught up in the history. I'm not sure this one is the best to showcase our procedures. It seems to be completely out of the ordinary."

She continued to skim the records.

"Oh, dear, it seems the child was removed from our jurisdiction and placed elsewhere, but there is no reason given."

She glanced up again.

"I'm afraid this is nothing like our usual way of handling things."

"How about we use it and one of your more routine cases to show how flexible the agency can be?" Adam suggested quickly. "Our angle could be that a small town's Social Services Agency has to be able to deal with a wide variety of situations."

"It does put us on par with Adamson, doesn't it?" Roberta said proudly. "Let me see who else we can showcase. I would need to get permission, of course, from the person in question."

"Of course. We'll start with Piper."

Half an hour later, Piper and Adam walked out of the building into the heat. She checked her watch.

"I have to go. I'm meeting Marjorie for lunch and I'll be late if I don't hurry," Piper said. "You were impressive. I couldn't have spun a tale like that. I need to study your technique."

He shrugged. "Whatever works, use it."

"I'm going to see Margaret later. Maybe she can give me some information. I can't believe I was born in Florida. Margaret knew. Why didn't she tell me?"

"See what she says and call me when you get home."

He wrote it on a notebook page, tore out the sheet and handed it to her. "Here's my number."

Piper hurried down the street, not wanting to examine how she felt. Margaret had told her over and over when she was growing up to leave well enough alone. She'd never listened. That hadn't changed—she was still searching.

Intellectually she knew she ran the risk of finding out her parents were as bad as Fiona's. But a small flicker of hope had her wishing they'd be wonderful people caught up in circumstances that had forced them to make hard decisions.

Today, she'd had her foundations shaken. First with Adam's suggestion that her birth date might not be exact, and now with the discovery she was originally from Florida, not Bradford. How could Bradford be listed on her birth certificate if she'd been born elsewhere? It had to mean Margaret lied. But why?

How and why had Margaret gone to Florida to get a foster child twenty-seven years ago? Margaret had the answers—if she'd only talk.

Marjorie was standing outside the police station. She smiled when she saw Piper and hurried to meet her.

"I thought you'd stood me up. Though if it were for that hunk you were with, I could understand."

"That's purely business."

Was Adam a hunk, Piper wondered. She was so used to great-looking guys in photo shoots that she never considered looks that important when she met someone new. Usually a man who was too handsome knew it. She dealt with enough self-centered males in her line of work. She wasn't looking for any in her personal life.

"I'd like that kind of business," Marjorie joked. "Want to eat at the café or are you up for a drive to the barbecue place?"

"Let's have barbecue. I don't get much of that in France."

"Too busy eating snails, I bet."

Marjorie pointed to a blue sedan.

"That's my car over there."

Lunch proved to be exactly what Piper needed to get her mind off the startling discoveries of the morning. Marjorie knew where everyone from their high school class had ended up and gave Piper a brief sketch of what each was doing. Only a few had remained in Bradford, mostly girls who had married local boys.

"What about you?" Piper asked. "I thought you'd be married by now."

"I *was* married—to Walter Hutchins. We divorced eighteen months later. He never grew up."

"I know how that goes. My first husband was the same."

"First?"

"I've been married twice," Piper said. "Once to a good ol'boy who never grew up. The second time to the world's greatest playboy. Why I thought he'd settle down with me, I'll never know. So now it's been there, done that, no more."

"Hey, I hear third time's the charm," Marjorie said.

"Or not. I'm not taking that risk again. I have a career I love, money in the bank and friends to do things with. I don't need a man."

"Maybe you don't need one, but they sure are fun to snuggle up with on a rainy afternoon," Marjorie teased.

"Oh, I might snuggle with one, but no more marriage."

For a split second an image of Adam flashed in her mind. Somehow she couldn't envision him snuggling with anyone. Hot and heavy sex, yes...

Sudden heat flushed her cheeks.

"I can't believe you and Cassie came back when Margaret got sick," Marjorie said, not noticing. "So the old stories aren't true?"

"That she was abusive? Not at all."

"You used to complain about her all the time."

"So did a lot of other teenagers about their parents. I still think she was too strict, but that was her way. She never hit any of us. I think she got a raw deal. And maybe while I'm here I'll find out who attacked Fiona."

"Fiona was bigger than Margaret by the time you girls left. I don't think she'd have stood for such treatment."

"Someone else beat her. I always thought it was that boy she dated a couple of times then dumped—Jack Denton. Remember him?"

"Sure do. He was a piece of work. Probably in the slammer somewhere by now. Sam's doing what he can to locate Fiona, you know."

"So I heard."

Piper looked at her friend.

"Don't you think it odd they didn't try to find other homes for us here? We only had another year of school before graduation. I bet I could have stayed with a family in town even if they weren't licensed foster-care people. Cassie could have moved in with Betsy's family."

"I heard Sam mumble something about slipshod work after he studied the files when Cassie first came back. It does seem odd, but it happened so long ago. Who knows? And now Sheriff Halstead is dead and gone, so he can't talk."

Piper had two quests—find her parents and clear Margaret's name. How likely was it she'd succeed with either?

"I can't believe Cassie started a catering service here," Marjorie said. "My aunt Caroline is using her for a party she's giving my uncle for his sixtieth birthday."

"After all our talk when we were kids, I'm surprised she came back here in Bradford," Piper mused. "All we talked about was escaping the town and making it in the big city. She did well in Boston, but this is home."

"Matt has something to do with her staying, I suspect," Marjorie said. "And you know, Bradford's not a bad place to call home."

Piper nodded, but she wondered if she would ever know the feeling of being home herself.

When it was time for Marjorie to return to work, she

dropped Piper at the convalescent hospital. Walking up to Margaret's room, Piper found the older woman asleep. She had two choices—wait until she awoke or go home and return later.

Feeling listless herself, she elected to sit in the waiting room. She idly leafed through some old magazines. Resting her head against the back of the chair, she closed her eyes, dozing a little. When she opened them, she looked around, restless.

Finding a bank of phones, she called Adam.

"Saunders."

"Did you find out anything?"

"No. I need a bit more information to get started. Any luck with Margaret?"

"She's sleeping. Or she was when I got here. I've been waiting awhile. I'll check on her again when we're through. Can we search birth certificates around my birth date? The date would have to be close, right?"

"I checked into that. A person can request his or her own certificate, giving the birth date. But if it's the wrong date, I'm not sure they'll conduct a search. Plus, you don't know what name you were registered under. What if Margaret called you Piper but your birth mother registered you as Susan?"

"It's worth a shot, isn't it?" she persisted.

"It's worth a shot."

"Maybe Margaret kept a file on me, or something," Piper said, thinking Cassie would have found it if there'd been one. Hadn't she said she'd gone through all Margaret's papers looking for the loan information a few weeks ago?

"How about anything new on Fiona?" Piper asked.

"I glanced through the file when I got back. Sam was right. The reports are sketchy and incomplete. There's no mention of who her assailant was, nor any followup for prosecution. It's as if Sheriff Halstead considered the entire situation closed once you girls left town."

"It's so unfair. Margaret never abused anyone. I want to do something so the whole town knows it."

"It's water under the bridge. Nobody will care now."

"I do. She needs to have her name totally cleared. We need to do something."

"Like what?"

"Can you do an exposé about the entire incident?"

Adam didn't respond at first.

"I can look into it."

"I know it's not the same as being in some war zone, but it's important to us. I would appreciate your help."

Piper hated asking him, and feared another rejection. But he was her best bet for getting more information. Look how much he'd gleaned this morning in the search for her parents.

"Stop by on your way back from the hospital and we'll discuss it," he said.

"Where does Sam live?"

Adam gave her directions. Piper hung up and went back to Margaret's floor.

The older woman was awake, watching television.

"Hi, Margaret," Piper said, glad to see she looked better, more alert.

Maybe she would pull through with no lingering handicap. Piper hoped so.

Margaret smiled lopsidedly and gave a slight nod. She lifted her hand and Piper took it as she sat in the chair next to the bed.

The second bed in the room was empty.

"Did your roommate go home?" Piper asked.

Margaret nodded once and squeezed her hand slightly.

"Good news or bad? Oops, let me rephrase that. Is it good to have the room to yourself?"

Margaret nodded and squeezed.

"Cassie will be by this evening. I'll come back with her then, but I wanted to talk to you alone."

Piper spoke slowly. She had to make sure her questions could be answered by yes or no. "Remember how I always wanted to know who my folks were?"

Margaret nodded once.

Piper wasn't sure, but it seemed the older woman's expression changed slightly.

"I never found out anything. I tried again when I was married to Billy Bob, but couldn't get any information. I've even listed myself on some adoption boards on the Internet, hoping my birth mother will see one of them and reply."

Margaret's attention was fixed on Piper.

"I may have a chance now. The sheriff has a friend

visiting who's a reporter. He has some ideas and is willing to help me research my past."

Margaret shook her head, squeezing Piper's hand harder than she ever had before, twice.

"Maybe nothing will pan out. But we've had some luck. We went to Social Services and I found out I'm from Florida, not Mississippi. You knew that. Mrs. Nelson at Social Services said I was in your care before I was registered with them."

Margaret shook her head, squeezing Piper's hand over and over.

"It's okay. Really. I know you think I'll find out I had parents like Fiona or worse. But it's something I need to know. Can you tell me anything at all? Did you ever hear anything about my parents?"

Margaret rolled her head back and forth on the pillow, her hand slipping from Piper's.

A nurse stepped in.

"What's going on here? Miss Margaret, you need to calm down."

She looked at Piper. "What happened?"

"She seems to object to a project I've started," Piper said slowly, standing.

She hadn't meant to upset Margaret. And the older woman was definitely worked up. Piper moved so the nurse could get next to the bed.

"It's okay, Margaret," Piper soothed. "Forget about it. I don't want you getting agitated. It's all right."

The nurse took Margaret's wrist to check her pulse, then positioned the arm cuff to take her blood pressure.

"You need to calm down, Miss Margaret. I'm sure whatever it is will be fine. But not if you get yourself upset."

Margaret tried to talk, but her speech was unintelligible. Her gaze never left Piper's and she spoke again. The tone sounded urgent, but Piper couldn't understand a word.

"Calm down. I won't talk about it again."

Piper silently vowed to keep her search private and not let Margaret get wind of it.

Her foster mother's reaction had confirmed something was wrong, which strengthened Piper's resolve. Maybe with Adam Saunders's help, she'd be able to unravel the mystery of her birth.

"Miss Margaret, if you don't calm down, you won't be allowed visitors," the nurse said firmly.

Margaret lay still, her eyes still locked with Piper's. Her breathing was rapid, and her skin had paled slightly.

Piper sat again and tried to smile.

"I'm sorry that upset you. Don't worry, I won't be doing anything you don't want. I had lunch with Marjorie Tamlin, remember her? She told me all about the kids I went to high school with."

For the rest of her visit, Piper regaled Margaret with some of the stories Marjorie had told her.

She left after a half hour. Walking along the tree-lined streets toward Sam Witt's house, she considered Margaret's reaction when she'd announced she was searching for her parents' identity. Strangest thing she'd ever seen. Was it simply frustration because she couldn't talk?

Maybe Margaret could clear up everything with a few words? Or was her reaction caused by something else? Piper knew Margaret hadn't liked her delving into the past. There had to be some way she could communicate with Margaret other than yes and no questions.

Sam's house was on a quiet street, third in from the corner. As she walked up to the shallow steps leading to the porch, she noticed the place was in perfect condition, recently painted.

Adam answered the door a moment after she knocked.

"Come on in. I've commandeered Sam's home office."

He limped back down a wide hallway, his cane thudding on the hardwood floor.

Taking only a moment to glimpse the masculine decor of the living room, Piper hurried after him.

"Is Sam married?" she asked when she entered the office.

"No, why?"

"I just wondered. Wow, for a home office, this is fantastic. Looks like he has a state-of-the art setup."

There were several computers, a fax machine and scanner.

"He works from home sometimes. What do you want to discuss first—Fiona or you?"

"Me."

"Figures," he said.

"Hey, this is something I've wanted to do for years."

"A birth certificate is not possible without more information," Adam informed her, sitting behind Sam's desk. "The only one you can get is the one you already have. I double-checked."

"How about hospitals?" Piper asked, sinking into the chair across from the desk.

"Do you mean in Orlando?"

She nodded. "I guess so. All these years I thought I was born in Mississippi."

"We need more to go on. What did Margaret tell you?"

"Nothing. In fact, she almost had another stroke when I talked about looking for my birth parents. She's definitely opposed to my search. What I can't figure out is why? I know they could be as bad as Bonnie and Clyde. I think I'm ready to deal with that. But chances are they were just ordinary people whose circumstances wouldn't allow them to keep a kid. Maybe they thought they were doing me a favor."

"Or your mother was some fourteen-year-old— only a kid herself," Adam suggested. "Do you think Margaret knows the story?"

Piper shook her head.

"I don't know. She never gave any indication she did when I was growing up. But then, she also didn't tell me she'd brought me here from Florida. Why would she lie on my delayed birth certificate?"

She leaned back in the chair, brooding.

"Sounds like there's something she doesn't want you to know," Adam observed.

"Like?"

"I haven't a clue."

"I wish we could have seen the information in my file. Do you think there's more that Mrs. Nelson didn't tell us?"

"Probably not. She seemed totally up-front."

"Unlike us."

"Hey, there might be a story here and that's all I told her."

"Right. I'm sure she can already see herself on prime time. Besides, she probably thought I already knew most of what was in the file. Maybe Margaret has paperwork on me. Surely she had to sign something when she first got me—or report to someone. I think Cassie pretty much went through her things, though, when she was looking for loan information. She didn't mention any personal files on any of us."

"Did you ask specifically?"

"No."

"Let's try that avenue. Also, look for any photos you don't recognize, or keepsakes Margaret never told you about. Maybe your mother left a locket with you when she turned you over to the authorities," Adam suggested.

"Not that I know of. Cassie found a photo album from when we were little. I think I was about three.

Maybe there's an earlier one when I was a baby. Margaret had me from infancy. Cassie arrived when she was four, and Fiona was in kindergarten, I think, when she first came."

"First came?"

"Her mother was in and out of drug rehab. When she was in, Fiona was with us. When she was out, and petitioned the courts, Fiona went back home."

"Tough life for a kid," Adam said.

"We all had it tough. I hope she's all right."

"You and Cassie have to accept we may never find her."

"I know. Like we may never find out who my parents were."

"It's early to give up," he said.

She looked at him.

"I'm not giving up. And it's not so early. I've been trying off and on since I was about ten and we had a project at school on finding out about our family."

"Living in France has to make searching more difficult."

"True. But I'd say being married slowed me down even more. Husbands take up a lot of time and energy."

"You're married?"

Adam didn't know why he should be surprised. She was a beautiful woman. Or maybe that's what surprised him—that she'd settled into something as ordinary as marriage.

"Not now. I married Billy Bob when I was eighteen. It didn't last long—less than a year."

"Then you went to France?" he asked, curious about her background.

"No, then I went to Manhattan. I love New York. I had the best time there."

She smiled the first genuine smile he thought he'd seen on her. Adam caught his breath. She was really extraordinarily lovely.

"*Then* you went to Paris," he tried to clarify.

"Right. Married again, to a dashing Frenchman who swept me off my feet." Her tone was sardonic.

He studied her, noting the subtle differences in her expression. She looked older suddenly, harder. Obviously neither marriage had been made in heaven.

"Still married?"

He knew so little about her. Before he met her, he hadn't paid much attention to the comments Matt had made about the girls from Bradford Hall. Now he wished he had.

"Nope, he left me for a younger version. Actually, that was two women ago. Jean-Paul is nothing if not fickle. Not that this has anything to do with my parents."

"No," Adam said. "Just curious."

"You're not married, are you?" she asked.

He shook his head.

"Not with your job."

Not with his job. And not that he'd found anyone he wanted to spend his life with. His mother and father had been married for more than thirty-five years. How many days was that, roughly? Twelve thousand and some? Twelve thousand breakfasts together, probably as many dinners.

He couldn't imagine wanting to spend so much time with one person. Where was the thrill of new experiences? Where was the adventure when you knew a person so well you could almost predict what they'd say?

"Earth to Adam," Piper said.

"What?"

He'd let his mind wander. Was he losing his focus in this one-horse town?

"I asked if you wanted to come to the house for dinner and talk to Cassie with me. Maybe she'll have suggestions about where to look. Or she might have come across something and didn't realize it was important."

"Will Matt be there?" he asked. If so, maybe he could get a little more information about Piper.

"Probably, they seemed joined at the hip. Or the lips."

Adam smiled at her tone. It must be hard hanging around lovers. Sam had filled him in a bit on Cassie and Matt's story.

When Piper left, he called Sam to tell him about dinner.

"Works for me," Sam said. "I have something to do tonight. So you don't have to entertain yourself."

"Thanks, Mother."

The sheriff laughed.

"Hey, if this means finding out the answer to the deep dark secret of what happened at Bradford Hall, then I'm all for it. That investigation was botched."

"You didn't give me much to go on," Adam complained.

"I copied everything in Fiona's file. I'll ask Marjorie to check around in case paperwork got cross-filed. But I'm thinking Sheriff Halstead either kept a lot of stuff in his head or never got to first base with that investigation."

"Seems odd Margaret Nunes didn't do more at the time to clear her name," Adam said. "If she hadn't done the deed."

"Oh, I don't believe she did it. Go visit the woman. She's sick now, but she was never a tall, strapping woman. Piper's tall, Cassie's tall, and I understand Fiona was, as well, and athletic to boot. Unless Margaret used a tire iron or baseball bat, she couldn't have hurt Fiona as badly as the photos show. Margaret's hands checked out clean, by the way."

"No abrasions," Adam guessed.

"None that were substantiated in the report."

"So why did they proceed? Why split up the girls and send them so far away?"

"Are you thinking there was more to the story than we know?" Sam asked, his voice taking on an intensity Adam hadn't expected.

"What do you think?"

"Absolutely. I've already started nosing around folks here in town. Don't want to spook anyone, but it's easy enough to segue into the subject when talking about Margaret's stroke. Any luck on Piper's birth parents?"

"Dead end so far. But I've got a couple more ideas."

"Nice of you to bring CNN here so Bradford gets national coverage," Sam drawled.

"What are you talking about?"

"Your interview with Roberta Nelson. It's all over town. I think she sees herself as the next TV news darling."

Adam laughed.

"It's still up in the air."

"Yeah, right. Let me know when you're ready to broadcast."

Adam gave a friendly suggestion to his friend and hung up. His foot ached a little, but not with the knife-edge sharpness he was used to. Maybe it was finally healing.

It was an hour later when he called the office in Atlanta. He wanted to keep his name out there. No forgetting Adam Saunders. While he was at it, he'd pick his boss's brain for suggestions on how to find a person who didn't want to be found.

5

Piper waited until Matt, Cassie and Adam were seated around the dinner table before telling them about Margaret's reaction to her visit that afternoon.

"Wow, what a surprise that must have been," Cassie said. "And scary. Why does she have such a strong reaction, do you suppose?"

"It's pretty clear she doesn't want me to search for my parents. Once I said I wouldn't do anything she didn't want me to, she calmed down. But you should have seen her—I was really worried. I thought she might have another stroke right there."

"So you aren't going to keep looking?" Matt asked.

"Not exactly," Piper hedged. "Actually, Adam is going to look. I'm going to be his assistant."

Matt and Cassie looked at Adam.

"I said I'll do what I can as long as I'm here—which isn't going to be long," he warned.

Piper wasn't buying it.

"A hotshot reporter like you can surely find out what I need before you leave. As well as find Fiona."

"Find Fiona?" Cassie asked.

"Sam's enlisted Adam's help in searching for

Fiona," Piper explained.

"More to keep me occupied and out of his hair than anything," Adam muttered.

"And I want to do something to show the world Margaret wasn't guilty," Piper added.

Matt raised his eyebrows. "Like what?"

"I don't know. I'm open for suggestions. How about a fund-raiser for her medical bills. If two of her former foster children are sponsoring it, wouldn't everyone know we care about her. We wouldn't come back here if she'd really been abusive."

"She's lived here all her life," Matt reminded her. "People should have known she didn't do it. I think the town's forgotten that incident. It never came up with the City Council when we petitioned for approvals."

"Which is odd, don't you think? Child abuse is a serious allegation," Adam said.

Piper nodded.

"If we never expose what really happened to Fiona, there'll always be lingering doubts. I say we find out what really happened and tell the world."

Cassie nodded. "I think we all got a raw deal."

"You're right," agreed Adam. "According to the files Sam dug up, the case was basically dropped once you girls were no longer in the county. Maybe more was going on than you suspected."

"Meaning?" Piper asked.

He shrugged.

"Corruption in the sheriff's office? Or maybe Halstead had more evidence pointing to Margaret and decided to conceal it to protect one of the town's own. You three weren't around to protest."

"Margaret was strict, but she was never abusive." Piper was adamant about that. "I want everyone to acknowledge it."

"A fund-raiser is a good idea, no matter what," Cassie suggested. "Margaret's medical expenses, even with Medicare, must be exorbitant."

"We need something that will draw lots of people," Piper said. "Make a big splash."

"Mention that a top French model and world-famous reporter will be there, and you'll draw a crowd," Matt said.

"I won't be here—" Adam started to say, but was drowned out by Piper's shout of joy.

"Terrific idea. I wonder if I could get some other models to come and put on a fashion show? I know a couple who live here in the States. Adam can talk about his most dangerous assignments...maybe bring in another celebrity. Cassie, you can cook...showcase all your fancy desserts. We could even have an auction."

Cassie laughed. "An auction?"

"Sure. We'll auction off your desserts like an old-fashioned box lunch. There are endless ideas."

"I like the box-lunch idea. Betsy and I could make the lunches and auction them off. It'd be great advertising for us."

"I'll call Enrique in the morning."

"Enrique?"

"He's my agent. He'll know who to ask for favors

and who owes us one. It'll be fabulous. Who can you bring, Adam?"

He hesitated. "Someone from New Orleans if I'm lucky. But I'm not sure I'll be here—"

Piper wasn't listening.

"Get someone famous so they'll attract a big crowd. Matt, what are you contributing?"

"I'll build the booth or auction block or runway. You name it."

"Does the town still have their Fourth of July celebration and fair?" Cassie asked.

He nodded.

"Let's do it in conjunction with that," Cassie suggested. "Everyone comes from miles around, so we'd be assured a big turnout."

"Great idea. That gives us a little over a month to get everything together and publicize the event. Now, how do we make sure everyone knows Margaret was innocent. We need proof by then."

Piper looked at Adam.

"No guarantees. Sam hasn't found anything new and he's been looking into the case longer than I have. But after dinner, I'd like to talk about what you two can remember about the night you were separated. Sometimes important details pop out simply through reminiscing."

"Good idea," Piper said. "I still think Jack Denton was the one who beat up Fiona. If we can prove that, then Margaret's name will be cleared."

"Who's Jack Denton?" Adam asked.

Matt quickly filled him in on the town's bad boy and his former relationship with Fiona.

"And if we can't prove it was him?" Cassie asked.

"Then we'll have to attack it from a different angle." Piper spoke directly to her friend. "I think we have enough credibility to be listened to this time. We're not sixteen and bewildered. We'll tell everyone Margaret was the best mother we could have had, and blame the sheriff's department for not investigating further."

"Works for me," Cassie murmured.

After dinner, Cassie and Piper talked about their last few weeks in Bradford twelve years ago. They had different takes on the same situations, from Margaret's relationship with the town banker to the wild bunch Fiona hung out with.

That last day seemed particularly hard for Cassie and Matt to talk about. It was the day Matt's sister had committed suicide and he'd blamed Cassie.

Adam appreciated how much these people wanted answers.

"I still think Denton is the best bet," Piper said at one point. "Did the reports say anything about him being questioned?"

Adam shook his head. "Tonight's the first I've heard his name."

"I don't know." Cassie looked doubtful. "They'd stopped seeing each other several weeks before."

"But he still harassed Fiona at school," Piper insisted. "She threatened to give him a black eye if he didn't stay way from her."

"When was this?"

"A couple days before she was beaten."

Adam jotted notes as they talked.

"Who actually came to take you from Margaret's house?" he asked.

It was Piper who answered.

"A deputy. He took us to city hall and questioned us separately. Then I was sent back to pack and picked up by another deputy and shipped off to Adamson."

Cassie nodded. "It was really late and I was sleeping on one of the benches at the sheriff's office when a lady from Social Services in Harrison County came and got me. We went by the house, but no one was there. I packed a suitcase full of my things and left."

"And Fiona?"

Both women shrugged. "I never saw Fiona or Cassie again until I got here on Monday," Piper said.

"Why do you think someone went to such great pains to keep the three of you from communicating?"

There was a moment's silence, then Piper said slowly, "To keep us from comparing notes and finding out the truth."

Adam nodded. "Bingo."

Adam accepted Matt's offer of a ride home. He'd purposely walked over for dinner, hoping Matt would drive him back to Sam's. He wanted to speak to Matt alone. He also had no desire to walk down that hill.

"Leg healing?" Matt asked as they drove down the long lane.

"I can walk on it, which is more than the surgeons first predicted. But I need it fully healed to get back to work."

"When does the cast come off?"

"In another couple of weeks. I'm seeing an orthopedist in New Orleans."

"You think we'll find Fiona by then?"

"No. Sam's done most of the groundwork and had no luck. But I'll do my best to throw anything I find into the mix. There's always the chance we've missed a lead somewhere. I hoped Cassie and Piper would come up with something tonight."

Adam tried to turn the conversation to Piper.

"You knew Cassie well back then, but what about Piper?"

Nothing like being up-front.

"Yeah, I knew both her and Fiona."

"She was pretty even then, I bet."

"Yeah, and knew it. She had boys flocking after her."

Adam suspected that much hadn't changed, except the boys were now men.

"Is she involved with anyone now?"

"Not from what Cassie tells me. She likes her life in Paris, and I guess after two bad marriages, she's sworn off men."

"Men or marriage?" Adam asked.

Matt glanced at him. "Interested?"

Adam shrugged.

"She's single, I'm single, and we're both stuck in this one-horse town for a few weeks. No offense."

"Hey, I'm only here because Cassie's here. I live in New Orleans."

"I can see the attraction. When are you and Cassie getting married?"

"She wants to wait until Margaret's back on her feet. In the meantime, there's enough work on the house to keep me coming by daily."

Matt described the renovations still required for the group home. He turned into the driveway of Sam's house and stopped, cutting the engine.

"Back to Piper. She's family, you know?" Matt said.

"I won't push if I'm not wanted."

Adam wasn't sure how much he wanted to get involved. But watching her talk, listening to her laugh had almost taken his breath away. To be intrigued by a woman this way was out of the ordinary for him. He suspected there was more to her than her blond beauty, and like any good investigative reporter, he wanted to learn all there was to know about Piper Morgan.

"She's grown up now," Matt said with a grin. "I think she can take care of herself."

"So what do you think about Adam?" Cassie asked as she finished the last of the dishes.

She was washing, Piper was drying and putting them back in the same place Margaret had always kept them.

Piper figured she had him pegged.

"He's bored. He's not likely to find any other challenges here, so why not help unravel a mystery or two. I give him a couple of weeks. Once his foot's healed, he'll be back in some foreign country so fast we won't see him for dust."

"So if we only get two weeks, I hope he can find something in that time."

"I'm trying not to get my hopes up."

"He found out you were born in Florida," Cassie reminded her. "That's a new fact. Piece the facts together one by one and something will turn up."

"He suggested we search for mementos or papers relating to me. Did you find anything like that when you were looking through Margaret's papers?"

Cassie shook her head.

"Now that you mention it, it's odd there weren't some kind of documents relating to the foster care. I think foster parents have to make reports, don't they? I'm sure Margaret would keep stuff like that. She seemed to keep everything else that ever came through this house."

"The question is where? Of course, as the workers move through the house doing the renovation, they're bound to overturn everything in the place. If they came across anything, would they know to tell us?"

"We can look ourselves, though I swear I've looked

everywhere already." Cassie frowned. "I'll tell Matt to let the men know we want any files or papers they find."

"You have plenty to do," Piper said, "while I, on the other hand, am a lady of leisure for a little while. I'll poke around and see what I can uncover."

"Don't forget those boxes in the attic I told you about. I didn't go through them all, just the one with my name on it. I think there was a box for each of us."

"Cool, let's go now."

Piper draped the damp dish towel over the edge of the sink and headed for the attic.

"You go on," Cassie said. "You don't need me for that. They're to the right at the top of the stairs."

A couple of minutes later Piper flicked on the single bulb that illuminated the attic and climbed the steep stairs. She remembered going up to the attic when she was a little girl. She and Cassie and Fiona had played dress-up on rainy afternoons.

If she remembered correctly, Margaret had had some dresses from as far back as the Civil War. Piper wondered if she had kept them all these years. She'd love to see them again.

The boxes were just where Cassie had said. Piper went over and pulled the one with her name on it away from the others. She knelt down and ripped the tape holding it closed, then slowly opened it. Inside were mementos from her teenage years, and a teddy bear from when she'd been a little girl.

Gently she lifted out the bear. Its black eyes stared

solemnly at her. For a moment she was swept back in time. She remembered being rocked by Margaret, cuddling her bear, after a fight with some girl at school. Vaguely Piper recalled sucking her thumb whenever she was upset.

She could almost feel Margaret's arms around her, her soothing voice telling Piper she was special and so loved.

How had that message gotten lost as she grew older? When she thought of growing up in Bradford, she remembered the fights with Margaret.

She needed to look beyond those and see the love the woman had so freely given.

Cassie was right, Margaret was the best mother they could have had.And Piper was ashamed at the trouble she'd caused her.

"I didn't know then how things would turn out," she said softly.

Placing the bear beside her, she dug further into the box. There were programs from school events, pictures of boys from the football team. Even a torn skirt she'd worn to a dance. She remembered when Margaret had made it for her. Piper had wanted the skirt several inches shorter, but Margaret had refused. On her way to the dance that night, Piper had rolled the waistband several times until the skirt was as short as she wanted.

But there were no other papers in the box, nothing that would give Piper a clue to her parentage.

Disappointed, she repacked the box, keeping the

bear out. As she pushed the carton back between the other two, she looked around the attic, hoping for a container that said something like "important papers." She smiled ruefully. No such luck.

It was growing late. She didn't want to stay in the hot, dusty room any longer. Another day would be soon enough to search.

Taking her bear with her, Piper returned to her room to prepare for bed. She felt more herself tonight. She'd enjoyed talking with Cassie and Matt. And Adam. He'd made her so angry when she first met him. Now she actually thought she might like the guy. He had a way of making her feel more alive than she had in a long time. Both of them led fast-paced lives in the public eye, and both had been temporarily sidelined. Maybe that's what seemed to draw them together.

Crawling into bed, Piper had to admit she was happy visiting Bradford–much more than she'd expected. Seeing Marjorie and hearing about former classmates had been fun. Even thinking about the annual Independence Day Picnic had made her feel nostalgic. How many years had the three foster sisters gone to the picnic, playing with friends, eating cotton candy until they were sick, sitting with Margaret on a blanket under the stars to watch the fireworks?

Simple pleasures brought happy memories.

The next morning Piper rose early to the sound of power saws and nail guns. She quickly showered and dressed, conscious all the while of the men on the main floor. She'd hoped to get out before they started, but she was more tired than she'd expected.

Walking into the kitchen a few moments later, Piper was surprised to see Cassie sipping coffee.

"I thought you'd be gone by now. Don't you have a catering gig today?"

"Betsy and I have a lunch assignment. But we did a lot of the prep work yesterday. I'm leaving soon. Have some coffee."

Piper took a cup and grimaced at the noise coming from the front of the house.

"I'm out of here," she said. "This would drive me nuts all day."

"I know. I blare the radio when I'm here cooking to try to drown out the noise. I'm hoping it'll be better when they move upstairs."

"Except then we'll be kicked out of our rooms. Are we moving up to the third floor?"

"Works for me."

"You could always stay at Matt's," Piper said.

Cassie shook her head.

"He's staying at his family's home. Too many bad memories of Dolores for me."

"I thought you two worked through that."

"We did, as far as our relationship is concerned. It's in the past. But I'm not comfortable going to that house."

"Lucky for me or you'd be living with him and I'd be on my own."

Cassie laughed.

"Never on your own, unless by choice. But I know what you mean. Matt's tied up tonight. Want to have dinner just the two of us?"

"Sure do."

"You and Adam don't have anything planned?" Cassie asked.

"Unlike some folks I could name, we are not joined at the hip. I probably won't even speak with him today."

The catch in her heart startled Piper, but she didn't want to think about it.

"What are you going to do today, then?"

"First stop, the bank. I need to get a local account and transfer some money so I can pay off Margaret's loan. Then I thought I'd find some friends whose parents have always lived in town and see if they'll tell me what they remember about Margaret bringing me here. Marjorie gave me the rundown on my old classmates. Did you hear that Suzanne Cotter ran off with a man old enough to be her father?"

Cassie laughed.

"Betsy keeps me up-to-date on all the happenings."

"Her parents have lived here a long time, right?"

"Sure. Her father's parents live over on Maple and I think her mother's folks live on Magnolia. Her family has been here since forever."

"Maybe I'll go talk with them one of these days. They might know more about my arrival in Bradford than younger people do."

"Good idea. But I'd start with Edith Harper," Cassie suggested. "She and Margaret have been friends since they were girls."

"Maybe Edith can tell us what happened between Margaret and the banker," Piper said.

"I'm so curious myself. I tried to find out more when I first heard about it, but came up with nothing. I still think it's strange they stopped seeing each other right around the time we left. Do you remember how often he was over?"

"Sure. We used to laugh behind their backs. At the time I thought it was so weird that anyone would be dating Margaret."

"I wonder if he was the love of her life," Cassie said dreamily.

"I hope not. Still, she never married. Surely someone would have seen her good points."

Piper finished her coffee and put the cup in the sink.

"Be back around supper time," Cassie said, gathering her box of special utensils and heading out the door.

Piper took her time walking to town. The bank wouldn't open until nine. She had more than a half hour to kill while waiting. Not particularly hungry, she nevertheless entered Ruby's Café and slipped into one of the vacant booths. Maybe she'd have some toast while she was waiting. By the rise in conversation, she was aware that she'd been noticed. She didn't really like the attention, *but* if gossip about her got people remembering, it might lead to important information about the day she arrived in Bradford.

Glancing around, she saw Sam and Adam at the counter, both putting away a huge breakfast.

As if her focus had tapped him on the shoulder, Adam looked back and saw her. He gestured to the empty seat next to his.

Ignoring the other customers, she crossed the café and slid onto the high stool.

"Good morning, gentlemen."

"Hey," Sam greeted her.

"You're up and out early," Adam commented.

"You try to rest while a bunch of guys are renovating a house, banging and sawing and yelling back and forth. Then there's the dust drifting everywhere—even upstairs."

She scanned the menu, aware of the curious looks of the other customers.

"Try the special, it'll fill you up for the day," Adam said.

She glanced at his plate, tempted to indulge in scrambled eggs with green peppers, onions, mushrooms, bacon and sausage. The stack of hotcakes alongside had her salivating. She usually ate toast and orange juice. If she ate a breakfast like his, she'd balloon up and never get another assignment.

"Just toast," she told the waitress, "and coffee."

"That's why you're so skinny," Adam said.

"It's called slim and it's required of a model."

"You're missing some really good cooking."

She'd done without in the past. Discipline was hard but necessary to keep her edge in a competitive industry.

She leaned forward to see Sam.

"Are you still looking for Fiona? Or have you abdicated to Adam?"

He shook his head, smiling slightly.

"It's not a high priority, you know. She's done nothing illegal that I know of."

"What are your plans for the day?" Adam asked. "Want to tackle Miss Nunes together?"

"I definitely do not! After yesterday, the last thing I want to do is even hint we're continuing the search. It's obvious Margaret knows more than she's telling, but she doesn't want me to know. Do you suppose my parents were killers or something?"

"Who knows? We could talk to her about Fiona and the last days you girls were here in Bradford."

"I don't know. Seems anything like that will upset her, and that's the last thing I want. Anyway, I plan to go to the bank this morning and open an account. Then I want to visit one of Margaret's oldest friends. She may know something."

"The banker?" Adam asked. "What's his name?"

"Allen McLennon," Sam said. "I talked to him a few months ago about the situation. He wasn't in town the day of the crime."

Piper leaned forward again.

"Where was he? From what I remember, he seemed to hang around Margaret all the time. We thought for sure he was going to ask her to marry him."

"I didn't get that impression. He wasn't mentioned in any of the reports and was only a casual friend of Margaret's from what I heard. He only found out what happened that day when he returned to town a week or so later. It was Cassie who told me he and Margaret were dating."

"Did he say why he stopped seeing Margaret?" Piper asked.

Sam shook his head.

"I didn't know to ask at the time. Like I said, it was Cassie who filled me in."

The waitress placed a plate of toast in front of Piper and refilled her coffee cup.

"Need anything else?" she asked as she slid the jam closer.

"This is fine, thank you."

"Thanks for stopping in," the woman said, nodding toward the rest of the room. "You're doing wonders for business."

Piper turned slightly and saw that the place was now crowded. For a moment it felt as if all eyes were on her. She turned back and grinned at the woman.

"Glad I could help."

When she wasn't working, Piper led a life of relative anonymity in Paris. It felt odd to be recognized in Bradford.

"You're used to it, I'm sure," Adam said.

She shrugged. "Not really. Without makeup, I'm pretty plain."

He looked at her.

"There is no way you'd ever be plain."

Piper was amazed at the warm feelings that washed through her at his compliment.

"Thank you."

"It's the truth."

"I'm heading out," Sam said, rising and putting some money beside his plate. "Catch you later."

"Have you found out anything else since yesterday?" she asked Adam when Sam had left.

"If you mean since last night when I went home to bed, no. I'll go with you this morning to talk to McLennon. If we can't find out more about your background, maybe we can learn something about what happened the day Fiona was beaten."

Piper nibbled on her toast, remembering how shocked she and Cassie had been to see Fiona.

"It was awful, you know. She was so angry she almost vibrated with it. I hope she made it and that she's living someplace nice and is as happy as a lark."

"You and Cassie did well, she probably did, too."

"You sound pretty sure of that. Haven't you heard how wild she was? Spend any time in this small town and you'll hear all about the girls from Bradford Hall."

"You three were rather notorious," he said. "But that's understandable."

"Now you're a shrink?"

"No, just someone who can see below the surface sometimes. Acting out was your way to rebel against the tough hand fate dealt."

"Maybe. But you're right. Cassie and I did okay. I hope Fiona did, too."

"Who is this friend of Miss Nunes's you plan to see?

"Call her Margaret, for goodness' sake. Edith Harper and Margaret grew up together. Cassie said she's seen Edith several times since she's been back, but she's never asked her about me and my past. She might know something that would help. Wouldn't you remember when your best friend decided to become a foster mother?"

"Can't imagine any of my friends doing that," Adam said.

She laughed, pushing away the empty plate. "Knowing you, why doesn't that surprise me?"

"Ready?"

She nodded. Before she could open her purse, Adam had placed a twenty on the counter. "Breakfast is on me," he said.

Piper thanked him and then waited while he stood. As soon as he had his balance, she led the way outside.

"Should you be walking so much?" she asked as they turned and headed toward the bank.

"I'm trying to get my mobility back as fast as I can."

"But shouldn't you give the muscles and bones time to heal before stressing them?"

"I don't have time to waste."

"Oh my, are we on a deadline?"

"There's nothing older than yesterday's news. Or yesterday's reporter. I can't afford to stay on the sidelines for long. You should understand that. What happens if you're out of the action for an extended time?"

"A dozen prettier and younger models would stand in line. I know what you're saying."

She had a feeling her visit to the States would be longer than she'd originally planned, yet she wasn't as concerned as she probably ought to be. Modeling was a job like any other. When it ended, she'd have to find something else. She hadn't a clue what it would be. But she didn't look on modeling as a life calling.

For a moment she almost envied Cassie. She'd found love and a more rewarding way to use her culinary talents.

Piper didn't think she could live in Bradford again. But it would be cool to live near Cassie, to talk every day, share secrets and dreams like they used to.

The bank was open by the time they arrived. Piper went straight to new accounts and quickly transacted her business. When she was finished, she rose, looking for Adam. He was standing at the far end of the lobby, talking with a woman at a desk behind a railing. Piper went to join them.

"McLennon is tied up for a little while," Adam told her. "Shall we wait?"

"How long?"

"Maybe another fifteen minutes, I'm not sure," the secretary said. "He's on a long-distance call."

"Let's wait so we don't have to come back."

Piper looked around and spotted some chairs

along one wall.

"We'll be over there," she told the secretary.

When they wcrc seated, she asked Adam how he figured interviewing Allen McLennon would help anything.

"We have a two-pronged plan here with regard to Fiona," he said. "First, you want to find her. Anything anyone might remember could help give us a new direction to try. Second, you want to clear Margaret's name. So more information about what happened to the initial charges might help. In fact, you should interview all her friends, find out as much as you can about the incident, and what happened afterward. You read the reports. It was a slipshod investigation from the get-go. Only in a small town would officials have the power to jerk kids from their foster home and send them packing. And I still don't get why you weren't allowed to communicate."

"I thought it horrible at the time, but everything happened so quickly. Questioning the decision didn't get me answers."

Adam shrugged. "It sure seems odd to me."

He stood up.

"The secretary is beckoning. I guess McLennon is available."

A couple of minutes later they were seated opposite the bank president in his plush office.

"What can I do for you?" he asked Adam, his attention flicking to Piper.

"You know Margaret Nunes—I understand you

were quite close once," Adam stated.

Allen seemed taken aback.

"We dated briefly a long time ago."

He stared at Piper.

"What's this about? Aren't you one of her foster girls?"

"Yes. I'm Piper Morgan. We're trying to find out more about the attack on Fiona Hunter and hoped Margaret's friends could help us out."

"It would help if you could give us your take on the situation surrounding the disposition of her foster children," Adam said.

"I wasn't here at the time," Allen told them. "I was out of town on business. I learned of the unfortunate incident upon my return. If you want any firsthand details, you'll have to talk to someone else, I'm afraid."

"Do you think Margaret beat that girl?" Adam asked.

McLennon shook his head.

"Of course not. Margaret is a small woman. As I remember, the girl—Fiona—was tall and athletic. She was stronger than Margaret and a known troublemaker. Got in with the wrong crowd if you ask me, then tried to lie her way out."

"How?"

"Accusing everyone in sight is my recollection," Allen said.

"Do you remember who she accused?" Adam asked.

Allen shook his head.

"Why did you stop seeing Margaret?" Piper asked.

The banker's expression changed slightly.

"We weren't suited. It was a mutual decision."

"What happened after the girls were sent away?" Adam asked.

"What do you mean?"

"With Margaret. With the investigation."

Again Allen shook his head.

"I don't know. Check with the sheriff's office. I stopped seeing Margaret and soon stopped listening to gossip."

"Formal charges were never made," Adam said. "Yet the girls were removed from Margaret's home without any notice. Seems strange, don't you think?"

"I think it all happened a long time ago. Those foster children are grown—" he looked at Piper directly "—and stirring things up isn't going to change the past. Let it alone."

"I want to find out what happened," Piper explained. "Margaret never hit any of us, ever and I want the record cleared for all time."

"She wasn't charged," Allen said.

"Were we the reason the two of you didn't get married?"

"Married?" Allen gave a bark of laughter. "I wouldn't have married Margaret Nunes, girls or no girls."

"You two seemed pretty close at one time."

"From a teenager's perspective maybe. We decided we didn't suit each other. I can't see at this late date how any of this is relevant."

"We're trying to get an accurate picture of what happened," Adam said, rising. "Appreciate your time."

Piper refrained from saying another word as she stormed out behind Adam. When they reached the sidewalk, she was fuming.

"He's a pig," she announced.

"Why so?"

"The way he said he'd never marry Margaret. They were close. It wasn't teenage fantasies. He brought her flowers and candy, took her to dinner, hung around the house a lot. You can't tell me he wouldn't have latched on to her if he'd been able to. I think she dumped him. He probably saw her as a good investment, owning that house and land. Wasn't he trying to get his hands on it earlier this spring before Cassie and Matt paid down the loan?"

Piper felt badly for Margaret, never finding love. Never marrying and having her own family. The woman had done a wonderful thing raising three children who were not her own.

"So, where to next?" Adam asked.

"Edith Harper's. If anyone knew what was going on back then, it has to be her."

6

"Where does Edith Harper live? Walking distance?"

Piper looked at Adam. She'd forgotten about his injury. The man never gave a hint of infirmity.

"I'm assuming she's still in the same house. It's not far, but we can drive if you like."

Adam pulled out a set of keys. "I have a rental, but I don't drive if I can help it." She took the keys as they walked back to Sam's.

When Piper pulled up in front of Edith Harper's home a little later, Adam whistled. It was a classic ante-bellum mansion, with white fluted columns, wraparound veranda and a manicured lawn that begged for children and dogs to run around on it.

"The Harpers were as rich as the Nunes at one time," Piper told him. "Or maybe I should say it the other way around. Margaret's father didn't contribute as much to the family coffers, as I heard as a kid. He ran the cotton mill in town, but didn't own it. When he died, the income dried up. Margaret had a harder time. The Harpers must have held on to their money. This place is gorgeous."

Piper knew Edith would be in a wheelchair. Cassie had explained that the older woman was plagued with arthritis. It seemed a shame that all her money could do nothing to improve her health.

When they were seated in the parlor, Edith asked them straight out the reason for their visit.

"It isn't often pretty young things like you come to visit an old woman like me," she said to Piper. "What can I help you with?"

"Cassie and I are looking for Fiona."

"So Cassie told me. I don't know where she went, honey. She was a wild one. Didn't take to rules and such. I declare, she sure gave Margaret a run for her money."

She smiled in remembrance.

"Not that Margaret wasn't up to it, mind. She knew you girls were a handful, but she loved you all."

"It was a shame the girls were taken away," Adam said.

Edith's eyes flashed.

"That was the crime if you ask me. Margaret never hit a soul. It about crushed her when those girls were taken. She couldn't contact them. Couldn't do anything to clear her name."

"Yet she was never charged with a crime," Adam said.

Edith nodded.

"There was no proof, just Fiona's accusations. Margaret would never do such a thing. Everyone knew that."

"Did she say who else Fiona accused?" Adam asked.

Edith shook her head.

"No. She never told me."

"But she gave you a hint, maybe. Or you suspected something?"

"It was a bad time," the older woman told him. "Nothing could be proved. And certain allegations are best left in the past. She mourned the loss of you girls, but she's got her second chance with this home Matt's starting. She was so looking forward to becoming involved with girls needing help again. I guess the stroke will end all that."

"She could recover enough to handle the job," Piper said, hoping that was true.

It was still too early to know how complete her recovery would be.

"But would she be well enough to handle such a stressful position long term? I have my doubts. She's not young anymore."

"Not so old, either," Piper said.

"It's good of you to say that. And she'll appreciate that it's coming from you."

"Why is that?" Adam asked. "Why Piper more than Cassie?"

"What?"

Edith looked confused.

"Not necessarily *more* than Cassie. Margaret wanted to find all three of you girls and have you come back to visit. I'm sure she's happy to see you and Cassie both."

"We're also looking for my birth parents," Piper told her.

Edith frowned.

"Oh, dear, I wouldn't do that."

"Why not?"

Piper hadn't expected that response.

"Best not to, honey. No good would come of it."

A rush of excitement swept through Piper.

"You know something, don't you? Please tell me what you know."

"I can't do that," Edith said. "I gave a promise a long time ago, and I'm not one to break promises. You turned out good. Your folks are long dead—at least your mother is. Let that be enough."

"You know who my parents were?" Piper asked, almost afraid of the answer.

"I don't know their names. Well, maybe I knew the mother's first name, but that was all. She died when you were a baby. Margaret raised you. What more do you need to know?"

"I need to know who my family is—or was. I need to feel connected, if only to someone buried in a cemetery. Who were they?"

"I can't tell you," Edith said.

"Can't or won't?" Adam demanded.

"Can't, won't, doesn't matter. I promised long ago. I will not break my word."

The woman seemed to grow stronger before their eyes.

Piper knew it was futile to pursue the subject. Edith wasn't budging on this one. At least not at this point. Could Piper find a way to make her reveal what she knew?

"Who did you promise? Margaret?"

"Doesn't matter whom I promised. I'm not going back on my word and that's my final say on the subject. Would you two like some tea? I can have Rosalee bring it out."

"That would be nice," Adam said.

Piper frowned at him. He seemed to be taking things calmly.

Edith knew her mother's name.

She was drowning with frustration. There had to be a way to get that information.

"Are you from around here?" Edith asked Adam.

"No, ma'am, my family is from Baton Rouge. I'm visiting Sam Witt."

"That young man's a much better sheriff than that Halstead fellow we had for so many years. He almost ruined Margaret."

"There wasn't any follow-up once the girls left Bradford," Adam commented.

Edith's housekeeper came in carrying a silver tray with cups and saucers, a silver teapot and plate of cookies.

"Thank you, Rosalee. You may put it on the table. I'll pour."

"You let me know if you want anything else, Mrs. Harper," Rosalee said.

She gave Piper a smile, nodded at Adam and quietly left the room.

"I don't know what I'd do without Rosalee," Edith said, carefully taking a cup in her gnarled hands and lifting the heavy silver teapot.

Piper held her breath, but Edith was capable of serving her guests.

Adam took the cup and saucer she offered and thanked his hostess.

"So what really happened to Fiona and why wasn't the case closed?" he asked. "There was plenty of evidence she'd been beaten badly. I'd think something would have been done about bringing charges."

"They took those girls from the only home they knew and sent them all away. Almost broke Margaret's heart. She was so distressed. She wouldn't talk about it much, but blamed herself. I told her she wasn't the one who did that awful deed and a person can't keep another person safe from every harm, much as we might wish to."

She handed Piper her cup and poured another for herself.

"What happened between Margaret and Allen McLennon?" Piper asked.

Edith kept her focus on her cup.

"They stopped seeing each other. I don't know for sure what happened. But she's never had a good word to say about him. I must say I don't care for the man, especially after he tried to foreclose on Margaret's home because she's in the hospital. Good thing Cassie fought him over that. I'm not up to doing it alone."

"Well, you and Cassie aren't alone anymore," Piper assured her. "I'm here."

"Didn't Cassie say there was some teenager Fiona stopped seeing that might have taken her rejection badly and gone after her?" Edith asked.

"Jack Denton," Piper said.

"I remember him."

Edith shook her head.

"That boy was never up to any good. Came from bad stock. He left town around the same time. Always suspected he'd run from his actions. Sheriff probably figured he'd done it, and if he was gone, no need for him to chase after him. His mother still lives over on the Branford Road. She's not much good, either."

"If that was the case, why not bring the girls back?" Adam asked.

Edith sighed.

"I have no idea how those things work. Maybe the authorities felt the girls were settled in their new homes and didn't want to disrupt them again. It would have done Margaret a world of good, let me tell you."

"How has Margaret managed over the years?" Piper asked, wishing to hear more about the woman who had raised her.

Her attitude had been undergoing a change since she'd returned to Bradford. Margaret was the only mother Piper'd ever known. She wished she'd been nicer to her when she'd lived with her. Piper hoped she could make it up to Margaret somehow. It wasn't too late.

Edith spoke for a little while about Margaret's life after the girls left, and how excited she was when Matt proposed a home for unwed teens.

Piper could tell Edith was growing tired, and glanced at Adam. He nodded, as if he'd read her mind. Piper wasn't sure she liked that possibility.

"We need to be going, Mrs. Harper," he said, setting the empty teacup down and standing. "Thank you for the information. I've enjoyed our visit."

"You stop messing with the past," Edith told Piper. "No good will come of it. If Margaret wanted you to know, she'd have told you long ago. Just be happy with the life you have. You've done right well by yourself."

Piper rose and leaned over to hug the older woman.

"If I turned out all right, it was due to Margaret."

"Of course. She knew a thing or two about raising girls. Come back and visit another time."

When they reached the car, Piper hit the top of the roof in frustration.

"I can't believe she knows the name of my mother and won't tell me."

"An honorable woman," Adam commented. "She gave her word and will abide by it. We'll find the answer ourselves."

Piper looked at him, hope blossoming despite the odds. "Do you really think so?"

"I'll do my best," he said.

She shivered in the hot sun. His look was intense,

his words almost a vow. She knew if her parents' identities could be discovered, Adam Saunders was the man to do it.

"Thank you. I know this is penny-ante stuff to you, but it means so much to me. Come on, I'll drive you back to Sam's."

"Mind stopping at the supermarket for a minute? I need to pick up some things."

Piper drove to the Winn-Dixie and parked in the crowded lot. The old brick store had been the primary grocery when she'd lived in Bradford and that didn't appear to have changed.

"Need help?" she asked as they entered the air-conditioned building.

"Push the cart, if you don't mind. It's not that easy with one hand."

Leaning on the cane, Adam headed for the produce section. Piper followed, looking around. American supermarkets were so different from the little specialty shops she patronized in Paris.

She missed getting fresh, warm bread and stopping for a café au lait on the Rue Montmartre. She didn't think Bradford even had an outdoor café. Maybe she'd check with Cassie or Betsy. That might be something else they could do. Piper could be their first customer. She loved people-watching.

Piper dutifully followed Adam as he went up one row and down another. When they reached the meat section, he paused, studying the various cuts of meat. Piper wandered past him, glancing at the packages of pork and chicken. She was glad Cassie had volunteered to do the cooking.

"Piper?"

She turned and smiled.

"Yes?"

A familiar-looking man was standing beside her.

"It's me, Norm Stanley. Remember?"

"Of course I do. How nice to see you."

Norm Stanley. She hoped her expression didn't reveal her shock. He'd been such a hunk on the football team. The two of them had been a hot item for a few months, until she'd moved on. Time hadn't been kind to Norm. His hair was receding and that muscular body had grown soft.

"I heard you were in town. Glad to run into you."

He almost preened.

"We should get together and talk over old times."

"Sorry, I'm a bit tied up."

She looked around for Adam. He was still back in the meat section. She had no intention of taking up with Norm again on any level.

"A cup of coffee won't take long. Maybe tomorrow?"

"No, I don't think so."

"Norm, we have more shopping to do."

A woman approached and glared at Piper.

"I'm *Mrs.* Stanley."

"This is Jessica, my wife," Norm said. "Heard you made it big in Paris while I'm still stuck here in Bradford. Working over at the hardware store. I'd like to hear about Europe. New Orleans is about as far as we ever get. I'm not surprised you're a model. You were always the prettiest girl in school."

Piper nodded politely and tried to avoid the daggers Jessica Stanley was shooting her way. She was sure the woman didn't relish her husband complimenting another woman—especially in front of her.

"If we need any hardware items, we'll drop by your store," Piper promised. "It's good to see you, but we're in a bit of a hurry."

Norm looked back down the aisle where Adam was standing watching them.

"Are you married?" he asked.

"That's my partner. We're here for Margaret Nunes. She's in the hospital you know. I've really got to run."

"Come on, Norm," his wife urged.

"Don't let us keep you," Adam said, coming up behind Piper and slipping an arm around her waist.

Piper was startled, but she caught on instantly. He had tossed a couple of steaks into the basket before he joined her.

"We're in a hurry ourselves."

He urged her toward the checkout.

"I'll call you," Norm said.

Piper didn't reply as she hustled to keep up with Adam. For an injured man, he moved swiftly.

"Thanks," she said when they were out of earshot. "It was getting uncomfortable."

"Old beau?" he asked.

"Yes. Emphasis on the *old*. Wow, he doesn't look anything like he did in high school."

"People change."

Piper glanced over her shoulder and saw Norm and his wife in a heated argument. If she'd stayed married to Billy Bob, that would have been her fate. Worse than death.

"I appreciate your backing me up," she said.

Adam's eyebrows rose.

"So we're partners now."

"Hardly. That was just a convenient excuse to avoid an unpleasant scene."

"Why not just tell the guy to get lost?"

"That's not exactly being small-town friendly."

"How 'friendly' were you planning to be with an old flame?"

"Get your mind out of the gutter, Saunders. I wouldn't touch the man with a ten-foot pole. I appreciate the backup, but keep the insinuations to yourself."

"I stand corrected," Adam said.

But Piper knew he didn't mean a word of it. Leaving him to pay for his groceries, she stormed out of the store.

When Piper pulled to a stop in Sam's driveway, Adam was torn. He was tired and his leg ached, but he hated to send her on her way. The air shimmered with anger. He knew he'd annoyed her with his suggestive remark, but he'd felt an unwarranted stab of jealousy at the thought of the men in Piper's past.

Now he didn't know how to clear the air.

"I'll help carry in the bags," she said. "Then I have to go."

"I'd appreciate it."

He looked at her, hit anew by how beautiful she was. No wonder that poor schmuck at the store had wanted to renew their relationship.

Piper hopped out of the car and picked up a bag and heading for the back door.

"I assume it's not locked," she said, walking ahead. "Who would burgle a sheriff's house?"

In only seconds she disappeared into the house.

Adam slowly climbed from the car and picked up a bag. The walkway was uneven, making it difficult to negotiate. He took his time, frustrated. Six months ago he wouldn't have given the bumpy sidewalk a thought. Now he had to approach every step as a potential disaster in waiting.

By the time the groceries were put away, his leg hurt so badly he could hardly stand. But stubbornness and pride made him ignore the discomfort.

"I've really got to go."

Piper folded the last bag and placed it on top of the pile on the counter.

"Where and why?"

She glared at him for a moment.

"Not that it's any of your business, but I'm expecting a call from my agent about the fund-raiser. I'm hoping there are some models in this area who would be willing to donate a little time to our cause. Are you still trying to find someone?"

"Might be able to get Michael Thomas," he said casually.

"Who's he?" she asked, leaning gracefully against the counter.

He didn't think she was deliberately posing. Such studied movements probably came naturally after so many years, but it had him thinking of moving closer and gazing down into those incredibly blue eyes. His leg might still be messed up, but the rest of him was in perfect working order.

"You don't know Michael Thomas?" he asked. He thought everyone knew the famous wide receiver for the New Orleans Saints.

"Should I?"

"He's a football player for the Saints."

"Probably be a great draw for little boys. And their fathers," she added. "Is he cute?"

"Does it matter?"

"Sure, if you want the mothers to come."

"I think women might be attracted to him. What's your type?"

She looked at him in surprise. Did she think he was asking for personal reasons?

"Not you," she said abruptly. "That was just a ploy at the market. I wasn't making a move on you."

"You've made that clear. And if I was out of line with my comments, I apologize."

"If?"

"Okay, I was and I do—apologize."

She looked away.

"I'd rather sulk than accept your apology."

Adam laughed.

"Hey, it's your call."

"I like tall, dark and mysterious men. Ones who show me a good time while they're around."

"While they're around doesn't sound like a very good prospect for a long-term relationship," he said, wondering why she'd described him.

"Been there, done that. Don't want to repeat past mistakes. I'm fine as a single career woman. I tried marriage twice and that's enough to know the revered state is not for me."

"I'd think you'd want to establish a family of your own," he said.

He had both parents living, a sister, brother-in-law and their kids, grandparents, aunts, uncles, cousins galore. What was it like to be totally alone in the world?

And what had gone wrong with her marriages? Was Piper too high-maintenance for a man to deal with, or was there something about the men she chose?

"I've thought about kids. But who knows what kind of parent I'd make? Not knowing anything about my own parents, maybe it's better to leave well enough alone, as Edith said."

"So you want to call off the search?"

She shook her head.

"Not on your life. But finding out about my past has no impact on my future."

She glanced at her watch.

"I've got to go. I might have already missed Enrique's call."

In a second, she was gone.

Adam leaned on his cane and thought about what had happened. He was intrigued by the mystery. To know that Edith Harper held the key to solving it was frustrating. But since she wouldn't talk, there were other ways to find answers. It might take longer than Piper wanted, but he had no doubt about the final outcome.

Sooner or later, they'd catch a break. One thing would lead to another and they'd find what they wanted to know.

Moving slowly to the bedroom, Adam ignored the pain in his leg. Despite his initial reaction at the library, he was attracted to Piper Morgan. She wasn't looking for happy-ever-after, and neither was he. As soon as his foot healed, he'd be back reporting the news wherever it happened.

And in a few weeks, she'd return to Paris, showing off the latest fashions and doing who knew what else.

But until then, they were both stuck in town. Why not see what chemistry might develop between them?

Michael Thomas called Adam later that day.

"Hey man, I checked my calendar and I can make the shindig you have going for that woman in the hospital," Michael said.

"Thanks, buddy, I appreciate it."

"I could even get Devine along if you think that would help," Randy said, referring to one of the running backs on the team.

"Heck yes. With the two of you here, we'd have everyone in six counties coming."

"Anything for an old friend. But I want a favor in return."

"Here it comes," Adam grumbled.

"Hey, it's only fair. I scratch your back, you scratch mine."

"So what is it?"

"There's a charity dinner given by the team in a couple of weeks. We each have a table to fill and I'm two short. One of my friends has to go out of town on business. It's one of our major fund-raisers and the money all goes to kids' charities. It'd be cool to have someone from CNN there. Bring a date, stay a few days in the Big Easy. We can catch up."

"So this event is prior to mine, I take it," Adam said.

Any later and he could be on his way back to work.

The minute Michael had said to bring a date, he'd thought of Piper. She'd have to agree if she wanted Michael to come to Bradford. His friend didn't know he'd just handed him a perfect solution for moving in on Piper.

"I'll have someone send you all the info," Michael told him. "What's your address?"

Adam gave it to him.

"You mobile yet?"

"I can walk a few steps."

"Yeah, well, no showing off. Just come and be prepared to be fawned over. But keep it humble, right?"

"You know me."

"Hey, if you steal my thunder, you're dead meat."

They talked for a few more minutes before ending the call. Adam phoned Piper as soon as he hung up.

Cassie answered.

"We've got Michael Thomas and Devine Ozigbo coming to the Fourth of July event," he said.

Her shriek almost made him deaf.

"How in the world did you pull that off? No, wait, don't tell me. I'll just stay impressed as can be. This is great. With you and Piper and two of the Saints, the town won't be able to hold everyone. We'll make a fortune. Can we charge just to have people look at you?"

For a split second Adam wished Piper showed some of the same hero worship. But he liked her the way she was—sophisticated, cool, and disinterested in long-term commitment.

"I hardly think so. But we'll come up with some way to cash in on their presence. There is a catch, however."

"Figures. It sounded too good to be true."

"Oh, it's true. Michael will keep his word. But they want me to attend one of their charity dinners in New Orleans. And bring a date."

"I hope you're not asking me," she said.

"I plan to ask Piper."

"She'll love to go!"

Adam almost laughed at Cassie's naiveté.

"Is she there?" he asked.

"She came home for a while earlier, took a phone call, then left. She said the noise from the construction was driving her crazy. She's tired and cranky and needs a nap. I don't know where she went, but I'll have her call you. Does she have your number?"

"Yes. Remind her when she gets back."

"Sure. Thanks again for volunteering and getting Michael and Devine. Oh, wow, wait until I tell Matt."

Piper sat quietly in the dimly lit room. Margaret was sleeping. She'd decided to visit when she couldn't rest at home, but if Margaret didn't wake up soon, Piper would fall asleep herself. She'd been leafing through some old magazines, looking at fashions, interested to see what was hot a few months back and now no longer in style.

Things changed so quickly. She should be worried about being out of the fast track while she was in Bradford. But like so many other things, it was too much effort. Would she ever get her old energy level back? She was used to being on the go all the time. Now a short visit with Edith Harper and a little grocery shopping had wiped her out. She glanced at the empty bed on the far side of the room. What would it hurt to lie down for a bit and catch up with her sleep.

Piper awoke a short time later. She stretched and sat up. Margaret was looking at her, amusement in her eyes. Piper hopped off the bed and smoothed the light coverlet. It was still clean for the next person assigned to the room.

Crossing to Margaret's bed, she smiled.

"Busted. I thought I'd take a short nap. The house is a mess and noisy to boot. I was desperate to get some sleep. Honestly, if Matt doesn't get that place finished soon, I'll have to take a hotel room."

Margaret nodded and glanced around her room.

"Or maybe I can check in here and share with you. That would be fun, wouldn't it?"

Margaret gave another nod.

"I visited with Edith this morning. I didn't know she was confined to a wheelchair. Poor thing. Arthritis must be a killer."

Piper did not plan to tell Margaret about her questions or her continued quest to find her parents. She almost felt betrayed by Margaret and her friend. When she'd been little there might have been reasons to shelter her from knowledge about her parents, but they didn't exist now. She wanted to know, but she wouldn't risk Margaret's health to find out. Best to search without Margaret's knowledge.

"What this town needs is a sidewalk café," Piper said, sitting beside Margaret's bed. "I love to get a coffee along the Rue Montmartre and watch people stroll by. There aren't as many people here as in Paris, but still, wouldn't that be fun? We could sip our café au lait and make comments about the people who pass by. At least here we'd know everybody."

Piper stayed with Margaret until her dinner arrived. Her walk back to the house was uneventful and hot, and she was glad to reach the shade of the big oak trees in front of the old place.

Cassie was in the kitchen. A delicious aroma filled the air.

"Something smells terrific," Piper said, glad not for the first time that Margaret had installed air-conditioning. "It's as hot outside as Marrakech," she moaned, pulling out a chair and sitting down.

"Dinner will be ready in about an hour. Want to take a shower first?"

"Sounds good. Did I tell you how much I appreciate your cooking? I don't do much at home. And your meals are better than a lot of top restaurants."

Cassie grinned.

"I worked in one of those in Boston. What do you expect?"

"And you like doing this? I feel I'm taking advantage."

"I love it. And I'm glad someone's around to appreciate my efforts."

"Like Matt doesn't?"

"Sure, but he has to say nice things, he's my fiancé."

"Why don't you two get married and be done with it?" Piper asked.

"I want to have Margaret at the wedding," Cassie replied simply.

"That would be nice. She'd love it."

Piper rose.

"I'll take my shower now. Let me know what I can do to help when I get back. I assume all the workers have gone."

"They finished up this floor today, which was a week ahead of schedule. Matt gave them tomorrow off, but come Wednesday, they start upstairs."

Piper headed for the stairs but stopped at the arch to the living room and looked around. She'd always loved this room. There was no furniture in it now, and she knew Matt planned to buy several sofas and chairs to create more than one conversation area. And there would be a quiet corner where girls could read or dream.

The dining room was ready, too. Margaret's long table and all the chairs were back in place for a family-style eating.

Piper tried to imagine the house filled with teens again, talking and laughing.

But only memories of her own years came. They'd usually eaten dinner in the dining room, breakfast and lunch in the kitchen. When they weren't arguing with Margaret about some restriction, there had been laughter and teasing. Her childhood hadn't been bad. Why had she remembered it that way? Only the last few months had been hard. It wasn't fair to let that overshadow all the other times.

She turned and headed up the stairs. How long could she stay? Long enough to get answers?

While taking her shower, Piper reviewed all she'd learned today. She couldn't have done it without Adam's help.

It was odd she didn't feel particularly sad to learn her mother was dead. That fact destroyed the fantasy she'd woven about her parents showing up for her someday, but now she knew why her mother, at least, couldn't have done so. She should have asked Edith if she was the cause of her mother's death. She hoped not.

And what had happened to her father?

Matt was with Cassie in the kitchen when Piper returned downstairs.

"Did you hear who Adam managed to get?" he asked.

"I think Piper knows, but not about the dinner."

Cassie turned from the oven with a pan of fresh-baked rolls in her hands.

"Dinner?" Piper repeated.

"In order for Michael and Devine to come here, Adam has to go to some charity dinner in New Orleans," Cassie told her. "He wants you to go with him. I said I thought you wouldn't mind. I was supposed to have you call him as soon as you got home, but I forgot until Matt came over. Sorry."

She gave a little grimace, but it soon morphed into a grin.

"I can't believe it. With you, Adam and two Saints,

we'll draw more people to the picnic than the town can hold!"

"Go with Adam to some dinner?"

Piper was pleased everyone seemed so excited about the football players, but what was this about going somewhere with Adam?

"He'll explain. Call him after dinner and get the scoop. Do you want to grab the dressing and salad from the fridge? I haven't mixed it yet—didn't want the greens to get soggy."

They ate dinner at the table in the kitchen, unlike when she and Cassie had been growing up, Piper thought. Margaret had felt formal dinners in the dining room with all the trimmings was one way to instill good manners.

"Do you think things would have been totally different if we'd stayed here until we graduated?" Piper asked.

Cassie tilted her head thoughtfully.

"Yes, I do. How different, I don't know. We talked about going to college in New Orleans, doing things there. I would never have become a chef, I don't think, if I'd followed through with that."

"You and Matt would probably have married right out of school and you would never have gone to New Orleans," Piper said.

Matt disagreed.

"The breach was too big back then. I hope things would have come around, but who's to know? What brought that up?"

"Visiting with Margaret today. I know I'm seeing her as one adult to another now, but I also remember when I was a kid. It's sort of odd. She really is a remarkable woman, but I never realized that as a teenager. I just wondered if I would have if I'd stayed here until I graduated."

"I think we needed some distance to gain that perspective," Cassie said. "Betsy never left. I'll ask her how she relates to her parents. Maybe all kids see their parents in a different light once they're adults."

"Maybe. I want to talk to Margaret's doctor next time he is there. I want some assurance she's going to be able to work at the teen home like she wants. I should have come back before."

"I'm not sure we were ready to come back before," Cassie said slowly. "I think this is the perfect time in my life and the best time in yours. I'm just glad it turned out the way it did. What if she'd died?"

Piper reached out and took Cassie's hand.

"That's a scary thought. We might have missed all this. Best friends forever."

"Best friends forever," Cassie repeated, squeezing back.

As soon as dinner was finished, Piper went to the phone at the base of the stairs rather than go get her phone in her room. She wanted to hear more about this dinner she had been asked to attend.

"Saunders," he said a moment later.

His voice sent shivers down her spine. She leaned against the railing and tried to ignore the awareness that seemed to spark any time he was near. Her defenses must be a little skewed from being ill, nothing more.

"What's this about a dinner?" she asked.

"No big deal. It's in a couple of weeks, in New Orleans. Michael wanted me to help him out with a charity event in return for him and Devine coming here."

"Who's Devine, by the way?"

"Devine Ozigbo. One of the best running backs in the business."

"Another football player I take it."

"If you were going to be in Mississippi long enough, I'd take you to a game. Your knowledge of football is woefully lacking."

"And you keep up with all the sports news in war zones?"

"Apparently more than you do in Paris. I don't have all the details about the dinner yet, but I'll let you know when I do."

"Maybe you should ask someone else."

"Why?"

"I don't know anything about football. Someone else would fit in better."

"Hey, I'm asking my friends to help out for your foster mother. The least you can do is reciprocate."

She wished he hadn't put it that way. She'd do anything for Margaret.

"You're right. I stand corrected."

"I've requested microfilm for the Orlando

newspapers for the three months around your birthday," he said. "The library can borrow it at no charge. I figure it's worth a shot getting the names of all the people who had a baby girl during that time period, and backtracking to see if those families are still intact."

"That sounds like a lot of work, and we don't know for sure I was born in Orlando."

"True, but it's a start. You have a better idea?"

"Get Edith Harper to talk."

"Okay, you work that angle, I'll work mine."

"I'll help. I can read microfilms, I guess."

"Your enthusiasm is overwhelming."

"I'm tired. Call me when the film gets here."

She hung up. Matt and Cassie were talking softly in the kitchen, so Piper went upstairs to bed. She wanted to yell and scream in frustration. Margaret had to know more than she'd ever let on. And Edith Harper did, as well.

Why wouldn't someone tell her the truth?

7

Piper and Cassie spent endless hours talking about everything under the sun. Piper sat in the kitchen when Cassie worked on new recipes. She went shopping with Cassie, surprised to find she recognized some of the longtime residents of Bradford. Twice she'd run into former classmates in the supermarket. Their exchanges were better than the one she'd had with Norm.

He'd called the house phone to invite her to coffee, but Piper had refused in no uncertain terms. He might be sincere about talking over old times, but she was not going to come between a man and his wife in any way.

"Idiot," she said as she hung up on him.

"Who?" Cassie asked, coming down the stairs.

"Norm Stanley. I told you about running into him the other day."

"You two were hot and heavy in high school. What's he doing now?"

"Working in a hardware store. I can't imagine what it was that attracted me to him back then."

"Ever think people have different stages in life? I

think my best time is just coming. I love my new business, I'm so in love with Matt I can't see straight. I feel my entire life has been leading up to this point."

"Think Norm's best time was in high school?"

"Maybe."

"Definitely in the case of Billy Bob Thompson. Gosh, I hope my best time wasn't when Jean-Paul and I were married. I think I was the happiest I've ever been during those three years."

"So are you unhappy now?"

Piper took a minute to consider. Slowly she shook her head.

"No, I'm not. I don't have all I want, but I have enough, and for the most part I'm happy with the way my life is going."

"Then either now is your best time or it's still ahead," Cassie said. "I think moving away made us see things differently. If we'd stayed, maybe you'd still find Norm hot."

Piper tried to envision what her life would be like if she'd never left Bradford. Uncomfortable with the direction of her thoughts, she followed Cassie into the kitchen.

"Are you going to see Margaret later?" Cassie asked as began pulling ingredients from the cupboards.

"Of course. You?"

"I'll tag along. I have the Chantress dinner so I can't go this evening."

Cassie had let Piper have the afternoon visits and taken the evening ones for the most part over the past week.

"There's no reason we can't go together every time," Piper said. "I'd be glad to have you along. It's hard to have a one-sided conversation—especially with all I'm keeping from Margaret. Questions about my parents keep popping into my mind."

"Any luck on that front?"

Cassie began to measure flour and salt into a large mixing bowl.

Piper sat at the table and watched.

"I've been through almost every box in the attic. There is lots of stuff from when we were kids, but nothing that looks like reports to Social Services or anything like that."

"I went through Margaret's papers in the breakfront in the dining room and the desk in her bedroom. Nothing there, either."

Cassie kept working as she talked.

"She probably kept things she didn't want us to see safely hidden away. We were nosy enough when we were little."

Cassie laughed.

"Remember that time Fiona played detective and was caught spying on us? Margaret had a hissy fit when she found out Fiona was taking pictures and taping conversations."

Piper laughed.

"Didn't Margaret erase the tapes and expose the film?"

"Yes. And Fiona was grounded for a week, I think.

But she still kept at it. I caught her more than once. I asked her if she was worried Margaret would catch her again, but she said she knew how to hide from Margaret."

"I can't believe we haven't seen her in twelve years—or each other."

Piper felt regret for the lost years.

"Not being able to even phone each other made it harder," Cassie said. "I still don't understand why our new foster homes were kept such a big secret."

"I should have tried to find you two long before now."

"Yet when we were first out of high school, didn't the world seem big and intimidating? It took all I had to hold myself together."

Piper nodded, remembering how alone she'd felt. She'd hoped Billy Bob would take care of her, but she'd sure been wrong. Even marriage to Jean-Paul hadn't made her life easier.

She'd learned she had to take care of herself.

"No update from Sam on the search for Fiona?" Cassie asked.

"No. I don't expect much more. How can a sheriff justify using law-enforcement resources to search for an innocent person? What are you making?"

"Lemon meringue pie."

"Are you still making a different dessert for every customer?"

"Yep. Betsy and I think it gives us a certain cachet. I ask for favorites and then go from there."

"What if two people have the same favorite?"

"Then first come, first serve. The loser has to go with her second favorite."

"I bet everyone loves that torte you made for us not too long ago," Piper said.

Despite the need to watch her weight, she'd had a second helping of the chocolate dessert.

"Everyone loves everything I fix," Cassie said smugly.

Piper laughed.

It felt good to sit with a friend without worrying about an upcoming shoot. She was slowly unwinding from the hectic pace of the past few years. Somehow her life in France seemed far away. She figured she could get used to this lazy lifestyle. Until the money ran out.

"I've had some funds transferred to an account at the local bank," she said. "Shall we go face the banker together? I'd love to see his face when we pay off the loan. I can't believe he wanted to sell the land and house to a developer for a golf course."

"Let's go later this week and take Edith with us. Then we can all go to the hospital and celebrate with Margaret. You know she'll insist on paying us both back."

"Maybe. I'm not worried about that. And if she doesn't, I sure don't plan to foreclose."

Cassie tilted her head slightly.

"Do you really have enough that you wouldn't miss such a large amount?"

"I really do. Want a loan yourself?"

"No, I'm doing pretty well. It's just, I don't know, for a rich person, you seem to live rather frugally. None of your clothes are particularly expensive. You don't wear any jewelry."

"We pinched pennies too much as kids for me to go wild with money. I did splurge when I was married to Jean-Paul, but the man can afford it. Once I was on my own, things changed. I refuse to be poor in my old age."

"I know we didn't have a lot of money, but I never really felt poor growing up, did you?"

"No. Sometimes I felt like an outsider. The only thing I could trade on was my looks. No family, hardly any friends besides you and Fiona."

"You had lots of friends," Cassie protested.

"There were a lot of people who hung around me, but I had few *friends*."

Her phone rang. Piper swiped it on while Cassie continued working.

"Piper?"

"Hi, Adam. Are the microfilms in?"

"No, they won't be here for another week or so. Sam's working tonight. I think Matt said Cassie is as well. Want to get a bite to eat together?"

"Go out?"

"You have to eat and so do I."

Piper thought about it. She'd like to discuss their search for Fiona and the one for her parents. Nothing much had been done about either over the past few days—at least not on her end.

And to be honest, she'd like to see Adam again.

"Okay."

"If you don't mind driving, Sam said there are a couple of good restaurants out on the New Orleans road."

"I know a few of the places, if they're still there," Piper said.

"Come around seven," he told her. "We can use my car. Sorry I can't get you, but my leg is bothering me today."

"You push yourself too much," she chided, remembering all the walking he'd been doing the other day.

"No pain, no gain. I need to get back in shape."

"Your body will heal at its own rate. Pushing too hard won't make you recover faster."

"What are you, a doctor?"

"No, just someone with common sense. See you at seven."

Piper hung up looked at Cassie.

"That was Adam."

"I guessed. What did he want?" Cassie asked.

She put the pie she'd just made in the oven and carefully closed the door.

"I hope this thing doesn't fall flat as a pancake."

"He and I are going out to dinner tonight."

"Oh?" Cassie looked at her and smiled. "Cool."

"It's not a date," Piper said quickly. "Just dinner and a discussion about the search we're doing."

"Uh-huh."

"What does that mean?

"We'll see what happens at the end of the evening. A kiss means it's a date."

"He's not going to kiss me, for heaven's sake."

Piper walked over to the sink and reached into the closest cupboard for a glass. She took her time filling it with water.

Would Adam kiss her? She didn't think so.

Sometimes he still acted as if he didn't really like her. And from things he'd said, he didn't seem to think too highly of her career.

Not that it mattered to her what he thought. Once they both left Bradford, it was unlikely they'd ever run into each other again.

"Where is he taking you?" Cassie asked.

"We're going Dutch," she said.

"Oh, excuse me."

Piper laughed, finishing her drink and putting the glass on the counter.

"I'm being silly. For some reason the thought of Adam kissing me struck me as funny."

"Hey, I think he's sexy. If I weren't so in love with Matt, I might be interested."

"He's not for me."

"I didn't say make a lifelong commitment. Go out and have some fun. You're going to be here for a few weeks, so why not enjoy yourself. Besides, you two have more in common than you think. He travels all over the world, you live in Europe. Both of you are probably bored to tears here in Bradford."

"I'm not bored," Piper protested. "I was thinking earlier how nice it is to relax and spend time with my best friend."

"For a while. But you'll be longing for the runway lights before long."

Piper shrugged. Cassie could be right about missing Paris. But Piper didn't think she was right about Adam Saunders.

"He's out of my league," she said.

"He's a guy, isn't he? He's in your league."

"It's *not* a date," she repeated.

"Tell me how he says good-night," Cassie retorted, laughing as she began to wash the bowls she'd used.

By the time Piper was ready to dress for dinner, she was convinced Adam had more in mind than simply eating together. If that's all he wanted, they could have met at Ruby's Café.

She looked at the few clothes she'd brought, mostly casual. How dressy were some of these restaurants? And what about the dinner Adam had asked her to attend in New Orleans? She'd have to get something new for that.

Settling on linen pants and a crop top, she brushed her hair until it gleamed. She applied just a smidge more makeup than she normally wore, then set off for their business dinner.

When she arrived at Sam Witt's house, Adam was

sitting on the porch. He came down the shallow steps when he saw her.

"Good evening," he said.

"Evening," she replied, feeling ridiculous at the butterflies fluttering in her stomach.

As she looked at him, Cassie's words echoed in her mind. Would he try to kiss her later?

He leaned on his cane, and from the lines etched near his mouth and eyes, she knew he was in pain.

"Want to postpone or get pizza?" she asked.

"I'm fine. I took some pain pills a little while ago. They'll kick in soon. The car's over here."

He handed her the keys, held the door for her and walked around to the passenger side.

"Cassie recommended two of the restaurants," Piper said as soon as he'd climbed in. "One is a seafood place, the other has a little bit of everything."

"You pick, you're driving."

"Then I'd love some fresh seafood."

"Sounds good. Any luck on the great quest?"

"I've been through almost all the boxes in the attic. Some hold memorabilia from when we lived here. Others contain things from Margaret's family. I felt like the worst trespasser when I searched through those. I think Margaret has a tendency to hoard everything—except papers relating to her foster children."

"Maybe we'll find out something from the newspapers. It's a long shot, but we might get lucky."

"So if we end up with a list of say fifty women who

had a baby girl in that time frame, what do we do next? Call all of them to see if they raised that child?"

"If we need to. We can cross-check with the obituaries. It could be some friend of the Nunes had a child and couldn't keep it for some reason—maybe the mother died at childbirth. There has to be something that enabled Margaret to take you."

"I had a thought. Her father was still alive then. Maybe there's something in his papers. He was a bit of a dictator from what people said. I was still a baby when he died, so I never knew him. I went through some of the family's boxes, but there's a lot more piled up there." Piper backed out of the driveway and headed for the restaurant.

"This car's bigger than I'm used to," she commented.

She'd noticed the difference the other day when she'd driven to Edith Harper's place.

"What kind of car do you have?"

"A small Peugeot, but it sits around more than I drive it. I travel a lot, and when I'm home, it's easier to take the metro. You travel yourself a lot."

"All the time. I don't even have an apartment. Get my mail from the office or my parents. I don't have a lot of bills to pay without a place to call my own."

"Is that why you're visiting Sam while you're convalescing? No place to stay?"

"Too much family. They treated me like I was never going to get better. My mother kept reminding me I could have been killed."

"So you could have."

"More than once. But that doesn't stop the need to report the news. The public has a right to know what's going on, good and bad."

"Mostly bad."

"When bad things happen, we report it."

"How long before you return?" she asked.

"As soon as this foot heals."

"And pushing yourself isn't going to make that foot get better any faster," she repeated.

"Sitting with it propped up and doing nothing isn't something I'm willing to do."

"Sounds like that's what the doctor ordered."

He didn't reply and Piper flicked a glance his way. She knew he must be impatient at the time it was taking to regain his mobility.

When they reached the restaurant, the parking lot was more than half-full. She insisted on stopping near the door to let Adam out. He grumbled, but finally got out of the car. Quickly parking, Piper hurried to join him.

His scowl didn't bode well for a pleasant dinner.

"I could have walked that distance," he said.

She slipped her arm through his and tugged him toward the door.

"Don't be such a baby. I'm hoping for a big platter of Gulf shrimp. What are you going to have?"

He stood still a moment, looking down at her. Slowly his muscles relaxed.

"I'm going for a captain's platter, some of

everything."

By the time they'd ordered, Adam's bad mood had faded. Piper couldn't help contrasting him to Billy Bob who could sulk for days. What had put that thought about her ex in her mind?

"I want some action," she said, unwilling to linger on the unpleasant image.

"What?" he asked, looking up in surprise.

"I'm desperate to find Fiona and my parents. I've been searching fruitlessly for my parents for years. And Margaret and Cassie and Sam have been trying to locate Fiona. No results in either case. How can people just disappear like that? I thought everyone here was always worried about the government knowing their every move."

"Propaganda. This is probably the easiest country to disappear in. If Fiona doesn't want to be found, she won't be. And we have made some gain in your case. We know your mother is dead. We know you came from Orlando."

"We don't know where my mother was from. She could have just arranged to have me there, and that's where Margaret picked me up."

"Could be. Given enough time, you can search the entire state." He narrowed his eyes. "Do I have something on my chin?"

Piper's gaze flew to his. Embarrassed to be caught staring, she could never tell him she'd been thinking about his mouth, the shape of his lips, the thought of him kissing her good-night.

Darn it, why had Cassie put that idea into her head?

"No, I was— Never mind. I'm wondering whether I should just give up and wait until Margaret's better, then ask her. I guess at this late date, a few more weeks or months won't really matter."

"I think everyone wants to know where they come from. Maybe Margaret has a safe-deposit box at the bank for official documents. You could ask her."

"I can't risk another reaction like last time. If we find something, okay. If not, then I'll figure out something else."

"Like what?"

"I don't know. Thumbscrews on Edith?"

He smiled at her joke and Piper actually felt her heart skip a beat.

Adam watched Piper savor the shrimp, fascinated by the rapturous delight on her face. Ever since they'd arrived, the other diners constantly glanced her way— men and women alike. To his surprise, she seemed completely oblivious to the attention. What made this woman tick?

"Tell me something about Piper Morgan," he said.

"What's to tell. I model clothes, I live in Paris. While I'm here, I want to find my roots."

"Tell me about your marriages."

He was curious about the kind of men that attracted her.

She frowned. "Not a subject I want to discuss."

"Humor me. I'm interested."

Her look was assessing. He could almost see the deliberation going on in her mind. She took another shrimp, dipped it into the butter and ate it.

"Billy Bob Thompson was the darling of Adamson High. He was the quarterback on the football team, which went to the state championship games two years running. His daddy owned the Chevy dealership in town. Proud as punch over his boy. And man, that boy was built. Tall, broad shoulders, sandy blond hair. I had a chip on my shoulder when I had to leave Bradford and move to Adamson. But Billy Bob pushed right through and claimed me as his girlfriend. Nothing serious, just parties and fun."

Adam had a picture of the good ol' boy she was describing.

And he didn't like him a bit.

"Then I turned eighteen and finished school. Do you know the foster-care system ends when a person turns eighteen? Doesn't matter if they have a place to live or a job. They're turned loose and have to fend for themselves. Now, a lot of people can do that, but it scared me to death. Cassie and I were talking about this earlier. She was scared, but her foster parents were really supportive. Imagine how it feels being alone in the world."

"Is that one of the reasons you want to find your parents?"

"Not so much now. Billy Bob proved to be a lifeline. He offered, I accepted. The first six months were a whirlwind of fun. But after a while, fun got tiring—at least for me. As far as I know, he's still partying up a storm."

"Don't you keep in touch?" He suspected there was more to this chapter of her life, but he didn't need to push. He'd get what he was after sooner or later.

"No. I filed for divorce and emotions ran high. Adamson is not a place I'd want to visit again. Anyway, I took off for New York."

Adam could picture the small-town, Southern teenager in New York. She was lucky she had ended up so successful. He wasn't sure he could have faced that city at eighteen or nineteen.

"So New York's where you met the Frenchman?" he asked.

"Jean-Paul Sartain. Sexiest man alive. And he knows it. I was so flattered by his attention. He's the reason I have my career. Took me to Paris, polished me up and pushed me to accept that first assignment."

"Nice man," Adam said, not liking this guy any more than Billy Bob.

Piper laughed.

"Your tone says otherwise. Actually, Jean-Paul *is* a nice guy. Generous to a fault, to me and everyone. He's rich as anything and flaunts money like crazy. Loves the adulation."

"Competing with you when you started doing so well must have hurt, then."

She went still, staring at him in surprise. She'd never considered Jean-Paul might have been hurt. She only remembered her own pain when they separated.

"I never thought of that. Do you really think so?"

He waved his arm in the air.

"Look around. Everyone in the place is watching you. They've probably never seen a more beautiful woman. I imagine that would be hard on the ego of a man used to being the center of attention."

Piper glanced around. Heads ducked and eyes were averted as she checked out the other patrons. She turned back to Adam.

"So, is it hard on your ego?"

He felt a spurt of amusement. This woman didn't have a clue.

"No."

"You're used to being the center of attention—broad-casting reports from war zones."

"I'm used to being on camera, but I'm not the center of attention. People are interested in the news, not me. There's a difference."

She thought it over and nodded.

"You're right. I never thought about Jean-Paul's reaction to my success. He pushed me to get into modeling. I thought he'd be happy when I did well."

"Instead?"

"He went off to find someone else to adore him."

"Tough."

Piper shrugged.

"I'm happy in my life. And I have some terrific memories. Anyway, enough about me. Tell me about the famous Adam Saunders. You've never been married, have you?"

"Came close once."

"How close?"

"I was almost engaged."

He hadn't thought about Deirdre and him as a couple in a long time. Would things have been different if he'd asked her to marry him?

"What happened?"

"Time and distance."

"What?"

"We never had any time together and were kept apart by our work."

"She's a reporter, too?"

"A very good one for the BBC. Likes the action as much as I do. I still see her from time to time."

"Absence makes the heart grow fonder," she teased.

"Out of sight, out of mind," he countered.

What he had felt for Deirdre had burned out a long time ago. He doubted that a marriage between them would have lasted.

"You're cynical," Piper said.

He did feel old, burned-out and cynical. The price for seeing so much misery firsthand. Bradford felt like an alien world to him. People here didn't have to worry about bombs or snipers. There was plenty of food to go around. Nice homes.

And it made Adam feel like a fish out of water.

"Just a realist. My job and marriage don't go well together. I can't imagine spending the rest of my life with one person. Can you?"

"Not after trying it twice. I think I'm happier alone. At least I don't have to pander to other egos. My own is demanding enough."

He didn't agree. So far he hadn't seen anything to suggest Piper had an inflated ego.

Quite the contrary. She had a sensitivity he hadn't expected. And she sure wasn't preening with all the attention that came her way.

"Finished?" he asked, noting the empty plate.

"I am and it was delicious."

"Want some dessert?"

She shook her head.

"I do have to watch what I eat to stay slim enough for the camera. Besides, I'm really full. I haven't had shrimp that good since I can't remember when."

"It's too early to call it a night," Adam said, not willing to spend the rest of the evening alone.

"We haven't talked about Fiona."

"I don't want to talk about Fiona. I want to learn more about you. What do you want out of life? Will you always live in Paris? How do you feel about Margaret from an adult perspective? What are your dreams?"

Piper felt surprised. Most people liked looking at her but didn't feel any need to delve below the surface. What did Adam want? This wasn't an interview, was it?

"Why?"

"The more I get to know you, the more you surprise me," he said.

"Because I'm not some dumb blonde?"

"You're definitely not dumb. And not just a pretty

face."

"Thank you. But I'm not into heart-to-hearts with passing strangers. I've already told you more than I have some of my friends in France. I think that's partly because I feel I've known you for a long time—I've seen you on television over the years. Gives people a false sense of connection."

"And the other part?"

"I'm following your suggestion—maybe if I talk about things, something might turn up. But there are limits."

"Cassie's out for the evening, Sam's at some meeting. I have no reason to go back to his house."

Piper held her breath, wondering what he was leading up to.

"So you're suggesting...?" she asked speculatively.

"How about I go back to the house with you and we start searching for any papers in Margaret's father's office."

"That room was cleared out for the renovations. I think a lot of the bigger pieces of furniture are in the garage out back. I can look, if you think that's a possibility."

"Two of us will be faster."

"Fine," she said. "Let's go."

This was definitely not what she'd expected.

And Piper was irritated at how disappointed she felt.

The ride home was silent. Adam seemed comfortable with the quiet, but Piper was not. She wanted to take him back to Sam's and spend the rest of the evening alone.

Perversely, she wanted more from Adam than he seemed interested in giving. Cassie was right. Piper and Adam were both here for a short time, so why not make the best of it?

"Tell me about being a war correspondent," she said as they drew closer to town.

"It's ugly."

"Are you talking at the library again tomorrow?"

"Yes. Are you coming?"

"I think so. Tell me something you won't be putting in your talk."

For the next few minutes he described the deprivation and danger, the heroics and horrors of the war.

She flinched at some of the images, but could vividly picture Adam slogging to get the story out.

"Quite a contrast to my life," she said at one point.

In comparison her own career seemed totally frivolous. Who cared about the latest fashions when children were dying? When lives were being lost?

Piper turned into the crushed-shell driveway and drove up to the front of the old brick house. Cutting the engine and the lights, she rolled down the window, letting in the sounds and smells of the night. In the distance she could hear a bullfrog in a pond, and the night breeze rustled the leaves on the trees.

"I'm glad you made it out alive," she said.

She opened the door and the harsh dome light lit up the car.

"Let's go search for those papers."

8

They entered the old house through the front door and Piper asked if Adam wanted coffee. When he said he did, she led the way into the kitchen.

"Where would you suggest beginning this search?" he asked, leaning against the table, resting his leg.

Piper filled the coffee maker with water and measured out the grounds.

"There's a formal study beyond the living room. It was almost sacrosanct, because it belonged to Mr. Nunes."

"Is that what you called him?"

"I didn't call him anything. He died when I was a baby. But that's how we referred to him. I don't think I even remember his first name. Margaret didn't talk about him a lot. We were never permitted in his office when we were young."

"So of course you spent as much time as possible in there."

Piper smiled and shrugged. "Fiona was the one who used to hide from Margaret in there. I don't think she was ever caught."

"Wouldn't Margaret have gone through her

father's things long ago and trashed anything she didn't need?"

"Not from what I saw upstairs in the attic. I think because the place is so big, the family saved everything. You take your coffee black?"

Adam nodded.

"What would have happened to you girls if she had married the banker?"

"We'd probably have been out on our ears. Can you see a newly married man wanting to take on three teenagers who weren't even related to him or his new wife? I've always wondered why they broke up, though."

"Why don't you ask Margaret?" he suggested.

"Kind of hard to phrase something like that with yes or no questions," she reminded him. "We'll just have to wait until she's better."

Piper led the way to the garage behind the old house. Opening one of the double doors, she felt for the light switch and turned it on. The dust covers on everything that had been moved from the house hid the individual pieces, yet their outlines were clearly visible. The huge desk sat near the back of the garage.

Adam walked past her and headed for the desk. Yanking the cover off, he moved around to open the drawers. There was a chair nearby he dragged over to sit on.

Piper put her coffee on the edge of the desk and went around to stand beside Adam. Reaching out, she pulled open the top drawer on the left side. Some papers had been tossed there along with a couple of pencils, but nothing else.

Meanwhile Adam began skimming through the drawers on the right side.

Three minutes later and they were done.

"Gee, that went well," she murmured, glancing around the garage. Across from the desk was a tall, old-fashioned wooden file cabinet, not covered by a drop cloth. Heading over, she opened the top drawer and peeked into some of the folders. Correspondence and papers from more than fifty years ago.

"Anything?" Adam asked.

"Nothing to do with me."

Running her fingertips along the tops of the files, she quickly skimmed through the rest, but found nothing.

She slammed the drawer shut and turned.

"This is a waste of time. It was always Margaret in charge of us, not her father. When I was younger, one of my friends told me that she'd heard her parents talking about how old man Nunes hadn't wanted Margaret to bring any children into the house. But she won that skirmish, I guess. So now we wait for the microfilm and hope it has something?"

"Might as well."

Adam slowly got up and started for the door.

"I'll be heading home, then. I'll call you when I hear from the library."

"Want to sit outside for a moment and enjoy the night air?" she asked, not wishing the evening to end just yet.

She was disappointed they hadn't found anything useful. Maybe there was no way to find out the truth unless Margaret revealed it.

Piper led Adam to the swing on the porch. Like most things in Margaret's house, it hadn't changed since her childhood.

"I appreciate your taking time to help me," she said sincerely.

"Gives me something to do while I wait."

"What if your foot doesn't heal enough for you to return to the danger zone?"

"I try not to think about that. There are other options besides being on the front line, but none of them appeal to me. I don't see a desk job in my future—or at least not for thirty years or so."

"You could be an anchor on the nightly news," she suggested. "That's not really a desk job."

"I want to be out uncovering the news, not reading someone else's reports."

"When will you know if you'll be able to return?"

"A few more weeks, with any luck. I *am* going back, you know."

He took her coffee cup and put it beside his on the table near the swing. He turned slightly to look at her.

Piper caught her breath, her eyes locked with his. Tension radiated between them both.

"I'm here a few more weeks. You're here until after the Fourth of July, then what? Back to Paris?"

She nodded.

"No one special in Paris?"

Piper shook her head.

"No one special for me anywhere," he said, drawing her closer and lowering his head to kiss her.

Piper hadn't been kissed in several months. His lips were warm against hers, moving with practiced ease. She didn't hesitate to return the pressure of lips against lips.

She was just getting into the kiss when he pulled back and looked at her. The faint lighting hid his expression, and she could only see the gleam in his eyes.

"Do you want me to leave?"

Piper put her arms around his neck and moved closer. "Now, why would you want to do that?" she asked.

Piper would have liked to sleep in the next morning, but by seven o'clock the workers were clomping up the stairs. They were starting on the second floor today, she remembered, turning over and hiding her head beneath the pillow. It wasn't fair, she grumbled to herself. She ought to be able to sleep in until noon if she wanted.

A few moments later a knock sounded on the door.

"What?" she called, not wanting to move.

Cassie opened the door and peeked in.

"They need us to get our stuff out so they can start on the en suite bathroom. Thought I'd give you a heads-up."

"So I really need to get out of bed, is that what you're telling me?" Piper muttered, still beneath the pillow.

She heard the door close, and a moment later the pillow was snatched away.

"You always loved to sleep in. If I do that, I feel the day is wasted. Come on, let's go see Margaret. I want to tell her about this next stage of construction. Give her something to look forward to."

Piper rolled over and sat up.

"Edith Harper knows about my birth parents and won't tell me anything. Margaret's a dead end. Any suggestions for what to do next?"

"What happened to Adam and his hotshot investigative skills?"

"He's still looking, but it's taking so long."

Cassie sat on the edge of the bed.

"You've been looking for almost twenty years and come up with dead ends. I'd say he's your only hope."

"It's so frustrating. I wish I had some truth serum to put in Edith Harper's tea."

Cassie laughed. "Once Margaret's better, pursue the issue. She can't keep the information from you now that you're an adult. And if your mother is really dead, what harm is there in knowing her identity?"

She leaned forward.

"So how did the date go last night? Did he kiss you?"

Piper lay back on the bed.

"You were right! He didn't go home until almost midnight."

"Pretty hot, huh?" Cassie teased. "Told you so. Are you going out again tonight?"

"No. I probably won't hear from him until the microfilm comes in."

Piper propped herself up on the headboard and gave Cassie the rundown on their search of the study furniture.

"So where do I look next?"

Cassie shook her head.

"The attic was the best bet, but since there's nothing there, we could ask Edith to check Margaret's safe-deposit box, if she has one. Edith has power of attorney."

"She'll refuse if she knows what we're after."

"You can charm your way around her. Aren't all models good actresses?"

Cassie tugged on the bedcovers.

"Get up and I'll fix us Belgian waffles for breakfast."

Piper groaned.

"Oh great. I'm going to gain a gazillion pounds and I'll never model again."

"You love Belgian waffles."

"I know. That's the problem."

"You're too thin, anyway," Cassie teased. "You need a few more curves."

"Just ruin my career," Piper sighed dramatically.

"Hardly. Hurry up."

Cassie left and Piper quickly dressed and made sure her room was tidied for when the workers came. They'd be moving the furniture out, but she didn't need to empty the dresser.

She and Cassie would be sharing a room on the third floor, while the new bathroom was built between the bedrooms. They'd have privacy, but no respite from the noise.

That afternoon Piper made sure she was at the library shortly before Adam was due to give his next talk. Word of mouth had publicized the event and the crowd was even larger than it had been the previous week.

She found a chair off to one side and sat, glad she'd come early. It wasn't long before the room was full and six people were standing in the back. The librarian came in with extra chairs.

Adam arrived promptly at two. He glanced around, looking a bit startled to see such a large crowd.

Piper slid down in her chair, not wanting him to see her right away. She wasn't sure why she'd come. He'd spoken so eloquently last night about the hardships of his work and the thrill. And he had told her things he'd never talk about today.

She loved to listen to him, and if she were honest, she actually missed him.

He held everyone in the palm of his hand as he described what went on behind the scenes and all the problems that came with working in remote and dangerous locations. The teenager who had been so interested last week was front and center this week as well. He had lots of questions. Finally Adam invited him to coffee later in the week so other people could get a question in.

Piper liked the way Adam handled himself. Once he looked right at her and for a split second she felt they shared a special bond. Then his gaze moved to the next person with a question. Did everyone feel special when he singled them out?

He was still surrounded by men and women wanting to speak with him when she slipped out. He never gave the impression of being impatient or in a hurry. What a gift he was giving to the people of Bradford, to share his experiences so generously.

Two days later Piper sat on the porch swing, trying to think of all the things she needed to do to get ready for the Fourth of July celebration. She also wanted to come up with an innocuous way to talk to some of the older residents in town who knew Margaret and might remember when Piper was brought to live at Bradford Hall. But memories of Adam's hot kisses the last time she'd sat on the porch intruded. She hadn't seen or heard from him since his talk at the library. Was something wrong?

She was annoyed he hadn't called, but then he had no real obligation to her. If they hadn't been thrown together by circumstances, they'd never have met.

But they had, darn it, and they'd gone out to dinner

and kissed. She'd like to see more of him, at least while she was in Bradford. They both knew they were in a hiatus from their normal lives. It wasn't as if she was going to fall in love with the man and have a heartbreak to deal with when he left. She'd learned that lesson before.

It was hot outside, but the dust and noise had driven her from the air-conditioned house. Even on the porch she could hear the whine of the saws and the pounding hammers. The weather forecast was for thunderstorms later in the day. She hoped they cooled things down. It was already too humid for her and she knew the summer would only get worse.

She felt restless. Maybe she should just call Betsy's mother and arrange a meeting. She had to start somewhere.

When the phone rang, she dashed inside.

"The microfilm's in," Adam said.

"Terrific. I'm bored to tears and can't even read a book with all the noise around here. I'll be at the library as soon as I can get there."

"The readers are in the back on the left, I'll see you there."

Not a word about their last meeting. Still, excitement flowed. She'd see Adam in a few minutes, and they'd start searching for a record of her birth.

Two hours later her enthusiasm had waned. Reading newspapers on microfilm strained the eyes and was boring. The birth announcements were in a different location each day, so the index had to be checked. A quick read and on to the next day. Piper took one month, Adam another. By the time they'd finished all the rolls, they each had a list of baby girls. Piper had twenty-six, Adam twenty-one. She had hoped for more.

"Go over the names and see if any are familiar," Adam said, sliding his list to her.

Piper read the names of the babies and mothers.

"None ring any bells," she said.

"That would've been too easy," he muttered.

He took both lists and rose.

"We'll turn in the film and head for the computers and check out death records. See if any of these women died that year."

The social security death index search did not turn up a single match.

"Dead end," she said.

"Cute. But there are other places to search."

"With the same results, probably."

"You give up too easily."

She shrugged. "In the greater scheme of things, I guess it really doesn't matter who my parents were. Knowing who gave me birth won't change the person I am."

"I'm not ready to quit."

She looked at him and knew she wasn't ready to give up either.

Besides, their search gave her the excuse to see more of Adam.

"It seems somewhat pointless to go through all these gyrations when Edith Harper and Margaret have the info we want."

"We have sources, but no way of making them talk. Come on, let's get out of here."

They walked out of the library into a blustery wind.

"It's going to storm," Piper predicted, as they hurried along the sidewalk.

"And soon from the looks of the sky," Adam added. "I wish you'd driven."

An ominous rumble of thunder rolled around them.

They were three blocks from the library when it started to rain.

"Shall we stop at the café?" she asked, huddling beneath an awning as the downpour increased.

"We can make a run for Sam's place. It isn't far. You go on ahead. I'll be there as soon as I can."

"You'll slip if you try to hurry," Piper said, not moving.

"I won't. Go on."

"I'll walk with you."

"No sense in both of us getting soaked."

"It's not cold. Actually, the rain feels good. Didn't you ever play in it when you were a kid?"

Adam shook his head in bemusement.

"That was different."

"Come on, let's get to Sam's."

As they walked, Piper lifted her face to the rain, letting it run freely down her cheeks. She blinked and shook the drops from her eyelashes.

"This is fun."

A bolt of lightning lit the sky to the left, followed almost immediately by a huge crack of thunder.

"Yikes, I'd forgotten about that," she said. "Let's get where it's safe."

They hurried as fast as Adam's injured leg permitted, but by the time they reached the safety of Sam's front porch, both were soaking wet.

Piper leaned over and wrung her hair out, then stood, pulling the wet shirt from her chest. "Now that the rain's cooled things down, it's not as warm as it was."

"Come inside. We'll get dry clothes."

She followed him inside Sam Witt's house. Looking at Adam, she was struck by how muscular he was. His shirt clung like a second skin, outlining the muscles of his chest and shoulders. Of course, he'd need to be fit to keep up with military personnel or emergency relief workers when reporting the news.

"I'll get you something to wear," Adam said, hobbling down the hall. "It'll be too big, but it'll do until your own clothes are dry."

Piper stayed by the front door, dripping onto the wooden floors. Once she'd changed, she'd find something to mop up the water before it did any damage.

When Adam returned, he'd shed his wet shirt. His skin was still damp, and the light dusting of dark hair on his chest gleamed. Piper swallowed hard, her eyes drawn to the splendid male physique.

"Here."

He handed her a towel and a cotton T-shirt.

She took it, raising her gaze to his. For the longest moment neither moved.

Then Adam raised his free hand and brushed back the wet hair from her cheek.

"You are so beautiful," he said.

"You are, too," she whispered.

When he lowered his head, she rose up on tiptoe to meet the kiss. Dropping the clothes and towel, she wrapped her arms around him and pressed her wet body against his. Instant heat. He pulled her tightly against him, deepening the kiss until Piper could think of nothing but Adam and the fact she was no longer cold from the rain.

He broke the kiss and leaned his forehead against hers.

"Sorry, but I need to get off my foot."

"By all means. Where shall we go?"

He hesitated a moment, looking deep into her eyes. "My bedroom is just down the hall," he said slowly.

Piper caught her breath. They were moving too fast. Much as she wanted to make love with Adam, she still hardly knew him. She found him fascinating, intriguing. But did that translate into trust?

"I'm rushing you," he said when she didn't speak.

"A bit. Is this something we both want?"

"It's something I want," he said. "But I don't intend to push the issue."

He stepped back and leaned on his cane.

"I meant it about my foot, though. I need to get off it before the pain escalates. Dry off in the hall bathroom. I'll change and then toss our clothes in the dryer."

He limped down the hall. Piper was tempted to follow him, to say to heck with her doubts and go for it. She knew he'd be as fantastic in bed as he was in front of the TV camera. But even though her body was screaming yes, she wasn't into casual sex.

She was afraid of getting involved with Adam. She liked to be on an even footing with men, and suspected he was a bit out of her league, no matter what Cassie said.

Taking the towel and shirt, she went into the guest bathroom and changed. The T-shirt was so big it fit like a baggy dress. She towel-dried her hair and left the towel on a rack, then bundled up her clothes and headed for the kitchen. Most likely, the laundry room was somewhere in the back of the house.

Adam was already in the kitchen, two tall glasses on the counter. He turned when she entered.

"Want some iced tea?" he asked. "It looks as if it's going to pour the rest of the afternoon."

The rain sheeted down. From time to time thunder sounded, growing gradually fainter each time. The main thrust of the storm was moving across the state.

"I'd love some. I can put these in the dryer, if you tell me where it is."

"Through that door."

That chore taken care of, Piper joined Adam at the small kitchen table. He was staring out the window, watching the rain. She took her glass and sipped, not so much to drink as to keep her hands from reaching out for the man across from her.

"So what next?"

"Maybe we should approach Margaret again," Adam said.

"I don't want to do that just yet. She's not well enough."

"We can get newspapers from other cities in Florida."

"I don't see how that would help. I'm not sure I'd recognize the names anyway. All the people I know in Margaret's life are here in Bradford. If she talked about former friends, I didn't pay attention. I wish I had, now."

"You still might not have made the connection."

"Not just for that reason. Margaret did so much for us. I should have been more interested in her as a person. How many people do you know who would take in three homeless girls and raise them. She tried so hard to keep us on the right path. Typical teenagers, we fought her every step of the way."

"I'll bet the three of you were cute when you were little," he teased.

Piper thought back to her earliest memories. Margaret had loved dressing them up and showing them off at church. She had taken them to swimming parties down by the river, made picnic lunches that

Piper still remembered. And she'd attended every school event.

Once again Piper felt guilty she'd stayed away so long.

"I should have come back after my first big success. To make sure she was doing all right. To tell her how much I appreciated her taking me on."

"Why didn't you?" Adam asked.

Piper shrugged.

"By then I was living in France. I'd come back once right after high school graduation, but I didn't get much of a welcome. That's when I went back to Adamson and married Billy Bob. I wanted to show the whole town I didn't need them. Only I was the one who found out being married meant nothing if I wasn't in love with the man."

"So you were in love with husband number two?"

"Yes, at least it felt like love. He really knows how to make a woman feel special and needed. Unfortunately, he doesn't know how to limit himself to his wife only."

The old hurt she'd felt when she'd discovered Jean-Paul with that other woman had taken a long time to fade.

"By then, I was working hard and barely had time to turn around, much less make a trip to Bradford."

"I still think we should tackle Margaret together," Adam said. "We can discuss Fiona and see if we get an opening to bring up your situation."

Piper felt certain this wasn't a good idea.

"I can't see her talking in front of a stranger. I think I'm stuck until she can communicate better. Do you know how hard it is to ask only yes or no questions?"

"Yes."

She laughed.

"Do you plan to marry again?"

Piper looked at him in surprise. Where had that question come from. "Why?"

Adam leaned forward, his gaze snaring hers.

"I'd like to get to know you more, see where this attraction leads. But I don't want any false hopes here. I'm not the marrying kind. As soon as I'm fit, I'll be back wherever the latest news is happening."

"I'm here through Independence Day, then I'll be returning to France."

Slowly she smiled.

"If you want to visit sometime, I'll show you the City of Lights. But I have no interest in marriage, either. I've tried it twice and it's not for me."

He held out his hand. Piper put hers into it, palm to palm.

Slowly he closed his fingers over hers and tugged gently. She rose from her chair. He pulled her down onto his lap and encircled her with his arms. The kiss was gentle and sweet, but Piper's blood heated instantly. There was no going back now.

9

Her cell phone chirped. Piper lifted her head, loath to leave the comfortable embrace of Adam's arms, but she was expecting Enrique to get back to her with names of models who could help at the fund-raiser. She was glad she'd remembered her phone today. Now she wasn't so sure.

"I need to get that," she said, slipping off his lap and going to the laundry room, where she'd left the phone when she put her clothes in the dryer.

"Hello?"

It was not Enrique, but her investment advisor. She immediately began speaking in French. He was not happy that she'd withdrawn such a large sum of money with no advance notice and wanted to know why she had done it. She liked Marc, and often took his advice, but it was her money to do with as she chose, and she carefully explained to him why she didn't owe him any explanations.

Adam had followed her to the door of the laundry room.

"Problem?" he asked, when she hung up.

"No."

She put the phone down.

"I didn't realize you spoke French so well."

She looked at him in surprise.

"I live in France—of course I speak the language."

"I've lived in other countries, but I never pick up more than enough to get by."

"But you're just visiting, I live there."

"Do you speak any other languages?"

"As a matter of fact, I do. German, Italian and Spanish."

"I'm impressed."

She considered that a moment.

"Why?"

He didn't respond. That hurt. Just because she had a pretty face didn't mean she didn't have a brain.

"You are so typically male. See a pretty woman and immediately assume she can't think."

She turned and opened the dryer, stopping the tumbling action. She snatched out her clothes, grabbed her phone and turned. Adam was still blocking the doorway.

"I'm getting dressed and heading out," she announced.

"I didn't mean to make you angry," he said slowly, reaching out to touch the bunched-up clothes. "They're still damp. Let them dry."

"No, thanks, I'm going."

"It's still raining."

"Then it won't matter if my clothes are damp, they'll just get wetter."

He didn't move and Piper wondered if she'd have to push him out of the way.

After a long moment, Adam stepped back and she swept past, heading for the small bathroom. In less than five minutes, she was out the door and trudging home in the downpour. Thankfully the heart of the storm had moved on and she didn't have to worry about lightning.

She knew she'd overreacted, but she didn't care.

Jean-Paul had thought she was dumb enough to put up with his unfaithfulness.

Billy Bob had figured she was only bright enough to do what he wanted.

She was a competent, successful businesswoman as well as a famous model.

Was that why she'd been so angry with Adam? Was she still worried about her past mistakes?

She didn't like that thought. What did she have to be scared about? She knew better than to get too involved with a rolling stone like Adam. He was a man who lived for the story—wherever that story was.

She had her own life and wasn't planning to alter it. It suited her perfectly.

When she reached the old house, she went right to her dresser, which was stored in the hall, to get dry clothes. The workmen were busy demolishing the walls between her bedroom and Fiona's old room. Taking her clothes, she went to the third floor. The bath there was an old-fashioned claw-foot tub with added shower, so she quickly stripped down and warmed up beneath the hot spray.

Dressing in fresh clothes, she decided to forget about Adam Saunders for the time being.

Piper called Betsy to see if her mother would talk with her about Margaret, but she didn't answer.

Piper tried the café next. Betsy was there. She gave Piper her mother's cell number and Piper made the call.

"I don't know if you remember me, Mrs. Fellows, I'm a friend of Betsy's from high school, Piper Morgan?"

"The supermodel. Honey, there isn't anyone in town who won't claim to remember you now. What can I do for you?"

"I wondered if I could come by for a few minutes. I wanted to ask you what you remember about Margaret bringing me here. It seems unusual for Margaret to have taken in a foster child—a baby—and I thought there might have been some gossip around town."

"There was always gossip about everyone in town, the Nunes included. Of course, I was pregnant with Betsy when you first arrived. And Margaret really was more of my mother's generation. Maybe you should talk with Mom."

"You think she would remember more?"

"Probably. Let me give you her number."

When Piper reached Betsy's grandmother, she invited Piper to stop by.

"I don't know all the details," Mrs. Shields warned her. "Margaret and I were never best friends. She was a year or two ahead of me in school, and the Nunes were a law unto themselves. Come on by and I'll let you know what I remember."

Mrs. Shields met Piper at the door. Betsy's grandparents' home was in an older part of town, with wide lawns and old trees. Her yard reminded Piper of the one at Bradford Hall, lots of flowers in colorful mixes.

"I do declare, you are even prettier than I remember," Mrs. Shields said when she opened the door for Piper. "Come in out of the rain. I know we need it, but I always figured it would work better if it rained between midnight and dawn and left the daylight hours in sunshine."

Piper smiled and stepped inside. The house was immaculate. A hint of apple seemed to fill the air.

"I appreciate your taking time to see me. I'm trying to find out where I came from and all, and hope you can help me out."

"Finding your roots, huh? That family history research is really popular these days. I heard Margaret can't talk. Can she write?"

Piper shook her head.

"She seems to be able to think clearly, but she has trouble processing thoughts into written or spoken words. The doctors are cautiously optimistic she'll get past that."

"Such a shame. I fixed us some iced tea. We'll sit in the front room and I'll tell you all I remember about Margaret Nunes and her family. The family will end with her, you know. I'm certain her father wanted a boy to carry on the family name. Men were much more into that kind of thing back then, don't you think?"

Piper nodded. She took the glass Mrs. Shields handed her and settled back on the sofa.

"I found out that Margaret took me in as a baby even before being approved as a foster parent. It started me thinking about the past and why such a thing would have been allowed. Or why Margaret would have even done it. Do you remember hearing about it?"

"Goodness, the Nunes were always fodder for the gossip mills. Old man Nunes was something of a tyrant. He ran the mill and didn't take kindly to anyone offering up ideas on improvement or modernization, though he'd sometimes take the advice ungraciously and implement change because of it. His wife died when she was young. I wonder if her being around longer would have changed things. He ruled that household with an iron fist. But he was generous with his daughter. He was always sending her off on trips. She went to England one summer, and another time was an exchange student in Paris, I think it was. Then she spent a spring in New York or some place up North. I was envious a time or two when she came back to school and talked about where she'd been."

"She never married, which I always thought was too bad," Piper said, hoping her comment might shed some light on the past.

"That's the truth. She dated a lot in high school, but

it never amounted to anything. Who wanted to have to deal with Mr. Nunes? By the time he died, she was middle-aged and already had you girls. I think y'all gave her lots of happiness."

"Maybe when we were younger, but I know we were hellions when we were teenagers," Piper said remorsefully.

Only now did she realize the full extent of the distress they must have caused Margaret. It was so unfair.

Mrs. Shields laughed.

"All teenagers are hellions at one time or another. I expect it was harder with three at once. But Margaret had strong principles. I'm sure she was up to it."

"You didn't see her much after graduation?"

"No, we didn't move in the same circles. Then I got married. Single women and married ones didn't intermix a lot—not so much in common anymore. Plus there was the financial differences in our situations. The Nunes had money, my folks didn't."

"Yet she had very little income when we were growing up."

"Oh, well, I expect most of the income came from her father running the mill. Once he died, things must have changed. Maybe he hadn't managed his investments well. She has that lovely old house, though."

"Do you remember when she brought me home?"

"I sure do."

Mrs. Shields smiled.

"Gossip ran wild that next month or so. No one ever expected Margaret Nunes to defy her father that way. Old man Nunes did not want children running around. But somehow she must have convinced him."

"He died when I was still a baby, didn't he?"

"That's what I recall. Nothing changed much. Margaret must have had *some* money from her father, because she never worked outside the home that I know of."

"Don't you find it odd that a spinster of about forty suddenly decided to foster three girls?"

"I'm not sure I do. I think when a woman turns that age, she really takes a long look at her life. Maybe Margaret knew she'd never have children of her own and wanted the experience of raising a child. It is fulfilling you know. I raised six. My daughter Martha only had Betsy and Phil, more's the pity. But two of my sons have four children each. I have seventeen grandchildren," she added proudly.

Piper felt a touch of envy at the woman's pride and happiness in her family. That was something Piper would never know. No babies, no grandchildren.

Unless at some time in the future she decided to adopt or foster children as Margaret had.

The idea surprised her. It wasn't something she'd considered before. Could she see herself taking care of a child? Raising him or her to be a responsible adult? Dealing with the problems of a teenager?

"Of course, the person you should talk to is Edith Harper. She and Margaret were best friends. She even went with Margaret on her summer tour of England.

Her family were the Parkersons, and they had money as well. Even though Edith married Bert Harper, she and Margaret remained close."

"I've spoken with Mrs. Harper," Piper said, hoping her frustration with that particular interview didn't show. "She wasn't able to help me."

"Let's see. There was a young girl who helped Margaret back then. I imagine it was a shock dealing with a newborn at her age. What was her name? I think it was Emiline Ruthers. If not, Rosalee over at Mrs. Harper's would know what her name was. You might see if you can find out anything further from Emiline. I don't know if she's still in town, but if she worked at the house, she'd know as much as anyone."

"Thanks, I'll try. I'm not having much luck locating my birth parents."

"I don't know who else to suggest if Emiline doesn't work out. Margaret had some other friends, but the family was private and I'm not sure how much she spoke about her personal affairs to others."

"Thank you for your time."

"Oh, don't go yet. Tell me about living in Paris. I've never been to Europe, but Paris is the city I'd like most to visit. Is it as wonderful as I think it is?"

Piper was glad to talk about her adopted city. And it was the least she could do to repay Mrs. Shields for the tip she'd given Piper.

As soon as she reached home, Piper went to the phone book to look up Emiline Ruthers. No listing. There was a T. Ruthers. She dialed that number.

"I'm looking for Emiline Ruthers," she said when a woman answered.

"She doesn't live here."

"Do you know where she is? I'd like to reach her."

"She married years ago and lives in Atlanta. Who is this?"

"Piper Morgan. I think she knew me when I was a baby. Margaret Nunes raised me."

"Oh, you're one of those girls. I reckon Emiline knew a lot about the goings-on there. She lives in Atlanta."

"Can you give me her phone number or address? I'd really like to touch base with her."

"Why?"

"I'm looking for my birth parents and hope she might know something."

"She doesn't."

"If I could just speak with her."

"Give me your number and I'll let her know you're looking to talk to her," the woman said.

Piper complied, wishing she could get Emiline's number directly and call her right now.

Why was nothing easy, she fumed as she hung up.

The house was quiet. The workmen had left for the day. Piper went to the kitchen, but there was nothing cooking. Cassie was on a job. Not that Piper needed Cassie to cook for her. She was perfectly capable of taking care of herself. It was just that she'd become used to having Cassie around.

Her phone rang. She quickly answered. Maybe Emiline Ruthers was calling.

Instead, she recognized Marjorie Tamlin.

"Piper, are you free tonight? A bunch of us wanted to get together with you to talk over old times and hear all about Paris."

"Who is the bunch?" Piper asked, thinking of Norm and his idea of getting together to hash over those same old times.

"Lulu and Connie, Pam if she can get a babysitter, and Julia. How about it. Won't it be fun?"

"Sounds like it," Piper said slowly.

It might be nice to see some of the girls she'd hung out with in high school.

And she could use a break from thinking about Adam and how much she was coming to rely on him.

"Okay, count me in. What time and where?"

Marjorie gave her the details.

"Learn anything new on your family?" she asked.

"Not yet."

"What about Fiona?"

"Nothing there either. Somebody's got to know something."

"Keep looking, I'm sure something will turn up. See you in a bit."

Piper no sooner put the receiver down than the phone rang again.

"Thanks for answering this time," Adam said.

He'd been trying to reach her ever since she had left earlier. She'd been hurt. He'd seen it in her eyes, though she'd acted as if it didn't matter.

Adam knew she was beautiful, and smart. Of course she'd speak French after living in France for so many years. Why had he been surprised?

He'd be lucky if she spoke to him again. Some serious fence-mending was required if he wanted to pursue the path they'd started down. And he did.

"Did you call before?" she asked.

"Several times, no answer. Then your line was busy. Look, I was an idiot. Sorry for the comment. It had nothing to do with you. Call it a side effect of the pain meds or something."

"Fine."

He waited for her to say more, but there was silence on the line.

"That's it?" he asked.

"I'll attribute your bad manners and insults to the medication. What else do you want?"

Darn, she was being difficult.

"To see you. How about dinner tonight? We can try one of the other restaurants Sam recommended."

"I'm busy."

"Doing what?"

"Not that it's any of your business, but I'm going out to dinner."

Adam didn't like the sharp prick of jealousy he felt.

"With Cassie and Matt?"

"No, with a friend," she said.

He'd told her he wanted to see more of her, see where their attraction led. But that didn't give him exclusive rights. He didn't want them, anyway. If something developed while they were in Bradford, fine–if not, equally fine.

He frowned. He was lying to himself.

"How about Saturday?"

"What about Saturday."

"Dinner," he said through gritted teeth.

She was deliberately baiting him.

"Isn't that charity dinner in New Orleans next Saturday?"

"Yes, you're still going, right?"

"Sure. But I need a dress, since I didn't bring anything like that with me. If Cassie's free, I need to go shopping this Saturday. So I don't know about dinner. I might be too tired."

He hadn't thought about clothes for the charity event. He didn't have anything suitable to wear, either.

"How about I take you shopping. I need to get one of my suits from my folks' place in Baton Rouge. I may even have the cast off by then. Be nice to wear a pair of pants that don't have one leg slit up the side."

"Think of it as sexy," she said in a throaty voice.

He thought of her as sexy.

Gripping the receiver, he regretted his stupid remark about her speaking French more than ever.

"You'd have to drive," he said, "but we can leave early in the morning and make a day of it—have dinner someplace in the Vieux Carre and enjoy some lazy jazz."

"How early? I don't know how late I'll be tonight."

"Not too early, then."

Did she have to remind him about her date?

"About ten?"

"You'll drive?"

"I'll see if Cassie will give me a ride to Sam's place and we'll take your car."

"It's a date."

She laughed and said goodbye.

Adam hung up, bemused. He was getting too involved. But she intrigued him. There was a lot more to Piper than he'd first thought. Discovering the different layers was a challenge he looked forward to.

Dinner that night proved to be more fun than Piper expected. Marjorie picked her up and drove to the restaurant. The others arrived soon after, and before long Piper felt as if she'd only been away a short time. These friends had never been as close as Fiona and Cassie, but they were girls from her past who knew what it was like growing up in Bradford.

Despite her enjoyment, the thought of seeing Adam early the next day hovered in her mind. She hoped they could manage to spend a day together without arguing.

Although the traditional Southern fare that the restaurant was known for was well prepared, the meal seemed secondary to the conversation, and everyone was talking at once, their group the last to leave the restaurant.

"Let's do this again next week," Connie suggested.

"Let's do it every week," Lulu said, hugging Piper. "Can't believe you stayed away so long!"

"I'm not going to be here much beyond Independence Day," Piper protested.

"Then every weekend until then," Lulu insisted. "And maybe you'll have to come back more often in the future."

The glow from the evening lasted all the way home. Piper thanked Marjorie for arranging dinner. It had been fascinating to see how the women had turned out, and as far as she could tell, they all seemed happy. Piper felt happy herself.

Life hadn't turned out half-bad for two of Margaret Nunes's foster girls.

Cassie dropped Piper at Sam's place a few minutes before ten o'clock the next morning.

"Why not get a car of your own?" she asked.

"Why, when I can use his rental? I only need to drive with Adam, it seems."

"When does his cast come off?"

"He goes in next week to that orthopedist in New Orleans. He's counting on it coming off then."

"So he'll be leaving soon?"

"As far as I know, he's here through Independence Day, same as me. He did promise to help with the fund raiser and roped those two Saints in. I can't see him being totally fit and ready to return to a disaster or war zone even by then."

"So we'll have at least another three weeks of his company," Cassie said.

"Looks like it."

Adam had the door open by the time Cassie drove off. The day was like the previous ones, hot and muggy. He came down the stairs and tossed her the keys.

"Ready when you are," he said, heading for the car.

Soon they were on the highway to New Orleans. Soft jazz played on the radio, and the air-conditioning kept the car cool. She could drive like this forever.

"Have fun last night?" he asked.

"I had a wonderful time," she said, glancing at him.

He stared straight ahead. Did he care or was he just making conversation?

"Where did you go?"

"To a restaurant near Bentonville. We shut the place down."

"Hard getting up this morning?"

She laughed softly.

"No. It was a small family restaurant, closed at eleven. I was in bed before midnight."

"Your own?"

She looked at him.

"Why, Adam Saunders, are you asking where I slept last night?"

"It's none of my business, I know," he said, avoiding her eyes.

"No, it's not. But if you care to know, I was in my

own bed. Marjorie didn't want to stay up and talk. After a full day at the sheriff's department, she was tired herself."

He swung around and looked at her.

"You went out with the sheriff's secretary?"

"And with Pam Stark, Lulu Evans and Connie Lightowler. All friends from high school. Who did you think I went out with?"

"You know perfectly well I thought you had a date with some guy."

Piper moved to pass a slower vehicle. When she slid back into the first lane, she looked at him for a second.

"I thought we were going to see where this mutual attraction would lead. How can you suggest I'd be seeing someone else?"

"Pull over and I'll show you where this attraction will lead."

She laughed, delighting in the rough emotion in his voice. If she'd ever doubted the intensity of his feelings for her, she didn't now.

"We're going shopping, and then having dinner in the Big Easy. Sounds like fun."

"Only because I'm doing it with you."

"Wow, no wonder you're good on the news—you have a way with words."

She was surprisingly touched by his comment.

"I'd rather have my way with you."

Piper felt a flush of heat wash through her. She knew he wanted her. He'd told her that before. But it was her own response that surprised her. She'd never felt such a powerful longing for anyone before. How would they spend the day shopping, surrounded by crowds, when they both would rather be someplace alone, just the two of them?

"Maybe we need some ground rules," she said pensively.

"Like?" He reached over and skimmed the back of his fingers down her cheek. "You're pretty when you drive..."

"And?"

"And when you're not driving. What kind of ground rules?"

"Exclusivity?" she asked.

"Fine by me. I'm not interested in anyone else at the moment. As long as it works both ways."

"Of course."

"What else?"

"No sex."

"*What?* I thought that was the entire point." Adam sounded horrified.

"I want to see if there's more to this than sex," she said firmly.

"I told you there'd be no forever after," he said.

"That's fine by me. Don't believe in it anymore. But I don't want what might prove to be a great friendship ruined by hopping into bed just because we feel this initial attraction."

"No sex ever?" he asked.

Piper flicked another glance his way.

"Maybe not forever, but for a little while. If I go to bed with someone, I want it to mean something. I did it the other way too many times when I was a kid and always ended up feeling used."

He was quiet and she wondered if she'd revealed more than he wanted to know. Or should know. Not that she cared. She was going into this with total honesty.

"You're quiet. Didn't you think there'd been other men in my life?"

"I'm trying not to think about it."

She laughed wryly.

"You knew I wasn't some shy young virgin."

"My guess is you were never shy a day in your life."

"But I was a virgin once, a long time ago. See, maybe this is a good thing. We're already running into a roadblock."

"I didn't say that."

"What did you expect?"

"I know you've had sex before. You were married so obviously. I just don't like thinking about you with someone else."

"There hasn't been anyone recently. I don't think I've had a date in months. And I'm very particular about what I do now."

"Okay, we take it slow for a while. Does slow include kisses?"

She thought about it for a moment. She could feel herself grow warm just thinking about the kisses they'd shared.

"Maybe a few kisses."

He ran his fingers over her arm, down to her wrist. "Touching?"

She drew a shaky breath.

"Okay, maybe touching, too. But no full body contact."

"You will let me know when it's appropriate, won't you? And make sure it's before July fourth!"

"I doubt I can last that long," she murmured.

"Good, because I know I can't."

He squeezed her hand slightly then let it go.

Tension shimmered between them. She was starting to care for this man, and while she wasn't looking for some long-term relationship, she didn't want things to get too complicated too fast.

Adam turned up the radio and they listened to music as the miles sped by.

"I want to start on Canal Street in the French Quarter," she said when they reached the city. "The stores there should have something I can wear."

"Let's eat first, then we'll have an uninterrupted afternoon to shop till we drop."

Piper found a parking lot as close to the French Quarter as she could. "You underestimate me if you think it's going to take me all afternoon to find a dress to wear."

"I've gone with my sister a time or two, so I know how long it will take."

Piper took his words as a challenge.

"Tell me about your sister, and I'll show you a different way to shop."

10

The restaurant they chose was near the parking lot. Piper knew they'd be doing enough walking in the afternoon without going farther to eat. She was aware of Adam's injuries, even though the man himself seemed to ignore them. Would he recover as swiftly as he seemed determined to do? There were some things that couldn't be altered no matter how determined a person was.

After they ordered, she said, "Tell me about that sister. Does she live in Louisiana?"

"Atlanta. She married a guy she met in college. Ed's a dentist. They have three kids." For the next several minutes, Adam told her about his sister and her family.

"Why didn't you stay with her to convalesce?" Piper asked.

"I did for a couple of weeks. Stayed with my folks, too, up in Baton Rouge. Too much mothering."

"So Sam's a better choice."

She couldn't imagine treating Adam as an invalid. He was far too independent to allow that for long.

"He sure doesn't try to mother me. I thought it'd be

like the old days. He and I went to school together. But Sam's changed."

"How so?"

Adam seemed to find it hard to put in words, but he talked about how different Sam's life was in Bradford from the one he'd led in New Orleans.

"You have to admit Bradford is quieter than this city."

"True. But Sam's older, now. You said his wife died. Maybe he wanted a change—to settle for a different kind of life."

"That's just it, why settle? He's only thirty-two. He could do anything he wanted."

"Maybe that's exactly what he's doing."

Adam shook his head. "I can't see it."

"That's because it's not the life for you. I can't see staying in Bradford forever, but Cassie seems to have flourished since she's returned. She and Matt are now talking about living there and having him commute when he has work in New Orleans. With the mini building boom in Bradford, he might just find enough work there to keep him more than busy. But to change the subject, when do you see the doctor?"

"Tuesday. The cast should come off then."

"And then what?"

"Walking support for a few weeks, and exercises to strengthen the muscles. I was planning to rent a place in New Orleans for that phase, but I'll stay with Sam and see about getting help from the local hospital in Bradford."

"Is Sam driving you in on Tuesday?" she asked.

Adam nodded. "It's hard for me to drive now, and I don't know how weak the foot and ankle will be when the cast comes off."

"How did you get the rental car to his place if you can't drive?"

"It's hard to drive, not impossible. My leg really hurt for two days afterward. I don't want to do that again until I'm ready."

When lunch was finished, they headed for St. Charles Street. The first store they went into had a sale in progress and was crowded.

"Not this one," Piper said, looking around at the merchandise.

They walked to the next one. It was almost empty of customers except for three giggling teenagers. Piper headed over to one of the display racks and began flipping through the dresses.

She picked out one and looked a minute longer. Choosing another, she turned just as one of the teenagers held up a bright red dress.

"Isn't this to die for?" she said to her friends. "I'm going to try it on."

"It's not for you," Piper said, without thinking.

"What?" The girl turned around and looked at Piper in surprise. "Who are you?"

"Just someone who knows about clothes. That dress is wrong for you."

"You're not my mother," the girl said as her friends drew closer.

Piper should have let the matter drop, but she knew the girl would not look good in that dress.

She walked over to the rack beside them. "You're getting something for a special event, right?"

"Prom," she muttered.

"Then you want something that will knock your date's socks off."

She pushed dress after dress along the rod, barely glancing at most of them. Finally she pulled out a lavender dress, held it up and looked at it front and back.

"Try this one," she said, offering it to the teen.

For a moment the girl hesitated.

"I'd take her advice if I were you," Adam said. "Monique is a model from Paris, so she knows clothes."

"A model?" one of the girls repeated, eyes wide.

"Paris?" the second squeaked.

Piper frowned at Adam.

"Yes, but I'm visiting family here. Try it on. What can it hurt?"

The girl took the dress and headed for the dressing room.

"I'll try these to see if one fits," Piper said, holding up the dresses she'd chosen for herself.

Five minutes later she decided to buy both. Just in case something else came up.

Stepping out of the dressing room, she ran into the teenager wearing the lavender dress. The girl smiled shyly at Piper.

"I look terrific in this dress."

"That's what you want. Call attention to yourself, not the clothes."

When her friends saw her, their eyes opened in awe.

"Oh, man, I want you to pick out a dress for me," one of the girls said.

Piper laughed. Adam looked amused.

"Okay," she said. "Come on. Are you all going to the prom?"

"Susie hasn't been asked yet," the first girl said, looking at the shortest of the three teenagers. "But I'm sure Jim will ask you, just be patient. You need to get a dress for when he does."

Half an hour later, Piper and Adam left the shop and three starry-eyed girls behind.

"Nice of you to help them out like that," Adam said. "They seemed to really appreciate the advice on makeup. They'll be fans for life."

"They're nice kids. I hope they have fun at the prom. But I'm glad I'm not a teenager. All those issues about guys and clothes and makeup."

Talking with the girls had given Piper the glimmer of an idea she wanted to discuss with Margaret. What if she and Cassie could work with the teenagers at the home Matt and Margaret were planning. Cassie could help with basic cooking skills, and she could advise them on fashion and makeup.

She couldn't wait to talk to Margaret about it.

"So I take it back," Adam said as they headed for the car. "You do shop faster than my sister."

"And we have most of the afternoon ahead if we're not returning home until after dinner," she said.

"It's too early to eat. Want to find a quiet bar where someone's playing sax and have a drink?"

"Sounds good to me."

They found an open-air bar where the music was slow and the service fast. Sipping their drinks, they watched people stroll by. Mostly tourists, Piper thought, hoping they were soaking up the ambience of the Quarter to take home and treasure.

She looked at Adam. He looked back.

"This is nice," she said.

She felt completely at ease, not as if she were on display, or had to make a favorable impression. How long since she'd been able to just be herself without thinking of her job?

He raised his glass in a silent toast and nodded.

The gunfire came from nowhere. Adam acted instinctively and dived for Piper, pulling her down with him, turning over the table and chairs in their way.

Other patrons dropped to the ground, as well, frantically looking around.

The shots came from farther up the street. Adam made sure he was between Piper and the direction of the gunfire. There were a couple more shots, then silence. One man raised his head to peer over a table.

"Is it safe?" a woman called from their right.

Adam gazed down into Piper's eyes. His adrenaline was coursing through his veins. For a moment it was like being back in Ukraine, though he didn't see any bodies or smell the blood. The acrid smell of gunpowder drifted in the air, though.

Sirens sounded, and in less time than it took Adam to pull Piper up, the street was filled with police cars.

"Whatever it was, I think we're safe," Adam said, watching the crowd gathering in the next block.

"You want to go see?" she asked.

He looked at her.

"I do, but only to report on what's going on. I'm not on assignment, so I'll try to restrain my curiosity."

"I bet a local news team will be on it in no time. But if you want to go, I'd love to see you in action. You're here, you might as well scoop the story."

He picked up his cane and started toward the crowd.

"If there's no more danger, we'll check it out. But if I tell you to duck, do it at once."

By the time they reached the scene of the shooting, police had a section of sidewalk closed. Two people lay on the ground, bleeding. Piper looked away, feeling her stomach turn. In only a second, Adam flashed his press card, stepped beneath the police tape and started talking to the cop guarding the scene.

Piper moved to one side, watching him as he asked question after question, first of the policeman, then witnesses to the shooting.

He was lost from her sight when the ambulance attendants arrived. One of the victims was dead, the other clung to life.

Piper shuddered, wishing she hadn't come here. Would Adam have left her at the bar? Maybe she should return. The waiter probably thought they'd stuck him with the bill.

A local news van careened to a stop, and a reporter and cameraman jumped out. When the reporter realized who was already there asking questions, he was elated.

Piper was close enough to hear his report.

"Ladies and gentlemen, this is a stroke of luck. With me is Adam Saunders, foreign reporter for CNN. How did you happen to be here at this time? What's been happening?"

Adam faced the camera and began reporting what he'd learned in the few minutes he'd been at the scene.

Piper was fascinated. Without a single note, he reported facts from the police and two of the witnesses. He did not name names, and he was calm and collected, talking to the television audience as if he were standing in front of them. His manner was cool, his delivery concise.

The young reporter beside him was almost delirious with excitement. When the report ended, he shook Adam's hand and offered to buy him a drink. By this time the police were asking people to clear the street.

The man was perfect for his job, Piper thought, leaning against the building as she waited for him. She hoped his foot healed enough for him to resume his work as soon as he wanted.

"You all right?" he asked, coming up to her a few moments later.

"Fine. And you're happy as a clam, aren't you?"

"It felt good."

The local reporter joined them.

"I'm Paul Casey, local news seven."

He shook her hand.

"The cameraman had to get the film to the studio, but I'm buying Adam a drink. You're with him? Can I buy you a drink, too?"

Piper smiled at the man's obvious hero worship.

"I'd love to share a drink with you both."

"We need to return to the bar we left to settle accounts."

Adam indicated the establishment down the block. The tables had been restored to their proper places, though few people were in sight.

Paul beamed.

"Great, just great."

They chose to sit outside, even though Piper felt a little apprehensive.

Adam and Paul discussed what they'd learned from the police while she sipped her drink, thankful that in her job the most dangerous aspect was the possibility of falling off a runway or too much sun exposure when an outdoor shoot took too long.

She listened as Paul asked Adam questions. She smiled at his energy and enthusiasm.

Adam looked older than his years, defined by cynicism, where as Paul still seemed the wide-eyed rookie, eager for new experiences and new challenges. Had Adam ever been that open and easy to read?

He looked at her. "You about ready to leave?"

"Sure."

She nodded to Paul.

"Not what I expected from an afternoon in New Orleans. Is it always this dangerous?"

"Crime happens everywhere," he said.

"Monique is a model from Paris," Adam announced.

She glared at him as Paul turned his attention to her, his eyes bright with excitement.

"Really? Would you consent to do an interview with me for a feature segment? I'm really trying to get noticed by the powers that be, and if I can show a wide range of abilities, they'll have to give me more assignments."

"I'm on vacation," Piper protested.

"It won't take long. I can get my cameraman and be back in just a few minutes."

"Maybe another time."

"We'll be here next week for the charity dinner the Saints are putting on," Adam told him. "Will you be covering that?"

"Not my assignment."

"Come anyway,"

Adam said, handing Paul his business card with a contact number.

"We'll give you an exclusive."

"Oh, man. Thanks!"

The reporter stood and reached out to shake Adam's hand, then grinned at Piper and headed back to work.

"We'll give him an exclusive?" she asked when Paul had gone.

"If you're going to be on TV, I thought you'd want to be dressed to the nines. Keep the image up."

"And you?"

"I want to be without a cast. I don't want people to suspect I won't be returning soon."

"Ah."

Adam looked at her questioningly.

"I hope you don't mind. I really wanted to give the kid a break."

Piper had to give him credit for honesty at least.

"It's still too early to eat dinner," she said. "What did you have planned for the rest of the afternoon?"

They were ambling down the sidewalk, away from the shooting scene and toward the parking lot.

"I thought a drive along the river. Change of scene from murder and mayhem."

"Good idea."

"You all right? You didn't have to get so close to the victims."

"I was watching you in action. You're a natural. I couldn't have given a report like that if I'd practiced an hour beforehand."

"It's my job."

"And you love it."

"I do."

They walked in silence for a moment.

Then Adam said, "Do you have a problem with that?"

"Maybe with the risks you take. Today you arrived immediately after the event, but I've seen you in war zones with mortars firing nearby. What if one struck you?"

"Then the newscast would have something else to report. I'm not as reckless as you seem to think. We have servicemen and women putting their lives on the line every day. I'm merely telling the world what's going on. And I take precautions."

"Do you?"

"I'm not self-destructive," he said mildly. "I'm looking for a Pulitzer and want to be alive to accept it."

Piper shivered a little. Until now she'd taken the reporting she saw on the nightly news for granted. Now that she actually knew someone on the front lines, she had a better appreciation for the dangers. She didn't want anything worse to happen to Adam than the land-mine incident he was recovering from.

As if they'd made an agreement, their conversation the rest of the afternoon was about noncontroversial topics. They commented on the gardens they saw from the road, the lazy pace of life people living on the banks of the slow-moving Mississippi seemed to enjoy, and the possibility of floods.

They ate dinner at a small Creole place near the quarter and headed for Bradford before it grew dark. Piper was feeling content as the miles sped by. She'd enjoyed the day, except for the shooting incident.

"A day for both of us," she murmured.

"What?"

"Just thinking. I had fun at the dress shop, you had fun at the shooting."

"Not so. I never enjoy seeing or reporting acts of violence. I merely report them."

"You love the reporting."

"Different matter entirely. I could be happy reporting on other news, like the launch of a new shuttle, or the discovery of a black hole somewhere beyond Pluto."

She had doubts about that. Those stories seemed so tame compared to war coverage. But maybe she was wrong. He'd been more committed to her search for her parents than she'd thought he'd be. When she'd first approached him for help, all she wanted was a few suggestions. His actual involvement was a plus.

"You're awfully quiet," he said.

"I'm thinking about my folks and the help you've given me. I know this has to be pretty tame stuff, but it means so much to me."

"I can understand that. I've thought how I would feel if I didn't know my parents or my sister. If I was alone in the world."

"I'm not alone," she insisted. "I have Cassie and Margaret. And Fiona, if we ever find her. Some ties are never broken, no matter how thin they're stretched."

When they reached Bradford, Adam suggested she go straight to Margaret's house and he'd drive the short distance to Sam's by himself. Piper pulled into the long driveway at Bradford Hall. The lights were on in the front.

"Guess Cassie's home," she said.

216 | BARBARA MCMAHON

"You sound disappointed."

"No. Well, a little. I thought we'd have some time together alone. It's still early."

"We can sit on the porch and listen to the crickets. I don't have a curfew."

She laughed.

"Me, either, though sometimes I expect Margaret to call me inside. We did have curfews growing up."

"Was Margaret strict?"

"We sure thought she was, but now I wonder if that was totally fair. She was doing her best to raise us right, and I think she did a good job. She instilled good values in us. I never had a problem fitting in with Jean-Paul's family and friends, thanks to the manners she'd drilled into us. She was from an old Southern family, where good manners were paramount."

They had made their way to the old swing on the porch and sat listening to the crickets as Adam had suggested.

Piper laid her dresses carefully over the railing.

The air was warm, but without the sticky heat of the day. Slowly Piper relaxed. The day had proved unexpected in many ways. And her feelings for Adam were changing. The more time she spent with him, the greater the attraction she felt for the man.

She didn't wish to repeat past mistakes, though. They were going to be together for such a short time. Should she take a chance and explore whatever he offered for the next few weeks or guard herself so she didn't risk being hurt?

She needed to talk to Cassie. She'd have some

sound advice.

Or maybe not. Cassie was so in love with Matt she figured everyone else should be in love, too.

Piper would have to trust her own instincts.

And what were they telling her about Adam? He was kind. Look how generous he'd been to Paul, inviting him to the charity event so he could get exclusive photos and an interview. She bet Adam would corral those football friends of his to be interviewed, as well.

He hadn't lost his cynicism, but he was big enough to open a few doors for a guy just starting out in his career.

She'd been impressed.

Cassie came out onto the porch.

"I thought I heard a car. What are you two doing out here? Want something cool to drink?"

"Nothing for me, thanks."

Adam stood up to leave.

"I'm heading for home."

"Thanks for the day in New Orleans," Piper said a little wistfully.

"Don't leave on my account," Cassie offered. "I'm not staying. I just wanted to tell Piper to lock up. I'm going up to our room."

"I need to be going," Adam insisted.

Cassie leaned against a post on the porch and watched as he limped to the car and drove off.

"Sorry if I sent him packing," she said.

"We weren't talking. Actually, I was trying to think of a way to get him to kiss me."

"Oh, darn. Now I'm really sorry for the interruption."

"We're supposed to be taking things slowly, but sometimes it feels too slow."

"You want to speed things up?"

"Am I being dumb? I'm here for another four weeks max. Then it's back to Paris. Adam said he'd stay until the Independence Day fund-raiser, then he's off to who knows where. It'd probably be better if we didn't get any more involved."

"Only?" Cassie asked.

"Only—I think I want him as much as he said he wants me."

Piper could hardly wait to see Margaret the next morning. She and Cassie had talked until late. She'd told Cassie about her idea of offering special classes for the teens at the home, and Cassie had loved the idea. Her only concern was who would teach the girls the styling skills, since Piper would be in Paris. Cassie volunteered to start a basic course in meal preparation and wanted to plan a schedule so the girls could get used to planning meals, grocery shopping and cooking for those staying at Bradford Hall.

Piper headed for the convalescent hospital as soon as she finished eating her breakfast of toast and tea. She caught Margaret before she was scheduled for physical therapy.

"Good morning!"

Piper gave her a hug and sat in the visitor's chair.

"Adam Saunders took me to New Orleans yesterday—sorry I couldn't come by. Cassie said she let you know."

Margaret nodded and said something that sounded almost like, *nice day.*

"I had a great day. Is it me or is your speech starting to come back?"

"Betta," Margaret said proudly.

"Terrific. In no time, you'll be able to fuss at us like you did when we were girls, remember."

"Nnnneed."

"I bet we did need it. Get well fast, Margaret. There's so much we can talk about."

Piper was amazed at how much clearer Margaret's speech sounded. Maybe she would make a complete recovery. Piper hoped so. She wanted Margaret around for a long time.

"I had a brilliant idea while I was shopping yesterday. I know you and Matt talked about taking in teenagers and making sure they got schooling and all. What about teaching them other things, too? Cassie could teach them to cook, and you could get someone to teach them about clothes and makeup, and someone else could handle budgeting. It's so important for women to know how to manage their money."

Margaret looked stricken for a moment and Piper remembered the loan.

"Everybody hits bad times once in a while."

"Hugh," Margaret said, nodding thoughtfully.

"Hugh? Who is that?" Piper asked.

Margaret shook her head in frustration and raised her good hand, pointing to Piper. "Hugh."

"Me? Oh, Margaret, I can't stay. My home's in Paris. My career, everything. I'd have to start all over in the States."

Margaret nodded rapidly, growing agitated.

"Okay, I'll think of something,"

Piper was once again worried that Margaret was becoming upset. But how could she make the kind of money she was used to if she stayed in the States? She needed that income to provide for her old age. Surely Margaret could understand that. They'd have to discuss it later, but not today.

For the rest of the visit, Piper expanded on her ideas, sharing the plans she and Cassie had come up with the night before. Piper was almost as caught up in making the home work as Matt and Cassie and Margaret. She knew that with Internet access they could keep in touch daily, but it wouldn't be the same as actually being here.

She could come visit in a few months, but by then the initial setup would be completed. They probably wouldn't need her help.

She couldn't think about that now. Neither she nor Cassie had told Margaret of their fund-raising plans. Or the fact that they planned to pay off the loan and bring Margaret the papers for a ceremonial burning.

Would Margaret be pleased or would pride make her angry at Piper's attempts to help?

For a moment she felt like a teenager again, unsure of what she was doing.

"Are you up to visitors besides family?" Piper asked.

Margaret nodded slowly.

"I want you to meet Adam Saunders. I'm sure you've seen him on TV reporting from trouble spots. He's staying with the sheriff and has been helping me—" oops, she almost revealed she was still looking for her mother, and she knew how Margaret would receive that news "—stay sane in this town," she finished lamely.

"He was injured overseas and is an old friend of Sheriff Witt's so he's convalescing here. He's giving lectures at the library on Wednesdays. I never thought he'd agree to do them, but I think he likes the interaction with people and he's discovered they're a lot more aware of current events than he expected."

Margaret nodded. "Mmmmeeee."

"I'll invite him the next time I come in the afternoon. You'll have to have the nurses put you in a pretty nightie and housecoat. He's a real hottie."

Piper was struck anew by how frail and elderly Margaret looked. Had she ever been considered a beauty? Her hair was iron-gray. Lines crisscrossed her face. Piper didn't remember her as particularly pretty. She did remember hugs when she'd been little. Treats like chocolate-chip cookies warm from the oven. Picnics with the four of them. Children tended to take people in their lives for granted. It was only now as she examined her past that she realized how special Margaret had been and still was.

She reached out and took the older woman's hand, clasping it firmly, startled by its fragility.

"Get well soon, Margaret. Cassie and I can't wait for you to come home. And the sheriff is looking for Fiona. If we find her, think what a reunion we'll have."

Margaret looked sad and moved her lips, but nothing came out.

The following Wednesday afternoon, Piper was one of the first at the library for Adam's talk. He and Sam had seen the orthopedist the previous day. She hoped things had gone well. He hadn't called her to report, not that he needed to. Yet he must know how interested she was.

"Hello, dear. My, you're looking much better than when I first saw you." Etta Williams peeped into the room. "I expect a bigger crowd today than last week. Mr. Saunders sure knows how to entertain a group."

"That he does," Piper murmured. She sat in the back, not wanting to attract any attention.

As the room filled up, she recognized others who had attended Adam's previous talks. The elderly man who loved to argue, the teenager who hung on every word, and the young woman who seemed to have eyes only for Adam, even though a wedding ring gleamed on her left hand. All were present and accounted for in the large crowd. Sam slipped in just before Adam and sat in the empty seat next to Piper.

"How're you doing?" he asked.

"Fine. You?"

"Still keeping the peace."

She smiled, impatient to see Adam.

He came into the room, leaning heavily on the cane. The cast was gone, and a Velcro-fastened support boot had taken its place.

"He got the cast off," Piper murmured.

"Yesterday. Doctor told him to take it easy, so I drove him this afternoon. Don't let him walk home. He thinks now that the cast is off, he'll be fit in no time. Not what the doctor said. He has PT to get through, and the prognosis wasn't as positive as Adam's claiming."

"Did you sit in on the appointment?"

"Actually I did."

She bet Adam loved that. He'd put whatever spin he wanted on the doctor's words, and she knew he'd resent Sam if his friend contradicted him.

As Adam sat down, he glanced around the room, his gaze lingering a second or two on Piper before moving on.

"So far I haven't discouraged you from coming. Thanks for the turnout. I hope today's talk will answer more of your questions about the moral rights of the press to report all the news, even though some people want to limit coverage, claiming it infringes on personal rights."

"This ought to be good," Piper said.

She remembered times when she and Jean-Paul went out to dinner and were plagued with reporters and paparazzi who distorted every word or gesture they made.

Her cell phone rang. She'd forgotten to switch it off for the talk. A couple of people turned and frowned at her. Piper checked the number, but it was one she didn't recognize. She was about to turn off the phone when she realized it was out of area.

"Excuse me," she said, nodding to Sam and quickly making her way to the end of the row. Once she was out of the room, she answer the call. "Hold on a minute, please."

She almost ran to the front door of the library and stood on the steps.

"Hello? This is Piper."

"This is Emiline Simmons. Used to be Emiline Ruthers. My sister-in-law said you were trying to reach me."

"Thanks for calling. Do you remember me?"

"Sure do, one of those foster girls Miss Margaret took in. The pretty one, as I recall. I haven't seen you since you were six."

"I'm the first one, I think. Margaret took me in when I was an infant. Do you remember that?"

"Sure do."

"Can you tell me anything about that time?"

"You cried a lot, didn't sleep through the night yet. I didn't have much care of you. Miss Margaret took it all on herself. She was tired for months, though, I do remember that."

"Do you remember how I came to stay there?"

There was silence for a moment.

Then Emiline said slowly, "I don't know exactly how that happened, but Miss Margaret got some bee in her bonnet about having you live with them. She and her daddy had words like I'd never heard in that house before. She yelled and screamed. He gave back as good as she did. They were always in his study, the door closed, so I couldn't hear all the words, but I sure do remember the yelling. That was before they put air-conditioning in that house and it was summertime. I could hear them through the opened windows. Not clear, but enough to know they was fighting."

"Do you know why?"

"Mr. Nunes, he didn't want no babies there. I heard him one time tell her to keep that child out of his sight."

"Margaret was a little old to want to take on an infant, don't you think? Was there some special reason she did?"

"Took a notion to have some kids around, she told me. Time that house had some laughter in it. Her daddy was a strict man, very proper and old-fashioned in his thinking. He hated having children in the house, and when Margaret took you in, I figured it hastened him to an early grave."

"Having a baby in the house killed him?" Piper asked skeptically.

"Maybe it was the fights, and all. I don't know. He

was never the same after Miss Margaret took you in. He was angry all the time. He threatened her once or twice about cutting off her money if she didn't do what he wanted."

"That's interesting," Piper said. "Margaret didn't have an income of her own?"

"She didn't work. Not outside the house. Once she took you in, though, she was a good mama. Taught you and that other one right from the first. Hard work raising kids, I have three of my own."

"She had three, too, counting Fiona."

"I got married when she was talking about that Fiona Hunter. I remember her folks. Bad."

"But Fiona wasn't. Do you have any idea why Margaret went out of state to get me? I wasn't even born in Mississippi."

"All I remember is she went off for a few days, came back with this baby and raised holy hell with her daddy to keep that child. That was you. First time I knew her to stand up to him about anything. He ruled that household until she brought you into it."

Piper asked a couple more questions, but Emiline didn't have much else to tell her. Piper thanked her for returning the call and hung up.

She was too restless to go back into the library, even though she liked hearing Adam talk. Instead she walked toward the park and sat in the shade near the playground. A couple of children were playing on the swings while their mothers chatted nearby.

Piper tried to make sense of Emiline's revelations.

Margaret had gone away and come back with Piper. Her father had been against Margaret caring for the children, but his daughter got her way. Why?

Talking to Emiline hadn't solved a thing. It had only raised more questions. She wanted to shake Edith Harper, make her reveal what she knew. Picking up her phone, she called the woman.

"Edith, it's Piper. Can I come over to talk with you?"

"Not today, girl. I'm in a lot of pain with my arthritis and just took some medication. I expect I'll be asleep in no time. What's happening with that loan?"

"My money was transferred. We can go to the bank anytime to pay it off."

"I think I'm in for a bad spell. Can we put if off until Monday? I'll get to the bank at nine. That do?"

"Sure. Maybe we'll have time to talk a little before we go to see Margaret."

"We'll see. How's she doing?"

"Better all the time. She was taking some steps with a walker yesterday."

"Is she talking yet?"

"A little."

Piper had had difficulty understanding her, but the nurses seemed to.

"She's tough. She'll lick this."

"I hope so."

Piper stayed in the park until she figured Adam would be finished his lecture, then she went back to the library. Her timing was good and she recognized people coming out the front door. She waited outside until the teenager left, knowing he was probably the last. Then she went to the meeting room. Adam and Etta were talking so she stood by the door.

He looked up and noticed her. Excusing himself, he limped over to Piper.

"I saw you leave."

"I got a call from Emiline Ruthers. Remember her?"

"Margaret's former maid?"

"Right."

They started to walk out of the library.

"What did she have to say?"

"Not much that was helpful. I wish Edith would just tell me what she knows."

"I don't think that's going to happen," Adam said. "What exactly did Emiline say?"

Piper sat on one of the benches near the library entrance. Sam had said Adam shouldn't be on his foot too long. When he sat beside her, she told him all she remembered about the conversation.

"So what made the docile daughter stand up to her lion of a father because of you?" he asked, looking at Piper.

"I have no idea."

"I can think of one or two. Needs some further investigation, though."

"Like what?"

"Like her father was having a little fun, got someone pregnant and then didn't want the kid.

Margaret found out and went to get it. That would explain why he acquiesced yet didn't want to be involved with the child."

"Me."

Adam nodded.

"So Margaret could be my half sister? That would be too weird. Any other ideas?"

"My money's on something like that."

"So now we need to talk to people who knew Mr. Nunes and see if they remember him being involved with a woman back then."

"My guess is that no one here knew anything about it. You haven't come across any gossip that hinted the baby was his, have you?"

"No. But maybe no one wanted to suggest that possibility to me."

"Could be. But I figure if Nunes was having a relationship, he'd make sure it was out of the townfolks' prying eyes."

So basically they'd reached another dead end, Piper thought. She looked at Adam.

"How's the leg?"

"Hurts more than I expected," he admitted. "I need to get it stronger faster."

"Let it rest, give it time to heal," she advised.

"I don't have a lot of time."

"You have until after Independence Day. You said you'd stay for the fund-raiser."

"Then I'm out of here. I need to be ready to return to work by July fifth."

She felt a pang at his words. He'd be leaving in only a few weeks. Back into action as he called it.

Back into danger more like. She shivered, afraid for him. Afraid of never seeing him again.

"Still, give yourself a few days to simply rest and heal," she said. "The cast just came off."

"I've got some work to keep me tied to a desk, mama hen," he teased.

"What? Researching this latest tidbit?"

"No, my editor at the network called to ask me to work on a series of commentaries for Roger Hamilton, our resident commentator."

"I thought he did his own commentaries."

"He outlines them, then they're farmed out for verification, enhancements, other insights. He compiles the information and bases his final version on that."

"It's like being a ghost writer?" she asked.

"No, more like an editor. The next series of commentaries will deal with the military and our involvement in different areas of the world."

"Why don't you do the commentaries?"

"Not my thing."

"Safer."

"Boring."

"Closer to home."

"Home is not where the action is."

She couldn't respond to that one.

"Fine, go get yourself killed."

Standing, she looked around for Sam.

"Wait here and I'll go find Sam."

"I don't need to wait for him. I'm perfectly capable of getting myself back to his placc. I don't need people treating me like an invalid."

Adam turned and began walking down the street.

Piper debated going after him but decided not to. She was annoyed enough with the man without watching him deliberately put his recovery at risk. Why were men so stubborn?

Or women, come to that. Edith didn't sound as if she would budge on her vow of silence. That left Margaret. Piper had to convince her former foster mother that she was entitled to know about her parents.

By the time she reached home, Piper was out of sorts with everyone. Margaret had refused to even look at her when Piper had brought up the subject of her parents.

Cassie was sitting on the porch when Piper walked up the driveway. She looked hot and tired too. From inside the house, the screech of a power saw could be heard. Piper sighed and went to sit beside her friend.

"They're still here, I hear," Piper said.

"Yeah. Matt said they'd be gone by dinnertime each day, but I think he meant dinner in California, not here. I wanted to try a new recipe for tiramisu, but didn't want sawdust and plaster in it. What have you been doing today?"

"Making enemies left and right."

"Who?"

"Adam's mad at me because I was concerned about his foot. Margaret because I want to know what she can tell me about my birth parents. Stay around long enough and I'm sure I'll make you angry as well."

Cassie laughed.

"Never. Oh, I forgot. There's a box for you just inside the door. It was delivered earlier. One of the guys signed for it."

Piper got the box and read the return address as she came back out.

"It's from Enrique."

Sitting down, she peeled off the tape and opened it. A note fluttered to the porch as she withdrew a midnight-blue dress.

Cassie scooped up the paper. "Oh, my goodness, what a beautiful dress."

Piper stood and held it up to her, smiling.

"It's a Versace. What does the note say?"

Cassie held it out. "I can't read it, it's in French."

Piper skimmed it and shook her head.

"Enrique says I have an image to uphold, and would I please wear this dress to the dinner and make sure everyone knows who the designer is."

"He sent you a Versace just to wear to dinner? What if you spill something on it?"

Cassie reached out and tentatively touched the shimmering fabric.

"I'm not going to spill anything on it. Enrique merely borrowed it, for show. He's always networking, keeping my name out there. But I'm not wearing it. I have a great dress I got in New Orleans."

The one Adam had helped her buy. It meant more to her than all the Versaces in the world.

"So what's the other one like? I can't wait to see you in it."

"Adam thinks I look great in it."

"Oh, like that, is it?"

Piper looked at her, startled.

"No, it's not what you're thinking. My home's in Paris, and his is wherever the action is. He said so today."

She carefully folded the dress and placed it back in the box, and put it on one of the chairs. She was annoyed at Enrique's intrusion into her time here in Bradford. Yet it helped her put things into focus. Rising, she walked to the edge of the porch and gazed over the lawn.

"I'm not made for a town like this, Cassie. You've found your niche. You and Matt will have a happy life together. And I expect you'll have a bunch of kids who will adore you both and always feel at home in Bradford."

"You could stay," Cassie said gently.

"No, I have nothing here. Except you. And Margaret. And after my badgering today, she's probably not feeling too kindly toward me."

"So find a nice guy and settle down," Cassie said.

"Someone like Norm? Can't you just see me?"

"I can see you with someone who makes you happy. Have a half-dozen kids to keep mine company. We'll build a family so large we'll have to eat in shifts at the holidays."

Piper turned and reached out to give Cassie a hug.

"You are the best family I could ever have had." She frowned. "Am I wrong to keep looking for the woman who gave me birth? To find out who my father was?"

Cassie shook her head.

"You'll find out someday. Keep the faith."

"Hey, we're heading out now."

One of Matt's men pushed open the screen and stuck his head out.

"But the water's off upstairs. Hope you don't mind."

"And if we do?" Piper asked.

He grinned.

"You're welcome to come over to my place to shower."

"In your dreams."

"You got that one right, babe. Free for a drink?"

Piper shook her head.

"She's taken," Cassie said, heading for the door. "And I want to get something started for dinner before Matt gets here."

Piper listened to the friendly banter between the man and Cassie as they headed toward the back of the house.

Could she really find a place for herself in Bradford?

11

On Saturday Piper took her time getting ready for the dinner in New Orleans. Adam had called on Friday to suggest they stay over at the hotel hosting the event to save making the return trip late at night.

She agreed, glad not to have to drive so late. His call had been brief and to the point. When she hung up, she wondered if he even noticed she'd been as curt. She wanted to ask how he was doing but feared another rebuff.

At least the water had been restored to the upper floors. She showered, and then styled her hair. Her makeup was not as dramatic as it would be if she were going under harsh runway lights, but much more than she normally wore. She planned to make sure Mr. Hotshot Foreign Reporter was the envy of every other man at the dinner.

The dress she'd bought in New Orleans was a dream.

She was ready ten minutes before Adam said he'd pick her up. She didn't know if he'd insist on driving.

A knock sounded on her door.

"Yes?"

Cassie peeped in. "Wow."

She came in and stared at Piper, eyes wide.

"Looking good?" Piper asked.

"Adam will die on the spot. Don't you dare let Matt see you. I'll lose him for sure."

Piper laughed.

"You're good for my ego. The only woman who registers with Matt is you."

"I came to see how you're doing. You sure you're okay with staying overnight?"

"Sure. This way I don't have to drive back when I'm tired."

Cassie smiled happily.

"Have a great time!"

When they heard voices from the first floor, Cassie picked up the small bag Piper had packed.

"Wait two minutes and then make your entrance."

Piper was transported back to their high school days when she and Cassie would have their dates wait in the foyer until they walked down the stairs. Fiona never played that game. She didn't dress up. But Piper had always loved making an entrance down the elegant old staircase.

Reaching the top of the stairs, Piper heard the men's voices. She peered down and saw Matt and Adam talking to Cassie.

Head up, shoulders back, Piper began her descent, her eyes locked on Adam to watch his reaction.

It was all any woman could hope for. He turned as she started down the steps, and immediately fell silent.

She didn't imagine the heat in his eyes as his eyes skimmed her from head to her ridiculous excuse for shoes and back up again. He couldn't look away. Piper felt his gaze on her face like a physical caress. She knew he wanted to touch, to taste, to feel.

"You look fantastic," he said, meeting her at the foot of the stairs.

"Thank you. You look mighty fine yourself."

He was wearing a pristine white dress shirt, dark maroon tie and dark charcoal suit. Unless she missed her guess, it was Italian. She wasn't the only one to appreciate fine clothing.

"Shall we?"

He offered her his free arm. Using his cane, he turned and they started for the door.

"I have Piper's bag," Matt said, taking it from Cassie.

The four of them went out onto the porch.

"Oh my," Piper said when she saw the luxurious stretch limousine in the driveway.

"I didn't want either of us to have to drive," Adam said as he escorted her to the back of the car.

The chauffeur was there with the door open.

"If I had known you were traveling in such style, I'd have joined you," Cassie said, patting the shiny car.

"You weren't invited," Matt said, handing the small suitcase to the chauffeur and pulling Cassie away from the car. "Besides, I have plans for us."

"Have fun," Cassie called out.

"You, too," Piper replied.

She turned to Adam as they headed down the driveway.

"This is a great idea. We have the limo tomorrow, too?"

"The chauffeur will pick us up at the hotel at ten. Unless we want to leave later."

"Sounds perfect. So how's your leg?"

"It's getting better," he said shortly.

"So you'll be back reporting in no time."

"That's right."

"There are some advantages to your job over mine. Viewers seem to like older reporters—they lend an air of wisdom to the news. But older models are quickly replaced by beautiful young things."

"You'll be the exception," Adam promised.

She patted his knee. "You can be charming when you want."

He captured her hand in his and brought it to his lips.

"And tonight I want."

There was no mistaking his meaning. Then she remembered their agreement.

"Did you reserve two rooms?" she asked.

"Yes, I did. And you're free to use either one."

"Umm."

Saturday night in the French Quarter was jumping. Tourists and locals alike crowded the sidewalks, enjoying the party atmosphere, and listening to the jazz that spilled out from every bar.

Their chauffeur drove up to the doors of the

opulent hotel where the event was taking place and they went inside. The lobby glittered with crystal chandeliers and gold leaf on the ceiling moldings. Tourists mingled with those attending the gala dinner, and there were as many flip-flops as Jimmy Choos.

They followed the signs to the ballroom. Dinner started at eight o'clock, but cocktails were being served. Adam's name was soon called as one of his friends recognized him.

Before long, several men had come over with their wives and girlfriends to greet him. He introduced Piper to everyone, making sure she was comfortable with his friends. Before long they were separated, but Piper didn't mind. She was used to holding her own at this kind of event.

Waiters circled with trays of champagne and Piper accepted a glass as she listened to a woman who was passionate about preserving the heritage of the Mississippi River.

When another couple joined their group and was introduced, she recognized one of the football players coming to Margaret's fund-raiser.

"Someone here to see us," Adam said, slipping his arm into hers.

Piper turned and smiled when she recognized Paul Casey and his cameraman.

"It was worth the wait to interview you," he said, his eyes never leaving Piper.

At his cameraman's prodding, he quickly set up the interview. Paul stammered out some questions and she answered them as honestly as she could. When Adam finished his share of the interview, Paul thanked them both profusely.

"He needs to develop a bit more cool around celebrities," Adam said when they turned back to the festivities.

"He's young and I thought he was sweet. You did a good thing for him."

"We were a package deal," Adam joked.

By the time dinner was served, Piper felt as if she'd held up her end of the bargain. She'd talked up designer fashions in general and her experiences as a model in Europe. Discussed changes needed in economic aid to some of the disadvantaged countries. And found herself studying Adam every opportunity she had.

"Are you enjoying yourself?" Adam asked when they were seated at their table.

Michael Thomas and his wife sat at Adam's left.

"I am. Are you?"

"It's good to see a lot of people I know. I didn't realize so many would be here tonight."

"Didn't you grow up in Baton Rouge? That's not so far from here."

He brushed a lock of hair from her cheek and leaned close.

"I'm the envy of every man here," he said softly.

She glowed with pleasure. She wanted him to be glad he'd invited her.

Dinner proved to be entertaining rather than tedious. Speakers gave humorous presentations instead of the usual earnest speeches about the charity. They did ask for contributions in addition to the cost of the tickets to the event, which Piper discovered ran a thousand dollars a person. By the time the speeches ended and the dancing started, more than two million dollars had been raised for the children's charity. Piper hoped the fund-raiser for Margaret would raise even a small fraction of that amount.

"Care to dance?" Adam asked when the music filled the huge ballroom.

"With your leg?"

"We'll find out."

He scooted back his chair and helped her from hers. They moved to the dance floor, and she turned into his arms. The music was bluesy and sweet, and the lights gradually dimmed, enhancing the ambience.

"I bet you don't get many nights like this in Kyiv," Piper said.

"None," Adam agreed, moving with the rhythm. "But I bet this is commonplace for you."

"Not really. I have to get a lot of sleep to make sure I don't look totally bagged for work. Photo shoots are often early in the morning to get the best light."

Over the past week Piper had regained her normal energy level, and tonight she danced with Adam and the other men at their table. A few others came over and asked, and Adam urged her to go ahead. She'd look over her partner's shoulder and see Adam in animated discussion with someone or other at their table. She was glad he didn't mind that she danced. She loved it.

Finally it was time to leave. Adam was leaning heavily on his cane. Piper walked on his uninjured side, wondering if he had done too much but knowing better than to voice the question. He'd just get annoyed. As he'd said, she wasn't his mother.

Her feelings were definitely growing stronger for Adam, but he seemed to be withdrawing. He made sure she knew there was no hope of a long-term commitment. Did he think she didn't understand? They were two people temporarily stranded in Bradford who had an undeniable chemistry. In less than four weeks they'd both be back in their separate worlds.

"We're staying upstairs," Adam said as they exited the ballroom. "I had the chauffeur check us in and have our bags taken to our rooms."

He stopped at the front desk and soon picked up two key cards. Limping heavily, he led the way to the elevators, which were crowded.

In the brighter lights of the lobby, Piper could see the lines of pain around his eyes and mouth. His leg was probably hurting more than he'd ever admit.

Piper knew how debilitating injuries could be and how much Adam wanted to get back to work. But stressing his injury was not the way to accomplish that goal.

They were the only people to get off on the eleventh floor.

"This way," Adam said, turning to the right. He stopped by a door and inserted the key. When it clicked open, Piper pushed it wide and flipped on the lights. She didn't recognize the small bag on the bed.

"Must be yours. That's not my case."

"Then we'll try the other."

She reached for the card and took it.

"I'll go along myself, Adam. You get off that foot."

Reaching up, she kissed him quickly on the mouth.

"Thanks for a great evening."

He swung his free arm around her waist, pulling her closer, returning the kiss.

His mouth moved hungrily against hers and she responded with an equal intensity. Her arms encircled his neck and she steadied herself before giving up to the delights of the kiss.

How long they stood there, locked in each other's arms, she wasn't sure. But Piper reveled in the touch of his skin, the magic of his mouth, and the burning heat that was slowly overtaking her.

Piper awoke to sunshine streaming in through the windows. The room was still cool thanks to the air-conditioning. She wished she wasn't waking up alone.

Piper yearned to be connected to another individual the way Cassie and Matt were. The way Betsy and her husband were. That special bond had been missing from Piper's marriages, which was probably why they both had ended so abruptly. Well, that and Jean-Paul's cheating.

She couldn't help thinking about Adam. He was different. Being with him made her feel more cherished and valued than ever before.

But she wouldn't dream of anything beyond the moment. She knew the rules.

Sadness welled up in her. It was going to be harder than she'd expected to say goodbye. The hope that he'd visit her in Paris sometime was the most she'd indulge herself. She had a life she liked and that was enough. She wasn't going to wish for the moon.

Slipping out of bed, she dressed quickly. As soon as she'd done that, she made her way downstairs to await the limo.

Adam saw her in the lobby when he stepped out of the elevator. He'd tried her room, but there'd been no answer. He hesitated a moment. She looked so alone sitting by herself, her small suitcase at her feet.

He thought back to last night. No one had let her be alone. Men and women had practically lined up to meet her. The cover-girl glamour had disappeared.

Today she looked like a beautiful woman, but not a famous model with star quality.

He preferred her today.

She smiled when he approached.

"Have you eaten?" he asked.

She shook her head.

"We have time before the limo arrives. The driver can wait if we're not finished by ten."

Something was wrong. He wasn't sure what, but it was more than his imagination. Following her as she headed for the hotel coffee shop, he was aware that his leg ached more than it had since the first days after the accident.

He knew he'd done too much. His doctor had warned him, but he had pushed ahead anyway. Now he was paying the price.

Their table was next to windows overlooking the pool and lush tropical landscaping. Piper studied the menu as if she had to memorize it. He knew what he wanted. Once their orders had been taken, he reached out and took her hand.

She looked up.

"Last night was fun. I enjoyed meeting all those people. For a man who travels, you have lots of friends around here. It was such a special evening. I really loved it."

"And now?"

Her smile was a little sad. It tore at his heart.

"But?" he prompted.

"But it can't last, can it? This growing feeling I have

for you. Special things never seem to last for me."

"It can last as long as we want it to."

"Or until July fifth, whichever comes first," she replied.

"We don't have to leave the day after the fund-raiser."

"I do. Enrique's complaining about rearranging shoots. He can be overly dramatic, but he's got a point. If I don't get back to work, someone else will be happy to step in for me. Then where would I be?"

She was right, of course. And he'd be leaving himself once he was fit for duty.

"How's the leg?" she asked.

"Fine."

It wasn't, but that was his fault for doing too much. He'd give it a rest today and be ready to start physical therapy at the hospital in Bradford tomorrow. He hoped a few more weeks would take care of it.

"Last night had to be a strain. You didn't need to dance so much."

"I wanted to dance with you. I won't walk much on it today. It'll be fine."

He didn't want to be babied by anyone—especially by Piper.

"Are you having second thoughts?" she asked quickly.

"No way. I want to see more of you. I like being with you."

That sounded like a come-on if he'd ever heard one. What was it about her that attracted him? Her looks, of course. But he was being truthful when he said he liked being with her. He liked the way she met life straight on, without pretense. The way she faced challenges and rallied around her friends when they needed help. And the way she kept going after her goals, no matter how many setbacks.

They finished eating in time to meet the limo at ten. Soon they were on their way back to Bradford. Piper stared out the window. Adam watched her in frustration. Something had definitely changed and he didn't like it.

When they reached Bradford Hall, Piper slid from the limo when the chauffeur opened the door.

"Thanks again for last night," she said, leaning back in and brushing a kiss across his mouth.

He watched her hurry inside, wishing he could run after her, race her up the stairs and find an empty bedroom.

It was Sunday, and Matt's car was in the driveway. No way was he going to have his wish come true.

"Home, James," he said, settling back against the seat. He still had a little more time to spend with Piper.

On Monday promptly at nine o'clock, Piper, Cassie and Edith Harper met at the bank. Piper had dressed as formally as her limited wardrobe allowed, meaning a dress and sandals, not shorts and a T-shirt. Cassie had dressed in linen pants and top.

Allen McLennon was available and they were immediately shown into his office. He couldn't stop staring at Piper, and once again she remembered how uncomfortable he'd made her feel when he had been seeing Margaret all those years ago. He'd stare at her as if she was a specimen. Gave her the creeps.

Cassie and Edith didn't seem to notice anything amiss. Edith came straight to the point.

"As you know, Allen, Margaret gave me her power of attorney. I'm here to pay off the balance of that loan you talked her into so we don't have it hanging over her head."

"It's not your loan, Mrs. Harper," he said. "The account has been brought current by Cassie and Matt. Regular payments shouldn't be hard for Margaret to make."

"We don't want her to have to worry about it at all," Piper said, reaching into her purse to take out her new checkbook.

"If you'll just tell me the amount, I'll write a check and that will be that."

"We would have to place a hold on foreign funds," he said.

"My account is at this bank. You'll see the funds are available. The balance, please?"

For a moment Piper wondered if he'd actually refuse, but with a disapproving glare, the banker lifted the phone and called the loan department for the current balance. He gave the figure to Piper a moment later.

She wrote the check and handed it to him with a

flourish.

"We'll wait for the final papers showing the loan paid in full," she said, settling back in her chair as if she had all the time in the world.

Cassie smiled and watched McLennon.

"Well, that's taken care of," Edith declared. "And a load off my mind." She perched on the edge of her chair like a little bird.

Allen rose, carrying the check.

"I'll take care of this," he said, skirting the desk and leaving his office.

"That guy gives me the creeps. He always has, even when we were teenagers," Piper said quietly, glancing over her shoulder to make sure he was out of range.

"He fancies himself, that's for sure," Edith said, smoothing her skirt with her gnarled arthritic fingers. "Comes from being president of the only bank in town. What he needs is some stiff competition."

"Isn't there a branch of another bank out at the new shopping mall?" Cassie asked.

"Yes," Edith said, "and they put one of those cash machines right in the parking lot across from city hall. Apparently anyone can get money when they need it. Seems to me the perfect target for robbers."

Piper looked around the office, impatient to leave. She couldn't wait to tell Margaret they'd removed all threat to the house and property. Now all Margaret had to do was get well enough to return home.

A few minutes later a woman from the loan department came into the office.

"Here we are. The loan has been paid in full." She beamed at them. "Who gets the documents?"

Edith held out her hands. "I'll take them. Where's Allen?"

"He was called away for a moment."

"Didn't want to face us," Piper muttered.

She stood up to go.

"Guess we know where we stand in the illustrious banker's eyes."

Cassie nodded. "Maybe I'll move my account to that bank at the mall."

The loan officer's eyes widened.

"We hope you'll continue to bank with us. We value your business."

Edith took the papers and handed them to Piper.

"You double-check everything. Then we'll leave."

Piper skimmed the document, noting the date and signatures. Nodding, she folded the papers and offered them to Edith.

"You keep them. Take them back to Margaret's place. She keeps important papers in her armoire in her bedroom. Put them there."

Her armoire?

Piper looked at Cassie, eyebrows raised in silent question. Cassie shook her head. No one had seen an armoire.

Though once Edith said it, Piper remembered the huge piece of furniture she'd seen as a child in Margaret's room near the window. Had she seen it most recently in the garage?

Piper was impatient to return home. But they had planned to visit the hospital and share the news with Margaret. Cultivating patience wasn't easy.

As they walked into the sunshine, Edith's faithful friend, Mr. Evans, stood near her car. "Need a ride, ladies?" he asked.

"We want to go to the convalescent hospital," Edith said, sliding into the front seat as he opened the door for her.

Piper and Cassie got into the back and in no time they arrived at the hospital.

As they were walking in, Piper saw Sam and Adam talking near one of the elevators.

Adam saw her and nodded.

"Wait for me," she told Cassie, then went to join the men.

"What are you doing here?" Adam asked, throwing a suspicious look at Sam.

"Don't look at me, man," Sam shot back. "I didn't tell her."

"Tell me what?" Piper asked.

"About his PT," Sam said. "I've got to go."

He touched the brim of his hat and left.

"I knew you were having physical therapy today," Piper said. "You told me at the dinner, remember? I could have given you a ride if I'd known."

"It's not for a while, but Sam's got someplace to go, so he dropped me off early."

"So you get to hang around here for a while. Fun."

"Yeah. Thought I'd get coffee at the cafeteria."

"Come with us. We're celebrating Margaret's liberation from the evil banker."

"Evil banker?"

"That's what I figure Allen McLennon is. Smarmy if nothing else. We paid off the loan this morning."

"Worth celebrating."

He glanced over at Cassie and Edith.

"I don't want to intrude."

"Come on. Mr. Evans will be happy for the male company. He's parking Edith's car and then will join us. Margaret's going to be so surprised."

A short time later they all crowded into Margaret's room. She sat in a chair near the window and seemed overwhelmed at first with so many people.

Piper introduced Adam, then told Margaret about paying off the loan.

If the older woman could have spoken clearly, Piper had a good idea she'd tell Piper off for taking such a drastic step without consulting her.

But the advantage of announcing it in front of everyone was that Margaret would have to act gracious. Piper had no doubt, however, that the next time the two of them were alone, Margaret would undoubtedly have a thing or two to say.

Piper hoped she'd be able to say it clearly.

Adam checked his watch after some time.

"I have to be going," he said. "My appointment is in five minutes."

"I'll come with you," Piper told him. "Margaret tires easily, so we all should leave."

"I'm ready," Cassie said, hopping off the bed. "I've got an appointment at lunch with another prospective client. We're almost ready for Betsy to quit her job at the café to work full-time with me."

She hugged Margaret and kissed her cheek.

"Be glad you're not home now. It's a mess with all the reconstruction, furniture being moved and all the dust in the air. It'll be a showplace by the time you get there."

"You young people run along," Edith said. "I want to talk to Margaret a little longer. If that is all right with you, Mr. Evans."

He nodded in complacent agreement.

Piper got off on the second floor with Adam.

"Don't you have things to do?" he asked as they walked to the physical therapy department.

"Sure, but I thought you could use a friend. I'll get a cab for us when you're ready to leave."

"I can walk back to Sam's."

"Ah, but I don't want you to return to Sam's. Guess what I found out? Edith said this morning that Margaret keeps all her important papers in an armoire. I think I saw it in the garage. It was in there, so it has to be hers, don't you think? Do you think we could just peek in it to see if there's anything?"

"Like private papers."

Piper frowned. She knew they were private, but if there was something to help her discover her parents, she wanted to see it.

The waiting room was empty except for a young girl sitting with her mother. Adam went to the desk to tell them he was there. He and Piper sat across the room from the other two occupants.

"How much physiotherapy do you have to do?" she asked.

"I'm not sure. I'm supposed to get some exercises, then come back a couple of times at least."

"Do you have full range of motion now?"

"No. The ankle was immobilized long enough to get stiff. I think that's what they'll be working on."

"So this is it, the last stage before your return to work."

He nodded. Reaching out, he took her hand in his, lacing their fingers.

"I have to go to Atlanta later this week. There's an important meeting I'm needed at. But I'll be here for the Fourth."

Piper didn't want him to go. It was childish, but panic flared. What if he was well enough to return to the international scene and start reporting again. Would the allure of the job prove to be stronger than a promise to be at a fund-raiser for a woman he'd only just met?

She realized he was champing at the bit to return to work. But she wanted to have the next few weeks together. She was counting on them.

12

When Adam rejoined her an hour later, she knew the session had been worse than he'd anticipated. He looked exhausted, and the pain lines she'd seen last Saturday night were there again.

"I'll call someone to pick us up," she said, jumping up when he came out. "Want to take a wheelchair to the curb?"

"No, I don't want a darn old wheelchair. Let's get out of here."

By the time they reached the old house, Piper was more concerned.

"Do you have your pain meds?" she asked when they walked up the shallow steps to the porch.

"I don't want them."

He hadn't said a word in the taxi, but his expression was surly. Piper wasn't sure she wanted to be around him.

"If you've got them, take them. There's no point feeling miserable. I'll get you some water."

The work on the second floor continued and the noise level prevented easy conversation. Piper got a glass of water and held it out to Adam.

He took the glass reluctantly, fished out a couple of pills and swallowed them. Setting down the glass, he turned and headed for the back door and the garage beyond.

"Is Margaret's room being renovated?" he asked.

"Not yet. They're still working on the bathroom between the rooms Fiona and I used to have. Margaret's room is at the far end of the hall, but I think they must have moved all the really heavy furniture at one time. Save having the movers come time and again."

Opening the garage doors, Piper could see the huge Victorian piece of furniture and went straight to it. Double doors stood closed above two deep drawers. She pulled out the top drawer. An old Bible rested on top of a pile of papers and file folders.

Adam dragged over the chair he'd used before and sat, resting his foot. "Let's see what's in here," he said.

In her excitement, Piper scooped everything up, not thinking to remove the Bible first. It slid off the stack and landed on the cement floor, two folders following. She put the rest in Adam's lap and stooped to retrieve the Bible. A yellowed newspaper clipping fluttered out. Piper picked it up.

"There's no date. It's from Orlando, though. Listen to this."

"Teen Death. A seventeen-year-old female from New Orleans was killed last night when the vehicle she was driving rammed a light pole on Atlantic Avenue. Preliminary reports indicate she was intoxicated and driving at excessive speeds. Death was instantaneous, according to Orlando Police. Her two-month-old daughter, safely secured in the back seat, survived. Police are withholding her name until notification of next of kin."

"Anything else in the Bible?" Adam asked, holding out his hand for the clipping.

Piper flipped through the pages and found another notice.

"Angela Harvesty killed in Florida," she read. "Angela Harvesty, 17, of 235 Parkside Drive in New Orleans was killed last Tuesday night in Orlando, Florida. A private funeral will be held tomorrow. In lieu of flowers, donations may be made to the Make-A-Wish Foundation."

He took the death notice and reread it.

"Can't tell what paper this one was from."

"Do you suppose Angela was my mother?" Piper wondered, a nervous tension in her voice. "That I was the two-month-old in the back? Piper Harvesty. Do you think that's my real name?"

"I don't know. It's more than we've had so far. Let me check into it and see what I can turn up. What about those letters?"

She picked up the stack, held together by a rubber band.

"They're addressed to William Nunes, no return address."

She slipped off the elastic and spread them out.

"From the postmarks on the envelopes, they're in

order and go back long before I was born."

She opened the top one and withdrew the sheet inside. She didn't feel as guilty reading Margaret's father's letters aloud.

"Carol said to thank you for the sweater set. Angela will look adorable in it. I wanted to let you know she's doing well. We celebrated her first birthday with friends, and from the cake smeared in her eyebrows and hair, I understand we passed with flying colors. She is a bit headstrong for one so young, but such a delight for Carol."

"It's signed 'Nathan.'"

"So Nathan and Carol felt William Nunes would want to know about Angela," Piper said. "Maybe your theory about Margaret's father having an illegitimate child was right. Could Angela have been his daughter?"

"Or they might just have been friends thanking him for a birthday gift. Let's see what the rest say."

Adam picked up the next envelope and scanned the contents.

One letter each year, always around November fifteenth. The brief missives followed the childhood of Angela Harvesty, from headstrong little girl to wild teenager. The tone of the notes changed from indulgence to frustration to anger. The last one said simply they were washing their hands of her.

"She would have just turned seventeen if these were all written on her birthday," Adam said. "The last one came six months before you were born."

"But no clear mention is ever made of any relationship," Piper said.

"We can try information in New Orleans to see if the Harvestys are still there," Adam suggested.

Piper opened a brown manila envelope and dumped out a couple dozen black-and-white photos. She looked through them, seeing one of Margaret when she was younger, standing beside a stern-looking older man.

"Her father, I suppose," she said, showing Adam.

There was one of an infant, wrapped in a blanket, asleep. No names or dates were on any of the photos. None of the other people looked even vaguely familiar to Piper. She scooped them up and put them back in the envelope, replacing everything back in the drawer except the clippings.

Piper pulled open the double doors of the armoire and looked at the boxes stacked there. The top one indicated yearbooks. She pulled it down, opening it. The top book was the yearbook from her sophomore year at Bradford High. The last year she was there. She leafed through the pages, stopping at the one with her class. Cassie was there, along with Fiona, Betsy, Lulu and Marjorie. And herself.

Adam looked over her shoulder.

"Cute."

"Makes you wonder how I ever became a model, doesn't it?"

"Shows you were experimenting. Now you've found your look. Are there any other year books?"

"We were gone by the time the one came out for our junior year. But here are some from elementary school."

More like magazines, these books were amateurish but covered grades one through eight. There were candid shots and individual black-and-white photos of each grade.

"I didn't know Margaret kept these," she said, flipping through one.

She handed it to Adam and withdrew another from the shelf.

"This was the first."

She smiled.

"We were so proud to be going to school."

She handed that one to Adam, as well.

"Mary Fiona Hunter," he said.

"What?" She looked at him, and then at the picture of six-year-old Fiona.

"She's listed as Mary Fiona Hunter," he said.

"That's funny. We always called her Fiona."

"If Mary is her legal name, maybe we need to be looking for her under that."

Piper stared at him. "You think it would be that simple?"

"Worth a shot. In the meantime, let's get to a phone and start with a few calls to any Harvestys listed. We can talk to Sam about Fiona later."

The information operator in New Orleans had no listing for Nathaniel Harvesty at Parkside Avenue.

There was only one listing for a Harvesty, Alfred on Merced Drive. Adam called the number, but only got an answering machine.

Adam then called Sam.

"Disney World," Piper said suddenly.

"What?"

"That's where Fiona wanted to go. We discussed moving to New Orleans, but she always wanted to go to Disney World. Maybe she's in Florida."

Adam conveyed the latest piece of information they had about Fiona to Sam.

"One more thing, can you run a check on a Nathaniel and Carol Harvesty? Twenty-eight years ago they lived at 235 Parkside Drive in New Orleans. I need to get in touch with them on another matter."

He listened for a moment than laughed.

"I figured it would brighten an otherwise dull day. Do what you can."

"What'd he say?" Piper asked when Adam hung up.

"He wanted to know if we thought he was running a missing persons' bureau. He's very conscious of the county's money."

"How much does it cost to run a driver's license check?"

"Probably a dime if that. Law enforcement agencies all have those reciprocal agreements."

"If the letters came to Mr. Nunes, do you suppose Margaret knew about them at the time? Knew about Angela?"

"Possibly. Or maybe she found the letters after her father's death."

"I bet the Harvestys could clear up a few things," she said. "How likely is it they died between then and now?"

"Depends on their age, but I think it's probably a good bet they're alive. Maybe they moved to Florida to retire."

"Funny. Maybe they live next door to Fiona."

"Cassie has her laptop with her, right?" Adam asked.

"Yes. She's doing a presentation to a prospective client."

"Then let's head back to Sam's. We'll use his, see what we can come up with on our own. And it's past time for lunch."

She reached for his free arm and looped hers through it, leaning against him slightly. She was sure not going to miss Adam when he left.

"Tell me about your upcoming meeting in Atlanta," Piper said when Adam seated her at the counter in Sam's kitchen and pulled out fixings for sandwiches. He sat on the stool and passed her the bread and cold cuts.

"It's about a realignment of assignments with a new unit being formed to fill in wherever needed. When a catastrophe happens or a war breaks out, we have dedicated reporters deployed. But if there are two major events at the same time, then we wind up short-handed. The thought is to have backup teams ready to be deployed at short notice. Men and women who normally have other assignments but who would be trained to cover a broader range of events and who could be mobilized in hours."

"And that affects you how?" she asked as she prepared the sandwiches.

He could have made his own, but he liked watching her assemble them, as if she were creating some gourmet feast.

"I've been asked to head it up."

Her face lit up and her eyes sparkled. She seemed as enthusiastic about the news as she'd have been if she'd just won some major prize herself.

"How wonderful. I'm happy for you, Adam. That sounds like a real coup."

"It sounds like they're putting me out to pasture in some desk job," he said.

"Or they're smart enough to make sure the best in the business helps establish the new group."

He thought about it for a minute. If the offer had come six months ago, before the land mine, would he have been as reluctant? Was he seeing hidden motives that weren't there?

"Go with an open mind, at least," she said, sliding the plate across the counter and bringing her own around to sit beside him. "You can always say no, right?"

"I suppose."

"When do you go?"

"Thursday, the meeting's Friday."

"I can give you a ride to the airport if you like."

He nodded.

"I appreciate that." Then a thought struck. "Want to come with me?"

"To Atlanta?"

"Sure. We can swing by Florida on our way home and see if we can find out anything more about Angela Harvesty."

He could see the idea held appeal.

"I would love it."

Adam felt a quiet satisfaction. He hadn't asked a woman to go with him on a trip in years. It wouldn't be all meetings in Atlanta.

"I'll get reservations." He looked at her, "Two rooms or one?"

She hesitated for so long he was afraid she was having second thoughts.

"Two should do," she said finally.

Piper was afraid to attach too much importance to the upcoming trip. She told Cassie it was to visit Florida to learn more about the woman they suspected was her mother.

She made sure she was at the library early on

Wednesday afternoon for Adam's lecture. As expected, the room was packed, with several people standing in the back. Adam began by telling the assembly this would be his last talk.

Amidst the groans and disappointment of the crowd, Piper felt her own heart drop. His cast was off, and he'd begun exercises to strengthen his foot and ankle. All things looked positive for an early return to work.

And if he took this new assignment, he could work behind a desk until he was fully mobile again.

She wondered if she'd be returning to Bradford alone after their trip to Florida. She wasn't ready to say goodbye to Adam yet. She wanted until the Fourth of July and would use all her powers of persuasion to make sure he gave her that much.

His question about the rooms had to mean something. She'd hesitated, but she'd laid out the ground rules. She felt closer to Adam than anyone besides Cassie. She wanted to believe it was because of his help in searching for her parents, but she knew it was more.

If they never found her parents, it wouldn't change things. She didn't see how they could make a relationship work. Long-distance affairs were doomed, yet it wasn't enough to make her give up hope.

Should she put her career on hold temporarily and move to wherever he was?

She knew she couldn't do that. She'd given up a lot

for Billy Bob and Jean-Paul. Which meant she needed to find a compromise that would work for both her and Adam. If he wanted the same thing she did.

The hotel in Atlanta was near the CNN headquarters and was frequently used by network personnel. Adam was recognized instantly and greeted by desk clerks and bellmen. Her room was spacious, with a huge California king-size bed, and overlooked downtown.

"Freshen up and we'll go out," Adam said before moving on to his room.

Had she chosen wrong, she wondered after the door closed. Should she have thrown caution to the wind and shared a room with him?

No. They had no long time future together. She'd take pleasure in the time they did have and bid him goodbye with no regrets.

She was ready when he knocked on her door.

"I'll be glad to get rid of this blasted cane. I feel like an old man hobbling along," he griped as they walked to the elevator.

"Well you don't look like an old man. Have patience,"

"Easy for you to say."

As they waited for the elevator, Piper reached up and kissed him on the cheek.

"Nice, but what for?" he asked.

"I'm happy to be here with you. Like you said the other day, I like being with you. I might think about

PIPER'S DISCOVERY | 267

changing our ground rules."

He drew her close. "You tell me how far you want to go, and we'll go there."

"What if I want more than just a weekend?" she asked.

"Do you?"

"I might."

"I might, as well."

She looked up, hope blossoming. "Really?"

"We can start with the weekend and see where it leads."

Hope deflated. But what had she expected? There was no way he was going to jump into a long-term relationship. At least he was honest.

Still, maybe this trip was a mistake.

His kiss made her forget her worries. She loved being kissed by Adam. Loved his touch, the scent of the man, the feel of his strong body against hers. But what would it be like when it all came to an end? Walking away from her first husband had been easy. Even leaving Jean-Paul hadn't been difficult once she'd discovered his infidelity. But leaving Adam would be an entirely different story.

The kiss intensified. Her body felt alive and she longed to be even closer to him. When he pulled back a few inches and looked at her, she saw reflected desire in his eyes.

The elevator arrived and the doors slid open.

"Still want to go out for dinner?" he asked. His voice was husky with emotion, and a coil of desire spiraled through him.

She sighed. "Yes."

When morning came, Piper was ready for breakfast when he knocked on her door. She knew he wanted to be early to the meeting and she didn't want to hold him up in any way.

He looked fit and rested. He hardly leaned on the cane.

"You look great," she said as they walked toward the elevator.

"I want to make sure I don't look like some damned invalid. I'm fighting for my career here."

"You'll be back in the trenches in no time."

He paused a moment and then looked over at Piper. She was surprised to see the bleakness in his eyes.

"There's no guarantee my foot will ever heal enough for me to resume my former life," he said slowly.

She was astonished. She thought everything was on track for his return to work in the field.

"I didn't know."

"I don't like admitting it, even to myself. But I've always made a point of being honest. I can't hide facts merely because I don't like them."

"Neither do you have to volunteer information if you're not asked," she snapped.

"I'll be asked. They want to know when I'm returning."

"So accept this position first. Give yourself as long

as you can to heal."

"Meaning?"

"Meaning it buys you some time. I think you've been pushing yourself too hard. Major injuries like yours don't heal overnight. But it doesn't mean you can't go back to work, just in another capacity. They obviously want you for this new position, and you're still their shining star. I'm sure you can return to foreign reporting once you're fully mobile again."

"I don't want to be stuck behind a desk," he said.

"Make that one of your terms for taking the new assignment. Once this new team is fully operational, you have the right to move on."

She shrugged.

"Who knows? You might like this assignment. You'll be the boss."

Piper wondered how she'd feel if she couldn't model any longer. That day would come sooner for her than if she were in most other professions, but she figured she had another four or five years to prepare for it. Then she'd have to find some other way to earn her living.

Adam stopped at a coffee bar before heading to the office. He was stalling and he knew it. Thinking about Piper made him feel guilty. He shouldn't have brought her. He had work to do, no time to spend with her. She could have met him in Florida, or even let him go there alone. Her being with him was an indulgence—one he couldn't resist.

The idea she'd planted took hold. This wasn't about the rest of his life. He'd listen to the proposal and decide if he'd take the position. Even so, it didn't have to be permanent.

He had to admit to a secret pleasure that they'd asked him. There were others who would be been equally good choices. Maybe his being sidelined had made him the first choice, rather than merit.

Don't be an idiot, he warned himself as he finished his espresso and headed for the CNN headquarters. Think of it as the honor Piper seems to think it is and give the powers that be a fair hearing.

Piper went to Neiman Marcus first. She loved the luxurious designer clothes they displayed. Before her work in the garment district, she hadn't had a clue about quality of fabric, smoothness of finished seams, attention to details. She only bought a few items of clothing each year, but she made sure they were made with care.

She also knew that for a lot of women, beautifully designed clothes were not an option, and not just for economic reasons. She'd long thought more women would buy designer fashions if they fit. Not everyone was rail thin. Runway models made the clothes look fabulous, but when women tried on the clothes in larger sizes, they looked very different.

However, if the clothes were designed specifically for the average women, with the same attention to creative detail and quality of fabric, it could revolutionize the industry.

Maybe she'd found the answer to her post-modeling dilemma. She could develop a line of high-end fashions for women who weren't built for a career on the runway.

Or maybe she'd be a consultant. Advising those teenagers in New Orleans a couple of weeks ago had been fun, and their appreciation was especially gratifying. Giving women direction on how to dress to their best advantage would be very rewarding.

Food for thought, but not today, she mused as she headed out to see more of Atlanta.

When her cell phone rang, Piper was sitting in a park, eating an ice-cream cone and watching children laughing and playing on the playground equipment.

"I'm through here. Where are you?" Adam said without preamble.

"I'm in a park but have no idea where. I'll hunt for a cab and return to the hotel and meet you there."

"Want to come by the office so I can introduce you around?" he suggested.

Piper was surprised Adam wanted to introduce her to his coworkers, but she wanted to meet the men and women who worked with him, most of them behind the scenes.

She met a dozen men and women who worked with Adam in some capacity. Then received a tour of the place and was intrigued by the satellite feeds, the amount of electronic equipment that was needed to bring the news from around the world to the newsroom to be broadcast worldwide.

"How did it go?" Piper whispered at one point when they were alone.

"Better than expected. I'll fill you in at dinner. I have a surprise for you, as well."

"What?"

"At dinner," he said, his eyes alight with teasing laughter.

"I hate waiting."

"Too bad. Aren't you always urging me to exercise patience? Here we are, this is Stan Burks's territory. Come and meet the man who juggles a thousand balls at once, yet keeps everything on time and on target."

Throughout the rest of the tour, Piper tried to figure out what had transpired at the meeting and what surprise Adam had for her. She heard him congratulated a dozen times over, but he wouldn't confirm his decision for her. He accepted the accolades with a modesty that surprised her. Adam was a star. She would have expected more ego from the man. He constantly surprised her.

"Give," she said when they were in a cab on the way back to the hotel.

"I've accepted the position. It starts next month. I don't have to stay in it beyond a year. That will give me plenty of time to get back on my feet. And the best thing is, I'll keep in touch with everyone in the field."

"The best of both worlds," she said.

"Close."

"That's the surprise?"

"No. I think I've got a lead on Fiona."

"What?"

Piper didn't bother to contain her excitement.

"That's fabulous. What is it? Do you know where she is? Can we call her now?"

"Easy. If the woman we've tentatively identified is your Fiona, she's living in Los Angeles."

"Oh my gracious, how did you do that? Just learning she might be Mary Fiona was enough?"

"That and the birth date you gave me. She's registered to vote there. We need to confirm, but I have a phone number. You can call her now if you like. That'll be the best way to find out if it's her."

He handed her a slip of paper with a 213 area code on it. Piper looked at it in amazement. Fiona!

She pulled her phone from her pocket and dialed the number.

"It's ringing," she said.

Her heart was pounding. Ever since she'd heard from Cassie, she'd been drawn back to the ties of childhood. She and Cassie both wanted so much to hear from Fiona. To see her. To have the girls from Bradford Hall reunited.

To her disappointment, the phone rang and rang.

"No answer," she said slowly as the connection moved to voice mail.

She didn't want to leave a message. She wanted to talk to her directly.

"You can try again later."

"It might not even be her," she said, her hope

fading.

"You won't know until you talk with her," Adam said.

"So close after so long. You think it's probably her, don't you?"

"I think so," Adam said with a grin. "Want to fly to L.A. to check it out?"

Piper laughed. "No, I can wait until she answers the phone."

Slipping her arms around him, she gave him a big squeeze.

"Thanks, Adam. Thanks so much."

The next morning they flew to Orlando as originally planned. There had been no answer at the number in Los Angeles, but Adam wouldn't let Piper be discouraged.

They headed straight to the police department to discuss the long-ago traffic accident. Piper knew that doors were being opened to her solely because of Adam.

From police records they learned that Angela Harvesty had been the driver, and with her was a young baby, as mentioned in the article. Angela had been drunk, and had had her license revoked several months prior. Obviously that hadn't stopped her from driving.

The report mentioned that the baby's grandparents, Nathaniel and Carol Harvesty had refused to take the infant.

Piper and Adam exchanged looks at that piece of information.

"Did they contact Mr. Nunes and ask him to come for her?" Piper asked.

"Says the baby was turned over to the Children Protection Unit," Adam said, reading further. "Let's follow up with that when we're done here."

The sad end of a young girl's life was so coldly recorded in the report. Piper shivered. This could be her mother.

"Not very loving grandparents, the Harvestys," Adam said when they closed the report. "It wasn't the baby's fault her mother was drinking."

"I wonder what they were like as parents?" Piper mused.

"We'll track them down and find out. Come on, let's see what we can dig up from CPS."

The file was not made available to them, despite Adam's best tactics, but the clerk came back and said merely that the baby's grandmother had claimed her and they'd released the child into her custody.

"So Carol Harvesty came without her husband," Piper said. "Wonder what happened there. And why she had to give the baby up. I'm that baby, aren't I?"

"We need to talk to her and get some answers. I got a woman at the office to check voter registrations. Both Carol and Nathan are living in Metairie. At least I think it's them. We'll swing by before returning to Bradford."

"The power of the press," she said.

"Never underestimate it."

"You go where no one else dares."

"Seems that way sometimes. The reality is most of the information is readily available if you know how to look for it."

Piper tried the Los Angeles number again.

"I wonder if she's on vacation and left her phone at home," she said. "I can't stand the thought of waiting two weeks and then finding out it's someone else."

"Then we'll just have to search for another lead."

"I want to find her before I have to return to Paris."

"You're sure you don't want to remain in Mississippi? You seem to like being close to Cassie."

"I love being with Cassie. And I expect to visit often or as often as my schedule will allow. But I have no job there. And I do have obligations to fulfill. Taking all this time has wreaked havoc with my schedule. I think I'll be working flat out until Christmas, but I've already told Enrique to hold those two weeks around the holidays open. I plan to return to celebrate with Margaret and Cassie and Matt."

"And Fiona, maybe, if you locate her."

"That would be so perfect. Where will you be Christmas?"

"Good question," he said. "It depends."

Piper almost invited him to return to Bradford. But they'd said no strings. Besides, he'd be caught up in the new job.

"Tell me about your favorite Christmas," she said.

He thought a moment.

"The one where I was ten. I got my first two-wheeler. It was a Norman Rockwell kind of Christmas.

All my grandparents were alive, so we had both sets at dinner. Alice wasn't the pest she later became. And I got what I wanted from Santa."

Piper laughed.

"I bet Alice adored you. What did you have for dinner?"

"The traditional ham and all the trimmings. And pecan pie for dessert. My mother makes the best pecan pie in the world."

"You wait until you try Cassie's," Piper said proudly. "She's the best cook in the world."

"You're prejudiced," Adam teased. "She's like a sister to you."

Piper rubbed the slight scar on her fingertip and nodded.

"And you're not biased about your mom? What is she like?"

She wanted to know all she could about the man she'd fallen for. Even if she never saw him again, knowing about him would make him seem closer.

They left Florida on an afternoon flight. Since it was Saturday, they were unable to visit the records division to look for her original birth certificate. Piper knew she was Angela Harvesty's child. She had to be. She still didn't know if Piper was the name her mother had given her, but now that she had her mother's name, surely she'd be able to locate the birth record.

Piper drove the rental car from the airport following the directions Adam gave. They stopped in Metairie in front of a small, neat ranch house. Roses were blooming in profusion, and the lawn was newly mowed.

Feeling butterflies again, Piper accompanied Adam up the short walkway. They rang the bell and waited.

An older woman answered. Her hair was still mostly brown, with ash highlights. She was trim and smaller than Piper.

"Yes?"

"Mrs. Harvesty?" Adam asked.

"That's right."

"I'm Adam Saunders and this is Piper Morgan. We're here on a family matter. Did you have a daughter named Angela?"

She lost her smile. "What is this about?"

"I think I have your granddaughter here," he said gently.

The woman looked at Piper for a long moment, then burst into tears.

13

"May we come in?" Adam asked.

She nodded and pushed open the screen door.

"My husband isn't home. He'd want to see her. Oh, my, you do look like Angela. I never thought I'd see you again."

She blotted her tears with the edge of her shirt and gestured for them to follow her into the living room.

"Please, sit down."

Her eyes never left Piper.

"You're so tall. Angela wasn't nearly that tall. How did you find me? I wanted to go to you so many times. You probably think we're terrible people, but it was so hard. Losing Angela, having to deal with her behavior for so many years, Nathaniel just wouldn't take it on again. We weren't that young. I'm sorry. Please, sit down."

Piper sat on the sofa, Adam next to her. He reached out a hand and enclosed hers firmly for support. Something she badly needed.

"Can you tell us a bit about what happened?" Adam asked.

Carol Harvesty sat in a chair to the right of the sofa.

Piper looked at her hostess. The woman must be in her seventies, but her skin was lovely, virtually unlined.

"Angela was always headstrong and wild. Even as a little girl, she got into more mischief than two other children would have. We encouraged her independence, but then realized we had created a problem child. We had waited so long for a baby and couldn't believe our good fortune when Angela came along."

She frowned.

"It proved too good to be true. She was a difficult child. And once she became a teenager, she was unmanageable. Drinking, carrying on with boys. Her father put his foot down, but she sneaked out behind our back."

Carol looked sad, remembering.

"All the happier memories were crowded out by her behavior the last couple of years. When we learned of her death, we were devastated. The last chance to build a close relationship, to undo some of the heartache of her teenage years was gone. Our only child was dead."

"But you had a grandchild," Adam said gently.

Piper had to give him credit. There was no sign of the hard-hearted reporter out to get a story. He was compassionate and empathetic, yet at the same time encouraged Carol Harvesty to tell her story.

Piper felt numb. She felt as if she were listening to the story of a stranger. Angela was her mother. But only because she gave Piper birth.

Margaret was her true mother. Why was it only now that she fully realized it? Margaret was the one who had walked the floor with her when she had croup. Margaret was the one who had attended every school event and cheered her girls on. Margaret's unfailing faith in her three girls had given Piper a confidence of her own.

She might have made a few wrong turns, but thanks to the strong grounding received from Margaret, she also knew how to make adjustments and get back on track.

Carol Harvesty was a stranger. She professed to have loved her daughter, yet had turned her back on her innocent grandchild and walked away.

"I know. I wanted to take her, but Nathaniel refused. He said bad blood would win out, and we couldn't risk another failure."

She stopped, stricken.

So they'd refused to give an innocent baby a chance?

"Do you know who my father was?" Piper asked.

"Not for certain. Angela was always with some wild boy or other. About the time she would have conceived, she was seeing a boy named Dax. I don't know his real name, or where he lived."

Maybe if the parents had taken more time to know about their daughter's friends, they could have helped steer her in a better direction, Piper thought.

"But she came sneaking in one night about the same time with another boy. We saw him as he drove off. It was Zach Tyler, the son of a business associate of my husband's."

"Where are these men now?" Adam asked.

She shrugged.

"I have no idea. Angela died twenty-eight years ago. We didn't keep up with the boys she knew. I tried to convince Nathaniel to let us take you home and raise you, but he was adamant."

"The report in Florida said the baby went into foster care, but then was taken home by her grandmother," Adam said. "That wasn't you?"

Carol stared at Piper for a long time. Sighing gently, she looked down at her hands.

"Margaret Nunes took her. Margaret is from a small town in Mississippi. She was Angela's birth mother, and when she heard we weren't taking the baby, she flew to Florida to claim her."

Piper stared at her, unable to comprehend the meaning of her words. Adam squeezed her hand, but she couldn't even respond.

"Margaret is my real grandmother?"

She'd longed for family her whole life. With one sentence, Margaret could have given her what she yearned for. Edith Harper knew. Who else in Bradford knew and refused to tell her? Refused even when as an adult she'd sought answers?

Carol nodded, swallowing hard.

"She became pregnant in high school. Her father was furious, but he didn't find out until too late to order an abortion. He had her sent away until the baby was born. She was such a precious child, Angela. We had wanted a baby for so long, but had given up hope. We were past the age most adoption agencies allow for parents. William Nunes and Nathaniel were business associates, and William proposed we adopt the child. We were so delighted. Only, it didn't turn out as we had hoped."

"Did Margaret get to see her daughter as she was growing up?" Adam asked.

Piper was grateful Adam was doing the questioning, for she couldn't seem to think. She actually felt a pain in her chest at the knowledge.

"Oh, no. William would never have allowed that. Nathaniel sent him a letter each year, telling him about Angela. But that was it. No contact."

"Not with William Nunes either? He was Angela's grandfather."

Carol shook her head.

There was silence for a moment. Then Adam asked if Mrs. Harvesty had any pictures of Angela.

"Yes. There are some albums. In the attic, I think. Oh, dear, it's been so long. And we moved, you know. We used to live in New Orleans, but after Angela died, well, we felt it best to move here."

Adam didn't respond. He seemed to be waiting for the woman to decide whether she could get the albums or not.

"I could go up and see if I can find them," Carol offered tentatively.

"We would appreciate that very much," he said.

"Can we help?"

"Come along. The attic has stairs and lights, but it's probably a mess. I don't think I've been up there in five years or more."

She led the way, talking the entire time.

"Nathaniel goes up there. That's where he stores tax records and all."

It took more than twenty minutes, but Adam located the box of old albums. Carol opened it and withdrew five albums, handing them to Adam. "I don't guess Nathaniel will want them. He never speaks of Angela anymore. I loved that child, and wish things had turned out differently."

She looked at Piper.

"I don't even know my granddaughter's name."

Adam waited a beat then answered when Piper remained silent. She probably looked as dazed as she felt.

"Her name is Piper Morgan. She works as a model in Paris. She's very successful. Has modeling work all over the world."

Carol eyed her uncertainly.

"Maybe Nathaniel was wrong about the bad blood. I wonder if your father *is* Zach Tyler. The Tylers are an old Louisiana family. Come from good breeding, you know."

Piper didn't care to hear any more from Carol Harvesty. She could tell the woman was still uncertain whether Piper had inherited her mother's "bad blood."

She walked down the stairs and out the front door

without saying a word. The entire interview seemed surreal. She wanted to go home, see Cassie and return some sanity back into her life.

She heard Adam thank the woman and promise to return the albums once Piper made copies of photos she wanted. Piper just wanted to get away.

"You okay?" he asked when he climbed into the passenger side of the car. The albums rested on the seat between them.

"No, I'm not."

"At least now you know," he said softly.

"Margaret's my grandmother. She's known that all my life and never once gave me a hint. What would be the harm in acknowledging that fact? She knew how much I longed for some family. Cassie and Fiona knew their parents. Every kid at school could recite their family history back to the Crusades. I was the odd one out. Why didn't she tell me!"

"You'll have to ask her that."

"Or just leave," she said bitterly. "I found out what I came for."

For a minute, she wished she could undo it all. Leave the past undisturbed, go on as she had been.

He looked at the albums, opening two, then handing her one. "Start here. She's a baby in these."

Almost against her will, Piper looked at the first page of the album. A baby wrapped in pink lay sleeping in someone's arms. She was so tiny.

"On top of everything, now I learn my mother was a slut."

"Hey, teen years are hard on everyone," Adam reminded her. "Cut her some slack. You only have one side of the story."

"Her parents don't even know who the father of her baby was."

"Which shows some lack on their part, don't you think? Mrs. Harvesty didn't say what they did when they found out she was pregnant. Do you think they were supportive?"

"Ha. I can't imagine that woman being supportive of anything if Nathaniel disapproves."

"She does seem intimidated by the man."

Despite her ambivalence about what she'd learned, Piper was intrigued with the photos in the book. Slowly she turned the page and saw her mother's life unfold. From tiny baby to toddler, to preschooler. Angela had had blond hair like Piper. Not like Margaret. Who had Angela's father been?

First day of school. Christmas with a tall tree and mounds of presents. Beaming parents. It looked like a happy family. Maybe there had been good times for Angela before everything crashed down.

Slowly Piper finished the book and reached for another.

"It must have been hard for a mother to give up her child," Adam said softly.

She looked at him. "Margaret?"

He nodded.

"Sounds to me she's another woman intimidated by a man. Only in this case it was her father.

Remember you said Emiline told you there was a big blowup when she brought the baby home? Maybe Margaret finally found enough backbone to stand up to her father. It was a few years later, but in the end she fought for you. That has to say something," he said.

She flipped through the other books. The last one showed a rebellious teenager wearing tight clothes, inappropriate makeup and a defiant attitude. The change was so drastic from the cute little girl of previous books that Piper's heart went out to her.

She could relate. Hadn't she coped during the teen years the same way—fighting against Margaret's rules?

"Do you think I'm like her?" she asked.

"I see a slight physical resemblance," Adam said.

"I slept around in high school. Then there was Billy Bob and Jean-Paul. Maybe I'm more like my mother than I want to be."

"Teens do reckless things. Do you sleep around now?"

She shook her head. "I told you, I swore off men after Jean-Paul." She tilted her head slightly. "Until you showed up."

"I'm flattered."

"It's temporary, I know. Let's get going. I want to talk to Cassie."

"And Margaret?" he asked.

"I don't know about that yet."

"Want to track down Dax and Zach Tyler? DNA testing can prove parental connection."

"Won't one of them be surprised to find out he has a daughter? I'll think about it. Maybe you can dig up info on them. Tracking down Zach Tyler should be easier. Then I'll decide if I want to continue the search. I'm feeling a bit blown away by everything. If one guy's a con and the other's a doctor, maybe I'll just pretend I'm the doc's daughter and let it go. It's funny, but I thought I'd feel something for her."

"Your mother?"

"No, Mrs. Harvesty. She raised my mother. She was Angela's adoptive mother. My grandmother. Yet I felt nothing. She's a stranger. So is the man whose sperm connected with Angela's egg. He doesn't even know a child exists, I bet. Why rock his boat? Maybe knowing who my parents are isn't that important after all."

"Talk to Margaret, find out more before closing down," Adam suggested.

She put the last album on the seat and started the engine. Soon they were on the highway, heading for Bradford.

Wouldn't Cassie be surprised at all she'd found out.

"I'll go with you to tell Cassie," Adam said. "Want me there for the confrontation with Margaret, too?"

"No, I want to do both alone."

She felt raw, exposed. What did Adam make of all this?

The ride home seemed to take only minutes, maybe because her thoughts were churning so fast. She drove straight to Sam's house and stopped.

Adam tried again to convince her to let him go home with her, but she refused. She wanted some time alone. When she arrived, the house was empty and dark. Taking her luggage and the albums, she entered through the kitchen. Cassie was working tonight. Saturday nights were the busiest for her fledgling company.

Piper left the albums on the kitchen table and went upstairs. She peeped into her old room. The men must have worked like crazy to have the ensuite bathroom finished. Painting and minor work still remained, but she could move back into her old room.

She ran water in the new tub. Maybe a hot bath would help her relax and gain some perspective. She wanted to rush over to the hospital and demand an explanation from Margaret. Not that she could browbeat the woman, but she'd insist on answers.

For a moment she regretted turning Adam away. Making love would drive the demons from her thoughts. Did that make her more like her mother? Using men? Why did Angela need to escape? Did she feel unwanted?

How could Margaret have given up her baby girl?

Piper tried to look at her situation objectively.

Margaret had been a teenager, with no home except her father's, no income. And it looked as if the father of her baby hadn't been able to marry her and make a family of their own. What choices had Margaret had?

When Angela was killed and no one stepped in to

take the baby, Margaret had made a choice. She'd fought with her father, and the experience and wisdom that came from being years older had enabled her to do what she wanted. Who was to say she hadn't fought for Angela and lost. The second time, she'd won.

Why not tell me?

Piper's thoughts went around and around, but everything came back to that one question.

Tomorrow, she'd find out.

Sleep didn't come easily. Piper tossed and turned, but her mind wouldn't shut down. She heard Cassie arrive home and almost got up to talk with her, but she knew her friend would be tired from the catering event. Morning would come soon enough.

When Piper woke, she knew it was later than she'd planned. That was hardly surprising, since it was almost dawn before she fell into a restless sleep. She rose and dressed. Breakfast, then the convalescent hospital. She wanted answers.

Walking into the kitchen, she stopped. Matt and Adam sat at the table, Cassie was humming at the stove. A wonderful aroma filled the air. Bacon sizzled. She saw the oven was on—biscuits, she knew. Her mouth watered.

"What is this? A conclave?" she asked, walking forward. She didn't need this. She wanted a quick bite and then she'd take off for the hospital.

"We heard you have news for us," Cassie said from the stove. "Spill."

Piper glared at Adam. "This is private."

Matt stood up. "If you want me to leave..."

"No, don't be silly," Piper said. "You're family."

"And I'm not?" Adam asked, raising his eyebrows in mock surprise.

"You already know."

She was grumpy. Lack of sleep. Pulling out a chair, she noticed the stack of albums on one of the empty chairs.

"I found out for sure Angela Harvesty was my mother. We visited her adoptive parents, got pictures and a brief history. They don't know who my father is, but my natural grandmother is Margaret."

The words came out in a rush.

Cassie froze, staring at her.

Matt sat back down with a whoosh.

After a long silent moment, Cassie turned back to the bacon.

"Don't say another word until I have breakfast on the table. I don't want to miss anything."

Matt brought Piper a cup of coffee.

Adam studied her, as if looking for signs that she was falling apart.

She was made of sterner stuff. Okay, the ideal parents who would someday come and claim her had been her own fiction. In her heart she'd known that all along. But somehow she'd hoped she would at least meet the woman who had given her life. Now she found out her mother had been a child herself when she died.

Cassie kept throwing glances her way, stirring the

bacon as if that would hurry the cooking. Piper could feel her concern. She knew Cassie was as stunned as she'd been to learn of her relationship to Margaret.

Finally breakfast was served. Cassie put the last plate down and sat beside Matt.

"Tell all."

Piper complied, giving all the facts as she knew them.

"I can't believe it. Why didn't Margaret say something?"

"Think a minute," Adam said. "She was a girl herself when she got pregnant. Obviously her father hushed it up. I asked Sam last night if he'd ever heard anything. Hey, he'll keep it confidential," he said when Piper glared at him.

She wasn't sure she wanted the entire world to know yet. If ever.

"Anyway, he's never heard a hint about it. And there's been a lot of discussion surrounding Margaret and her girls because of the scandal with Fiona. So she gave up her baby. That's what a lot of teens do. She hadn't even finished high school at that point. How could she support herself and a baby?"

"That wasn't the case when I came to live with her," Piper said.

"No, but she was still dependent on her father. Still lived in his house. My guess is they came to an agreement. Remember Emiline said they were fighting for weeks? My theory is he agreed to let her keep the baby as long as she kept the relationship secret.

Margaret must have told Edith. She's been a faithful friend over the years. I guess I have to admire that."

Matt nodded.

"Honor is strong in the South. Comes from Reconstruction, I think, when we didn't have much else."

"Once her father was dead, she could have said something," Piper stubbornly insisted. "She knew I was looking for family. She must have known how much I wanted to belong somewhere."

"Maybe, or maybe not," Adam said. "You need to ask her."

Piper shivered. She wasn't sure she wanted to face Margaret anymore. What would she say? How could Margaret have denied her the family she'd wanted so badly?

"We all wanted to belong somewhere," Cassie said slowly. "Margaret did her best to make us feel loved here. Remember when we were younger? We followed her traditions at birthdays and Christmas, and they became ours. I still make gingerbread at my birthday. And I always have pecan pie at holidays. She taught us about her family, gave us pride in who we were and encouraged us to do what we wanted while respecting others."

Piper thought back to the stories Margaret had told about her mother and father and her grandparents. The residents of Bradford had suffered hardships during the Depression and wild times at the mill when it was in full production. She had shared a family history with three children who didn't know theirs. She had instilled pride and determination in her three girls.

"If you hadn't been taken away so abruptly, if you all had finished growing up here, you might see things differently," Adam said. "Teenage years are hard enough within a stable family. You three lost that when the state separated you. Who knows, maybe Margaret planned to tell you the truth when you turned eighteen."

"You need to get the rest of the answers from Margaret," Matt said.

Cassie nodded.

"I know."

Piper felt her anger subsiding.

Adam reached out and took her hand, squeezing it gently.

"Scared?"

She resented the way he could read her so easily. How had he come to know her so well?

"A little," she confessed, reluctant to admit it.

"I'd be, too," Cassie said. "Want me to go with you?"

Piper shook her head.

"This is something I want to do alone. As soon as I finish eating, I'll go."

Could she stretch breakfast until Thursday? She was nervous about talking to Margaret. But her determination to find the truth was stronger. She needed to learn about her family.

When breakfast was finished, Piper rose, almost feeling sick to her stomach at the task ahead.

"Walking?" Adam asked.

She nodded. It'd take longer to reach the hospital that way.

"I'll walk with you a bit. There's something I want to ask you."

He smiled at Cassie.

"Thanks for breakfast. You beat Ruby's by a mile."

"Thank you, kind sir. Tell all your friends I cater breakfasts, too."

"Breakfast in bed?" Matt asked.

"Only for special customers," she said, then blushed at the look in his eye.

Piper envied them once again. She glanced at Adam. He was studying her closely, but she couldn't read his expression.

"Let's get this over with," she said.

They headed out. When they reached the sidewalk, Adam put his hand on her arm and stopped her.

"Let me say what I have to say now. Timing's bad, but I need the answer to make plans. I know we talked about seeing where this attraction would lead. And God knows I've never thought about settling down. I mean, can you imagine seeing the same person every day for the rest of your life? When I used to think about that, I'd get panicky and want to bolt."

She nodded. Was he ending their time together already? She wasn't ready. She wanted to count on his support while she discovered the truth of her background. Was he dumping her because of what they'd learned yesterday?

"We said no strings," she reminded him, tilting her chin slightly.

She was nothing if not strong. He'd never guess how much his leaving would hurt.

He looked away.

"Yeah, well, I want to change that."

He turned back to her, narrowing his eyes slightly as if to assess her response better.

"Change it to what?"

Adam took a deep breath.

"Piper, what do you think about getting married. To me?"

She stared at him.

Had she heard him correctly?

Adam Saunders wanted to *marry* her?

"I can't do that. I've been married. Twice. I'm not cut out for marriage. And after learning what I did yesterday, maybe I can understand why."

"What do you mean?"

"Look at my background. Margaret didn't marry, and neither did Angela. I tried it and it didn't take either time. Maybe Mrs. Harvesty's right. Bad blood will out—or bad genes, at least."

She turned and hurried down the street, feeling as if her heart would explode. Adam wanted to marry her. For a second she let herself imagine being with him for the rest of her life. It would be glorious.

But not for him. In no time he'd grow bored with

her, as Jean-Paul had, and look for someone else. She couldn't stand that again. Adam knew women all over the world, exciting reporters, glamorous newscasters, competent and sophisticated network women who had so much to offer a man like him. How could she compete?

"Piper."

She looked over her shoulder. He was hurrying after her. She wanted to run away, but stopped. He'd reinjure his leg if he kept up that pace.

When he reached her, he took her arm again, more firmly this time.

"Is that a no?" he asked.

She laughed, her heart breaking.

"Yes, it's a no. Thank you for asking me, but it would never work."

"Why not?"

"For a hundred reasons."

"Give them to me one by one and I'll counter all of them. Unless you don't love me."

She stared at him.

She loved him.

She'd known it was happening, but tried to pass it off as mere physical attraction.

"We're so different."

"Opposites attract," he countered.

"I live in France."

"That's part of the reason I need an answer soon. I have the option of setting up the new task force wherever I want. I thought Paris would give us the advantage—in Europe, close to the Middle East. The only area that would be a long commute is the Far East. We can work around that. Next."

Piper shook her head.

"Adam, I'm honored, truly. But you'd get tired of me in a while and—"

"I've never felt like this before. Never felt that I'd like to be part of someone's life. To have them share mine. To grow old together. I see that with you, Piper. Marry me."

He gave a lopsided grin.

"What have you got to lose?"

My heart.

Before she could say another word, he pulled her closer and kissed her.

"If you can't say yes now, think about it, okay?"

She nodded, heart pounding. She wanted to ignore her reservations, but she couldn't. There was too much going on now to think calmly and sensibly.

Had he misread her? Adam wondered. He had no doubts about his own feelings for Piper. They were different from anything he'd ever felt before. He and Deirdre had had much in common, but somehow he'd never envisioned a long-term future with her.

With Piper, he could see shared adventures, a future with children, lifelong friends, and one day— when they retired—maybe they'd return to Bradford to sit on a porch with Sam or Matt and Cassie.

He could admit it now. His stay in this town—and Piper herself—had completely changed the way he looked at life.

Apparently Piper didn't share his vision.

Or did she need time?

A lot had happened in the past couple of days. The recent revelations had knocked her off balance.

But he wasn't giving up. He wasn't accepting no for an answer.

"Come on, I'll go to the hospital with you. If you want me to stay in the hall while you talk to Margaret, I'll wait there. But I don't want you to be alone."

"I want to go alone."

"Not today."

They walked a block in silence.

"You didn't ask me to marry you to make me feel better, did you?" she asked.

"Of course not. I want you for my wife. And I'll need a better reason than the ones you've given so far before I accept your rejection. I think about you all the time. I've told you things I've never told anyone else. I'm in love with you. And that's something I never thought I'd say."

His hand slipped down, and he laced his fingers through hers. Slowly they headed toward the hospital.

When Piper walked into Margaret's room, Adam stayed at the doorway. She hadn't asked him to wait outside, but neither had she indicated she wanted him with her. He watched as she squared her shoulders and walked across the room to where Margaret sat on a chair, looking out the window. The view was of huge old trees, veils of Spanish moss dripping from their branches. If she had been closer to the window, she might have seen the lush gardens on the hospital grounds below.

Adam wished he knew the outcome of this meeting. He couldn't stand the thought of Piper being hurt any more than she was already. She'd been on her own for years, building a successful career. She was a strong woman.

Yet he wanted to protect her from disappointments and sadness. Keep her smiling and happy. No one who knew him would ever believe he could have such feelings—he was surprised himself.

Now he understood why Sam hadn't started dating again. If Piper said no, Adam knew he'd never find anyone who would make him feel this way.

Margaret turned when she heard Piper's step and smiled.

Adam thought her smile was more symmetrical. She was making progress in her recovery. According to Piper, Margaret was using a walker. It was only her communication skills that were slow in coming back.

Piper pulled over another chair and sat next to Margaret.

"I visited Carol Harvesty yesterday," she said gently. "She told me that you're my natural grandmother. I wondered why you never told me yourself."

Adam gave her credit. He wouldn't have been so kind, but would have gone in with guns blazing, demanding answers, tossing accusations. He tensed, waiting for Margaret's response.

Don't let her hurt Piper, he prayed.

Margaret's eyes widened slightly, then she dropped her head, averting her eyes from Piper.

Slowly reaching out, Piper touched her hand.

"I was sad to learn my birth mother died so young. She was just a child. I wish you had told me about her and about you. I'm so glad you came for me. What would have become of me if you hadn't?"

Margaret raised her head slightly, looking at Piper. Even from across the room, Adam could see the hope, the longing, the love.

"I'm sorry for your stroke, Margaret. But it was the best thing to happen for us all. Cassie and I are back now, and we're going to find Fiona. We're a family. A real and true family."

Piper reached out to gather the older woman into her arms, holding her tightly in a hug.

Adam wondered how Piper felt, knowing for the first time that she embraced her own grandmother. Her own flesh and blood.

Piper had found her family.

14

Piper sat back and smiled at Margaret. When the older woman glanced toward the door, Piper turned. Adam was still leaning against the jamb.

"I'm fine," she said. "Thanks for coming with me."

"But you don't need me, right?"

"Margaret and I need to talk," she said, reaching out to pat Margaret's hand.

"But I—"

"Thanks for all your help. I wouldn't know about Margaret and Angela and everything if not for you. But I can take it from here."

It was as clear a dismissal as he'd ever heard.

She had what she wanted. She hadn't asked for anything he hadn't been willing to give.

"Then I'll go."

He nodded to Margaret and took another long look at Piper.

"But we have things to discuss before too much longer."

The hospital hallway seemed endless. He wasn't sure how long it took before he was outside in the sunshine.

Thanks for all your help.

Her entire world had turned upside down. He knew that. Maybe he needed to do something to show her he fit right into that overturned life.

Slowly he returned to Sam's house. He'd call his boss and get started on the new assignment. His mind began to focus on the tasks ahead. Who did he want on the team? How much leeway was his boss giving him to determine who was on board? He wanted to plan the logistics, then prepare some appropriate drills so they'd be ready the first time a real event hit.

He had a plan—for both his professional and his personal life. But first he needed access to the computer. He quickened his pace.

Piper couldn't understand Margaret. She was trying to communicate, and Piper could see the frustration in her eyes. But the sounds coming from her mouth made no sense.

"We have lots of time to talk about it," Piper said soothingly. She was relieved to see Margaret appeared willing to discuss the situation and didn't stonewall her or become distraught.

"Ah, good morning, Miss Nunes." A cheery nurse came in with a wheelchair. "Time for PT."

Piper rose and stood to one side as the nurse helped Margaret into the chair.

"My, you seem full of energy this morning," the nurse commented.

Margaret tried to speak, but the sounds were garbled.

"We'll be working on speech later. Maybe you'll feel like writing some of what you're trying to say. Remember we worked on writing yesterday?"

More sounds came, and this time Margaret seemed angry.

"I know it's slow, but it gets the job done. Every one's in such a hurry these days."

"Write me a letter, Margaret," Piper said. "I'll be back later today to read it."

She hadn't known Margaret's writing skills were far enough along to be legible. Maybe communication was possible after all.

Piper went as far as the elevator with them, parting when Margaret and the nurse took an up car. Piper waited for one going down and returned to the lobby.

She didn't have any more answers now than she'd had before she arrived. But she would by the end of the day.

Cassie went with Piper to the hospital in the late afternoon. She was almost as anxious to learn about Margaret's past as Piper was.

Margaret was in bed, and she appeared wan and tired. On the tray over her lap was a notebook, and she was laboriously writing in it. When she saw them, she looked up and smiled.

At least she seemed glad to see them, Piper thought with relief.

"Cassie knows as much as I do," she told Margaret.

Margaret nodded. She put down the pencil and pushed the notebook toward Piper.

With a glance at Cassie, who pulled two chairs close to the bed, Piper picked up the notebook, sat and read aloud.

The letters were more printed than written. And uneven and shaky. But legible.

"Dearest Piper, I have so many regrets for the things left undone over the years. I never regretted you, darling child. You know my father forced me to give up my precious baby. I only held her once. She was so adorable. I thought I would die when I never got to see her again. I didn't know he got reports. He didn't tell me. I found out when I discovered the letters one spring cleaning a couple of years before he died. He was angry, so was I. I always did what he wanted, but he never forgave me for Angela. I loved her, though.

"I couldn't marry her father. I couldn't earn my own living then, because I was still in school. When I got older, I should have moved away. But I stayed with my father, making my home with him, dependent on him. Heartbreak kept me from dating. I fell in love with a boy named Joshua, and he died in Vietnam.

After I found the letters, I lived for those yearly reports on Angela.

When the Harvestys told about her wild behavior, I thought if she'd had her true mother's love, she'd have turned out better. Maybe not, but those were my thoughts.

Her adopted father called mine when she died. He was fed up and didn't plan to do anything with the baby—you. I couldn't let history repeat itself. I was determined to bring you home where you would be loved. My father said no. But I was older. I didn't have a job, but I could get one. I didn't have a place to live, but I could find one. Finally he gave in, and agreed on the condition I promised never to tell anyone who you were.

My father was a proud man. Scandal was too much for him. I kept my promise, though I longed to claim you over and over. In my heart, I was always your grandmother. I love you, Piper.

Forgive an old woman's failings. You have a fine family background. Joshua Cannon was your grandfather. His family goes back for generations in Mississippi, and even includes a state senator.

As for your father, I'm sure—

Here the writing stopped.

Piper hugged the notebook to her chest and looked at Margaret.

"Someday, when you can talk easily, you'll have to tell me the entire story in detail. Especially about my grandfather."

"And me," Cassie said, her eyes teary. "I can't believe you're Piper's grandmother. I'm so glad you took her in and then wanted more kids. Where would Fiona and I have been without you?"

"I don't want to get your hopes up," Piper told them, "but Adam may have found Fiona. Drat, he's got the number on his phone. We've been trying to get in touch with a Mary Fiona Hunter, same age as Fiona, who lives in Los Angeles. No one answers and I never leave a message, wanting to talk to her first. I'll have to call Adam and get the number."

Margaret seemed happier than she had since Piper arrived in Bradford. The deception must have weighed heavily on her all these years.

Piper had a lot more to discover. She wanted to know about Joshua Cannon and how her grandparents had fallen in love. How tragic he'd died young. Would Margaret and he have had a large family had they married?

And Angela, how different would her life have been? Would she have been as wild and rebellious?

The past couldn't be changed. Piper wished she'd known earlier, but was grateful to finally learn the truth. Surrounded by her family, Margaret and Cassie, she truly felt she was home.

"We need you at home, Margaret," Cassie said. "There's so much to talk about. You'll have to show Piper all the old family pictures, and she's got albums from the Harvestys. Do you have any pictures of her grandfather?"

Margaret nodded.

"If the woman in Los Angeles is our Fiona, maybe she can fly out for a visit right away," Piper said. "We'd all be together again."

Piper ran up the steps to Sam's porch and knocked on the door. Cassie followed.

Sam opened the screen and looked at them. "Ladies," he said.

"Can I see Adam?" Piper asked. "I need to get something from him."

"He's gone," Sam said.

"Gone where?" she asked.

"I'm not sure. Either Atlanta or New York. He was talking about his new assignment and where he might locate the office, and who he had to call, and a dozen other things."

"Gone?" Piper repeated. "He left?"

Sam nodded.

"With a message for you. He'll be in touch for that talk. You know what he means?"

Piper let out her breath, not realizing she'd hoped for more when Sam said he had a message.

"He left because I didn't say yes," she said slowly.

"To what?" Cassie asked.

"To marrying him."

"Adam asked you to marry him?"

Sam was genuinely surprised.

Piper nodded.

"And you turned him down?"

Cassie seemed equally shocked.

Piper shook her head, a slow ache building in the region of her heart. Swallowing hard, she tried to think. All that churned in her mind was the fact Adam was gone.

"No, I didn't say yes. He caught me by surprise, and I just found out about Margaret and Angela and all."

"Are you sure he asked you to marry him?" Sam asked.

"Will you marry me is pretty hard to miss," Piper said curtly. "It wouldn't have worked. I've already failed at two marriages. We're so different. He has a dangerous job and lives for excitement. I want routine and safety. I live in Paris, he lives out of a suitcase. I can't risk more heartbreak."

Oh, but she yearned for Adam to come home to, to share her life with, to grow old together. If she wasn't so scared.

"How dumb can you get?" Cassie sounded disgusted. "He loves you, you love him, the rest can be worked out."

"There was no reason for Adam to hang around," Piper said, "and all the reasons in the world to leave. If he really cared for me, why stay after I didn't accept his proposal. I must have hurt his feelings. He probably thinks I don't want him."

It wasn't true. She wanted him so much she ached.

"Maybe you'd better think this through, Piper," Cassie urged her gently. "Oh, honey, you've always wanted a family. Now you know Margaret's your grandmother. You can have a husband, children, grandchildren of your own. You have a heritage to pass on, family stories. Don't throw away your chance at happiness. It's so rarely given."

Each word was a blow to Piper's heart.

"And happiness can be snatched away in a heartbeat," Sam said slowly. "My wife died two years ago, and I'd give anything to have her back for ten minutes."

"Adam isn't some redneck good ol'boy or some fancy French playboy," Cassie said, coming closer and giving her a hug. "He's a hardworking man who took time to help a stranger find her family. He's nothing like your first two husbands. Take a chance, honey. Besides, I'd love to have him for a brother-in-law."

Piper clutched her head between her hands.

"I don't know what to do."

"Do you love him?" Cassie asked.

She nodded.

"But I never told him."

Cassie rolled her eyes in exasperation.

"Then call him and tell him yes!"

In only seconds Piper dialed Adam's number.

"Saunders."

She caught her breath. It was do-or-die time.

"I love you," she said shakily. "Don't leave."

"Piper?"

"I want to reconsider."

"Piper, does that mean yes?"

"It means maybe."

"Yes. Just say it," he urged.

"Do you love me?"

"Like crazy, more than I thought I would ever love anyone. Say yes."

"Yes. Come home."

"I'm at the airport. I'll be there as soon as I can make it. Piper, I love you."

Tears gathered in her eyes. Slowly she ended the call and looked at the two facing her. Her heart was about to burst from her chest.

"He's coming home. I guess I'm going to marry him after all."

Two nights later and Adam, Matt and Cassie sat around the picnic table in the backyard of Bradford Hall.

"So you're sure you won't be settling in Bradford," Cassie said for the twentieth time.

"I've still got my assignments in Europe, at least through the end of the year. We'll come to visit at Christmas. But once the Independence Day events are over, I have to get back to work," Piper confirmed.

"The wheels are in motion to open our new office in Paris," Adam said. "I'll need a crash course in French, but since most of our work will be done in English, I'll manage. The position's for at least a year. After that, who knows. Maybe I'll transfer to New Orleans, if I can get my wife to move back."

"Margaret was happy with the news we're getting married, don't you think?" Piper asked again.

"Yes," Cassie assured her. "Another incentive for her to get better quickly. The home will be ready to open soon, and my wedding and now yours are waiting for her recovery."

"I do *not* want a double wedding ceremony," Piper said firmly.

"Are you kidding. If you were there beside me, who would look at me. I get first dibs, though. Matt and I have been engaged longer."

"Okay. You go on a Saturday morning and I'll do Saturday afternoon and we'll have one heck of a reception Saturday night."

"Did you call that number again?" Adam asked.

"Yes, no answer," Piper told him. "Are you sure it's an active phone?"

"Keep trying. If that's not your Fiona, we'll keep searching. If she's alive, we'll find her."

Piper nodded, looking at Cassie and Matt and then her beloved Adam.

She still had moments when panic seemed close. She hoped their marriage would last forever. For her part, she knew she'd never find another man to love the way she loved Adam. He swore he loved her, and she believed him.

After finding her family, finding love and happiness when she least expected it, Piper was beginning to believe in happy endings.

If you liked **Cassie's Return**,
you may enjoy *Billionaire's Betrothal*,
book 1 in the *Gold Gate Romance* series.

If you enjoyed **Cassie's Return**,
please consider leaving a review.

More books by Barbara McMahon

Bradford Hall

Cassie's Return

Piper's Discovery

Golden Gate Romance Series

Billionaire's Betrothal

Her Not So Empty Nest

Dakota's Hero

One Special Kiss

Finding a Wife for Tanner

The CEO's Baby

Love Times Three

Office Charade

Cowboys of Wildcat Creek

Valentine's Cowboy Rescue

Holly's Reluctant Cowboy

Shelly and the Cowboy

A Cowboy for Eliza

Kristi's Cowboy Hero

Sweet Reunion Romance Collection

Unexpected Reunion

Unanticipated Reunion

Unpredictable Reunion

The Talmadge Sisters

Letters to Caroline

Trusting Abby

Michelle's Marriage Deal

The Harts of Texas Series

Rebel Heart

Reckless Heart

Tangled Hearts

A Sweet Clean Christmas Romance Collection

The Christmas Cop

A Teaspoon of Mistletoe

The Cowboy's Special Christmas

The Christmas Locket

A Soldier's Christmas

A Key West Christmas

Cowboy Heroes Series

The Cowboy Next Door
Cowboy's Bride
One Stubborn Cowboy
Crazy About a Cowboy
Never Doubt a Cowboy

Cowboy Marshal
Summer Cowboy
Second Chance Cowboy
Movie Star Cowboy

Tropical Escape Series

Island Rendezvous
Come into the Sun

Island Paradise

Rocky Point Series

Rocky Point Legacy
Rocky Point Reunion
Rocky Point Promise

Rocky Point Hero
Rocky Point Inn
Rocky Point Dawn

The Ultimate Billionaires

The Cynical Sheikh
Falling for the Sheikh

A Sheikh of Her Own
The Unforgettable Sheikh

Sweet Romance Stand-alone Collection

Because of You
Cowboy Charade
I'll Take Forever
Jared's Promise
Mail Order Bride
Not Really Married

Sweet Meant To Be
The Cowboy Comes Home
The Paper Marriage
Trusting Jake
The Banished Bride